GREED

To Mom + Patti,
Enjoy my first
novel! Thanks for your
support.

Love,
Dunk

GREED

An Eli Hockney Novel

DEREK PACIFICO

Pacificop Press

CONTENTS

To my wife Johanna, who was just as much a part of the department as I was. She suffered when I was down, rejoiced in my success, and supported me through all the trials and tribulations of the various shifts, divisions, and assignments the department had to offer. Cops' wives are a special breed, but they broke the mold after mine.

Prologue

The San Bernardino County Sheriff's Department is one of the premier, if not the premier, law enforcement agencies on the West Coast. While the Los Angeles Police Department and the Los Angeles County Sheriff's Department are more famous for being depicted countless times in television and movies, it is often the SBSD that is called on by sheriffs and chiefs of police across the country to assist in investigations and provide first-class training.

The sheriff of San Bernardino County is a gregarious yet humble man who can quiet a room with his mere presence. When attending a conference of law enforcement officials, the SBSD sheriff is the one everyone wants to meet and seek advice from, and when he speaks, everyone listens.

Thus, the San Bernardino County Sheriff's Homicide Detail is the elite of all investigative units. Their members designed, developed, and continue to deliver the only two-week interactive homicide school on the West Coast.

Only sixteen homicide detectives in the detail are responsible for investigating all the murders, suspicious deaths, in-custody deaths, and officer-involved shootings in a single county that is roughly the size of the state of New Jersey. The fact that they can proudly report a consistent clearance rate of 90% or above is almost unheard of in large law enforcement agencies with half the crime.

Understaffed and paid far less than every other Southern California Sheriff's Department, the members of SBSD don't stay because they can't go anywhere else; they stay because they would never want to work anywhere else. SBSD is a family of tough deputies who often are forced to respond to bar fights and domestic disputes all by themselves, while their friends in Los Angeles respond to similar calls for service with easily up to four two-man cars. SBSD deputies have earned their unpublished motto, *"One riot; one deputy."*

Based on real events...

The Early Years

The afternoon sun beat down on the Little League field in Rancho Cucamonga, California, the Inland Empire's jewel city that only a few decades ago was nothing but grapevines and rural living. It had become the epicenter of high-end shopping, dining, and entertainment in San Bernardino County, the largest county in the contiguous United States. At a little over 20,000 square miles, SBC is larger than the nine smallest states or, to put it another way, larger than the four smallest states combined.

A group of boys thirteen and under in white baseball pants, cleats, matching hats, and miscellaneous T-shirts were practicing their grounders and playing catch while their coaches got all the gear set up. A young boy of foreign descent stared at them from behind the chain-link fence.

"Can I play?" asked the young boy with a thick accent.

"Um, we aren't playing, we're practicing," replied Eli Hockney, one of the more gifted players on the Rancho Cucamonga Dodgers 13U ball team.

"Can I practice?"

"Yeah, I don't know. We're a team you have to try out for."

The boy dropped his head and sulked off before Eli stopped him. Looking the boy up and down, he saw that his clothing was tattered, and his sandals were worn nearly through.

"Hey, what's your name?" he asked.

"Avi."

"Where you from?"

"India."

"Indiana?"

"No. India. It's a big country far from here. But I live here now."

"Do you know how to play baseball?"

"I don't know. I have never tried."

Eli's partner, growing impatient, shouted at him, "Hey, Eli! You coming back?"

"Yeah, hang on."

"I have seen many baseball games on television," the boy from India said.

Eli handed him his glove. "Here, try this on. You're right-handed, I hope."

"Does it matter?"

"I guess we'll find out."

Eli ran backward a few paces and tossed Avi the ball. He caught it quite easily. Eli pointed to the other player some distance away and said, "Can you throw the ball to him?"

Avi reached back and threw the baseball like a natural, straight to the other player's glove. Looks were exchanged between Eli and his friends. Avi had some skill.

They threw back and forth a few times before Eli saw a marked San Bernardino County Sheriff's Patrol Unit pull into the parking lot. His dad, Deputy Ernest "Ernie" Hockney, had come by during his swing shift to see his son's practice.

"Hey, Avi, go over with Steven and keep playing catch. I'll be right back."

Eli ran to the driver's door to chat it up with his pop.

"Hey, son. How's practice?"

"We're just getting started, but it's good."

"School?"

"Yeah, fine, Dad. It's school."

"Who's that?"

"I dunno really. He just showed up. Said he's never played before, but he can throw pretty good." Eli continued, "I think he's poor, though. Said he just moved here from India. Asked to play, but doesn't know how. I mean, look at him. He's in shorts and sandals. I don't think he can make *our* team."

"Well, don't be so sure. Looks like he's got a decent arm. Can he hit?"

"I have no idea. He seriously just walked up like five minutes ago."

"Listen, son, we've talked about this kind of thing before. Just because someone doesn't have money doesn't mean they don't have talent or value. I know plenty of stupid rich people, while some of the best and smartest people I've ever met can barely pay for groceries. Money isn't everything."

"Yeah, I know." Eli took a moment to ponder his father's words. "Hey, so, if he does want to play, and Coach lets him, I doubt he has a glove or other stuff. Can I give him my practice glove?"

"Wow, boy, I'm proud of you for thinking that way. Son, if he wants to play and can make the team, give him your better glove, and I'll get you a brand-new one this weekend."

"Seriously?"

"Yeah. Listen, we do all right. Not rich, but we're far better off than most people on the planet. Besides, I'm hearing the overtime in homicide is crazy."

"Oh, that's right, you start Monday, don't you?" Eli grinned. "Do I have to call you detective now?"

"Detective, sir! If you know what's good for you."

"Yeah, sure, like *that's* gonna happen."

The father and son laughed a moment together, until they were interrupted by the bark of the unit radio. "11-Paul-4?"

Deputy Hockney grabbed his microphone. "Paul-4."

Dispatch replied, "11-Paul-4, a four-ninety-point-five at Walmart. Security has two juvies in custody for shoplifting video games."

Deputy Hockney gave his son the fatherly look that Eli knew all too well to say, *See why I'm on you all the time about stuff*, then he replied into his radio mic, "10-4, en route from Rutherford Park."

"Better not be any of your friends," Deputy Hockney said to his son.

"Yeah, better not be, but my friends are all right here on the field."

"All right, I've got to go. Be good for your mom and don't hassle her about a shower and your homework."

"I won't, I won't. Go to work and put away some criminals, will ya?"

With that, Eli backed away from the patrol unit, and his father put it in Drive to pull away, but not before he called, "Love you, boy!"

"Love you, Dad!" Eli replied as he ran back to the field to rejoin his friends and coaches.

Deputy Hockney pulled out of the parking lot and turned onto the street parallel to the ball field and gave a couple of toots of the siren to the great pleasure of the young baseball players and their coaches alike.

When Eli reached the group, they were on one knee listening to their team meeting before practice. Coach Larry liked to speak to the kids about sportsmanship, leadership, and teamwork before each practice, even if for just a couple of seconds to get everyone thinking on the same page and to reiterate his motto: *Take care of each other, take care of yourselves.*

Sometimes, team meetings were like nice Sunday school sermons. Other times, they were disciplinary reminders of how teams who don't support each other are doomed for failure. When one of those speeches started off the meeting, the kids knew they were in for some serious sweating. Thankfully, this day's speech wasn't starting off with a forecast of wind sprints. Instead, it started with an introduction.

"Boys, this young man here is Avi. He's from a country called India. Does anyone know where that is?" Coach Larry asked.

The players blinked and stared, openmouthed, no one responding.

"Wow, okay, I guess we don't teach geography anymore in school. So, listen, can anyone tell me what sport is super popular in India?"

Coach Larry waited briefly for an answer, and some of the players shouted, "Baseball!"

"Nope. Soccer. But there, they call it football. Avi tells me he's played ever since he can remember, just like many of you have with baseball.

Soccer players"—Larry looked at Avi—"football players can usually out-run most other folks. How's your speed?"

"Good," Avi replied sheepishly.

"Well, let's warm up with a footrace, shall we?" Noticing that Avi wasn't wearing sports shoes, Coach Larry backtracked. "Oh, we'll have to put that off for today..."

"No, it's okay." Avi stood and kicked off his sandals. "We only wear sports shoes in games. We practice without."

The kids all looked at each other and snickered.

"Hey!" A firm word and a glare from the coach quieted the players who might have thought to be rude. "All right, then. Up and on your feet. Shoulder to shoulder right here at second base. When I say go, you will all sprint toward center field, hit the fence, turn around, and sprint back."

The boys lined up shoulder to shoulder, with Eli and Avi in the center of the line, splitting the group equally. Eli was one of the captains of the team, his athletic ability unquestionable. Coach Larry raised his hand and shouted for the boys to sprint off.

Immediately, Eli, Avi, and two others led the pack of boys sprinting with all their might toward the center field fence two hundred feet in the distance.

The sound of deep exhales and pounding feet was the only thing heard as the boys rushed toward the fence. Eli and Avi were in the lead. They hit the fence at the same time, but in the turnaround on the warning track, Avi's feet slipped on the sandier dirt, whereas Eli's cleats allowed him to keep his feet underneath him and take a lead of a few yards before Avi regained his balance and got himself back up to speed.

The distance between Eli and Avi for half the distance back to second base had been a respectable fifteen feet, but with the end goal in sight, Avi poured on the speed and passed Eli, who hadn't slowed one bit. They crossed second base and their coach with Avi leading the end of the race by ten feet.

Coach Larry smiled. Rarely, if ever, had anyone beaten Eli in a footrace, and certainly never by someone not wearing shoes. Eli too was impressed.

Avi reached out to shake hands with Eli to congratulate him on a well-run race. Puzzled by the adult gesture, Eli held his hand out, then shook Avi's. Then he put his hand up for a high-five and induced a great clapping smack from his new friend.

Eli and Avi walked back to the dugout together, where Eli had his gear bag. He reached in and pulled out an older black Wilson baseball glove. He held it in his right hand and then handed Avi the newer Rawlings two-tone brown glove. It was one season old, in good but not new condition.

Eli only had to make it a few more days and then he and his father would go to Dick's Sporting Goods, where he'd be able to get a new glove and spend a glorious weekend working in the new leather. His father would have the whole weekend off, wouldn't have to sleep late to make his shift, and they could get in some serious catch. Eli's father loved to hit baseballs to him on an empty infield. Come next practice Monday afternoon, his glove would be good and worked in and ready for whatever the coaches could throw at him.

***

"Finally!"

"Are you done with your geometry?" Eli's mother asked while she was finishing up the dishes.

"Yeah, but I've still got that stupid essay."

"What's stupid about it?"

"I have to do it," Eli replied with gloom.

His homework depression was interrupted by his baby sister's gleeful shouts. "Daddy, Daddy!" She stood on the living room couch looking through the window with a view to the street in front of their home.

A couple of marked sheriff's units were parked in front of the house, followed by a few dark unmarked SUVs, unmistakably driven by the command staff. Moments later, uniformed and suited men rang the doorbell.

Mrs. Hockney walked to the front door, wiping her hands dry with the dish towel. Opening it, she found her husband's captain, the deputy chief of patrol operations, and the station watch commander standing there, all looking solemn. An unfamiliar, kind-looking man also stood with the men. The brass crucifix on his lapel caught her eye. She didn't know him, but she knew only too well what his special insignia represented. He was a member of the chaplain corps, and that could mean only one thing.

Without a word being spoken, Linda Hockney began shaking, and her eyes welled with tears. Captain McKenzie opened his mouth to speak, but no words came out. His eyes were red and dripping with tears. He cleared his throat and opened his mouth once more. "Linda...I'm sorry."

"Tom?" Linda looked to the more familiar Sergeant Thomas Miller.

Miller's eyes too were red and filled with tears. He held out his arms and took one step forward. Linda fell into his arms in the embrace of a friend.

Eli didn't fully understand what was happening, but he knew enough to realize that something terrible had happened. Never had he ever imagined that when he said goodbye to his father a few hours earlier that he wouldn't be coming back home ever again. There would be no more catch. There would be no more unofficial rides in the police car. There would be no more loving embrace from his father who'd supported him, mentored him, and pushed him to be the best that he could be.

***

The movers had everything loaded and now pulled down the rear door of the truck. Linda stood on the driveway with some neighbors, tearfully hugging and saying their goodbyes. A Century 21 sign with the words SOLD emblazoned in red and white was implanted in the grass behind them.

Eli and his baby sister, Emily, came out of their home one last time. He carried a cardboard box on top of which was his black practice glove, while his sister dragged a stuffed toy lion. Eli put his box into the rear of the minivan and then helped Sissy into her car seat and buckled her in. Eli climbed up into the front passenger seat, having been promoted to the shotgun position against his will.

After a short drive across town, the Hockneys met up with the movers at the tiny apartment complex on the south side of the city. The narrow driveway led to a carport-only parking area. The gray stucco, cookie-cutter apartment complex was triple stacked, with each floor having multiple apartments. Everyone was either below or above someone else. Stone stairs, the shin killers, as they would come to be known, ascended with two turns for each floor, making the trek to the second floor a miserable hike, especially with a BMX bike in tow.

The apartments, although not fully ghetto, were for lower-income families. Graffiti decorated the dumpsters, not every light functioned, litter removal didn't seem to have the highest priority, and yard maintenance was a lower priority still. A small strip of grass in between the parking curbs ran the length of the parking lot.

Stepping out of the minivan, Eli unlocked his sister's car seat and let her out. She was blissfully unaware of what was really happening. She grabbed her stuffed lion, named Oscar, and followed her mom upstairs behind the movers, who had the first pieces of furniture in their arms.

Eli went to the back of the van and opened the rear door. He took out his baseball glove and a ball. He firmly pulled his Dodgers hat down on his head and then walked out to the grass strip. He tossed the ball high into the afternoon sky. The sun was still high and nearly blinded him as he tried to catch the ball. He could hear the sounds of the game in his head.

All Grown Up

The sun was shining so brightly, he wasn't sure he'd catch the ball. Eli put his glove between the sun and his face, blocking the light from blinding him until the last moment, when the ball finally fell from the sky and landed in his glove, making the final out of the inning.

At twenty-eight, Eli had grown into a serious athlete after years of playing baseball for both his state-championship-winning high school and two years on scholarship at college before tearing the labrum in his shoulder, which permanently ended his baseball career. As painful as the injury, surgeries, and recoveries were, and as disappointing as it was that his professional baseball career had come to an end before it got started, Eli answered the call he felt deep in his soul. He was now Deputy Sheriff Elijah Hockney of the San Bernardino County Sheriff's Department.

Cheers erupted from his teammates, also fellow deputies in this men's league baseball tournament. They were in serious competition with the San Bernardino County Fire Department, who had the deputies down by one score going into the final inning.

"All right, boys, let's tie it up right here!" Eli exclaimed with confidence that it could and would be done. "Bobby, you're up, right?"

Although no money rode on this game, no state championships, and no scholarships, the competition was intense.

Eli didn't like to lose—at anything. After two outs were racked up by his teammates, one on a pop-up to right field and the second a ground out to short, it was his team's last chance to get something going. Avi got ready to take the plate. He and Eli had grown up best friends and were patrol shift partners.

Avi started toward the plate when Eli stopped him. "Hey, wait. Avi, come here really quick."

"I know, I know, swing for the fences."

"No, actually. Bunt."

"What, with two outs? Are you nuts?"

"Dude, no one bunts better than you. They won't be expecting it, and with your speed, you're sure to get on."

"Are you sure?"

Eli pushed Avi toward the plate. "Absolutely. You got this, bro."

"Okay, but just single me home. Don't try to hero this thing."

Avi took the first pitch as part of the sneak-bunt plan. Thankfully, it was clearly way off the plate and called a ball. The pitcher was a little slower in this last inning, making it the perfect scenario for Avi to lay down a flawless bunt toward third base. He squared up and tapped a little dribbler to his left, right down the third base line.

Caught off guard, the fire department's third baseman had a long run to try to scoop up the ball. He got to it in time to make a throw to first base, but it was going to be close. Seeing Avi's speed in full force, the third baseman rushed the throw, and it flew wildly past the first baseman, allowing Avi to make it into second base standing.

It was up to Eli to just lay down a single anywhere, and Avi could score. Sensing the fatigue in the arm of the firefighter who had now pitched seven innings, Eli was confident that if he got the pitch he wanted, he could end this game with one swing. He had batted cleanup most of his baseball career, from Little League to high school and college.

And these were just firefighters, for God's sake, not the Yankees. This at-bat would finally put to rest the debate over who was the better team. The fire guys had only won last year on an error by a rookie baller on the sheriff's side. Therefore, in Eli's opinion, they hadn't actually beaten the deputies. It was time to shut them up with one swing.

The first pitch came in low and outside. Eli didn't bite. He smiled to himself and thought that if the next pitch came in a little more over the plate, he could take the ball the other way for an easy homer. This wasn't a professional field. The near fences at this park were only roughly 300 feet.

"Put some grass stains on the ball, Eli!" shouted Avi in support.

The next pitch came in a little high, and Eli got lucky by fouling off the pitch behind him. Had he popped it up, the game would have been over. But he was still alive with a one and one count. Luck was on his side one more time with the next pitch.

The pitching firefighter probably should have been taken out a few batters ago, but he wasn't. He intended to throw a fast ball to the inside, but instead, the ball floated over home plate and looked like a cantaloupe to Eli. He swung his bat in near perfect form and struck the ball solid. It was a moonshot, causing the center fielder to sprint for the fence. Jumping up higher than seemed humanly possible, the center-fielder snagged the ball as it cleared the fence, robbing Eli of a walk-off homer and ending the game in favor of the fire department.

Avi had made the turn around third and was almost home when he saw his team drop their heads when the third out was made. Jogging toward second base, Eli was shocked to see the ball caught and that he was the third out. Game over.

"So there you have it, boys," exclaimed a firefighter. "We have better schedules, better pay, love and respect from the public, and we get the ladies too. Wow, it must suck to be a deputy."

"Screw you, Jeff," teased back one of the deputies. The back-and-forth continued for a bit, players from both sides getting themselves even more fired up. But cooler heads prevailed, and Eli was able to shuttle his guys back into the dugout to pack up and leave.

Avi held his comments until he and Eli were back at the station in the locker room. Coming out of the shower wrapped in a towel, Eli made his way to his locker. Avi was ahead of him, having already donned his tan-and-green uniform.

"Hey, sorry about the fly out. I really thought it was going to go yard," Eli said.

"Yeah, I don't care about the game," Avi replied with his head down, focused on weaving his ear and mic cord through his uniform shirt before connecting it to his radio.

"Then what? I can tell you're pissed at me."

"No Eli, I'm not pissed..."

"Come on, then, what? Smalls, you're killing me!" Eli was hoping the quote from *The Sandlot* would crack a smile across his friend's face.

"Are you sure you're okay?" Avi asked with a concerned look. He knew it was coming up on the fifteenth anniversary of Eli's father's murder. The on-duty killing had never been solved. The elder Deputy Hockney had pulled over what turned out to be an unreported stolen car driven by an unknown suspect who was determined not to go to jail, or back to prison. The moment the deputy walked up to the door, the suspect shot him in the head and simply drove away. No chase, no helicopters, no manhunt. Because the traffic stop occurred on a neighborhood street, it was a couple of minutes before anyone drove up to discover the officer down. He hadn't even been on the stop long enough without radio contact for dispatch to have any concerns or request a status check.

Without a description of the gender, race, or any other identifying characteristics, the homicide team had zero suspect leads. No one was talking. Not one peep out of any neighborhood. The stolen car was found abandoned a few blocks away, but forensics wasn't able to locate any fingerprints that didn't belong to the household from which it was stolen.

"Yeah, I'm fine," Eli replied with a hint of annoyance. "I just got under the ball a little."

"You know that's not what I mean. Listen, I don't care about the game. But I am a little worried about you."

"Why?"

"Look at you," he replied.

Eli Hockney's physique was that of an underwear model. He spent most of his off-duty time in the gym, training in martial arts, and entering into CrossFit games. Most men would be jealous of his physique and aspire to reach that level of physical fitness. But Avi wasn't jealous. He was also in good shape. He knew there was more to it than simple healthy living.

"What's wrong with the way I look?"

"Nothing. You're perfect. That's what concerns me."

"Dude, you are seriously losing it right now."

Eli had gotten his underwear, socks, and uniform pants on and was lacing up his boots, but remained shirtless while Avi continued. "Look, you're in spectacular physical shape, and that's a good thing."

"So?"

"You put together a county-wide emergency services men's baseball league, something that's never been tried before, and it's successful. Hugely successful."

"And?"

"You got deputy of the year last year, you're number one out of the station for promotion to detective..."

"Yeah, so what's wrong with hard work and success?"

"Nothing. Never mind. Forget I said anything. Get dressed and let's go to briefing."

"Hang on," Eli called to Avi, who was about to walk away. "What's your point?"

"Nothing. I'm just tired from the game."

"Bullshit! Spill it."

Avi kept his head buried in his locker for a few moments then took a deep breath and blew it out quickly through pursed lips. "I worry that it will never be enough for you. Nothing ever is. You have to have the best of everything that you can afford, or not afford. You have to be the best at everything, or otherwise you think you're a failure."

"What the—" Eli stammered for the right comeback.

"You know I love you like a brother, always have, so I'm going to say this one time." Avi took a careful cleansing breath before continuing, "He is already proud of you."

"Don't go there, Avi," Eli replied tersely while shoving his arms through his T-shirt and yanking it over his head. "That's not why—"

"It's not? Now I'm calling bullshit. You don't think for one second we all don't know you live under your father's shadow? You don't think we all see that you crawled there all by yourself? No one pushed you there. Not your mom, not me, not the sheriff. Stop trying to make sure what happened to your father isn't going to happen to you. Because it's not."

Eli was stunned. No one had ever held a psychological mirror to his face before.

"We've got your back," Avi continued softly, "and all you have to do is relax just a little and let yourself enjoy life every once in a while. Either that or your head is going to fucking explode."

"What makes you think I'm not enjoying life?" Eli scoffed as he threw his bulletproof vest over his head and stretched over the Velcro straps snugly.

"When was the last time you had a girlfriend?"

"Dude, you know I get plenty of action."

"That's sex. When was the last time you've had a real relationship with a nice girl?"

"Seriously, Avi, this has got to be the worst conversation you and I have ever had. You really don't know what the fuck you're talking about. Let me finish putting on the monkey suit, and I'll see you in briefing."

When he was fully uniformed, Eli walked out of the empty locker room to head toward briefing. But before he got there, he heard his name being called.

"Hockney, get in here," Sergeant Fred Williams ordered.

Eli stopped in his tracks for a moment. Having heard the tone and seeing the sergeant's face, he feared something he'd done in the past few days or even a week ago had come back to bite him in the ass. He couldn't think of anything that had gone too awry. His sarcasm and attempts at being pithy had often gotten him in hot water with citizens who complained about his tone and lack of tact.

"What's up, Sarge? Whoa!" Eli was surprised that the station commander, Captain Ron Whitaker, and Lieutenant Horace Beemer were also in the watch commander's office with Sergeant Williams. They all had stern looks about them. Their arms were crossed, and whatever was being said was immediately hushed upon Eli's entrance, which unnerved him.

What had he done so wrong that it conjured up the entire station command staff in one small room? Just how badly had he screwed up?

"Want to explain yourself?" Captain Whitaker asked.

"Um..."

"I hear there was some sort of kerfuffle at the ballpark earlier today," Lieutenant Beemer added.

"Well, we lost the game, and sure there was some trash talking, but nobody threw any blows. I don't understand. What—"

"We'll ask the questions, Deputy Hockney. And whether you remain Deputy Hockney is a question for another day at this point," Captain Whitaker said, sucking all the air out of the room.

"Sir, I don't..." Eli stammered, sweat forming on his forehead.

Then a booming voice came over the telephone speaker. "Aw, come on, guys. That's enough."

Everyone but Eli started laughing, clearly pleased that they'd sweated the young deputy. It took Eli a moment to recognize the voice he just heard. "Holy shit, is that the sheriff?"

"Yeah, son, it's Miller. Hey, Ron, you guys are mean! If you're ever lucky enough to be up for another promotion, I'll remember what you did here today to one of our finer deputies."

"Well, that makes me safe from retribution, boss. I think you and I have reached our highest rank on this department," Whitaker joked.

"So, hey, Eli, I don't know if you know I was one of your dad's sergeants back in the day," Sheriff Miller continued.

"I remember, sir. I've never forgotten when you came to the house that night."

"Neither will I."

The room's mood changed dramatically. The captain, lieutenant, and sergeant had been younger deputies or just coming on the department when Deputy Ernest Hockney was killed, and none of them had known him or worked with him.

"Are you calling because we're coming up on the fifteenth, sir?" Eli politely asked the sheriff.

"Wow, is it fifteen years already? No, Eli, that's not why I'm calling you, or letting these knuckleheads mess with you. I'm calling to promote you to the rank of detective, effective Saturday the eighth at midnight sharp. How does that sound?"

Cheering erupted from fellow deputies who had gathered secretly behind Eli in the hallway. They'd been prompted to quietly listen in by the watch commander, who had slipped out to bring in the crew.

"That's awesome, sir, thank you!" Eli said, smiling from ear to ear. When the noise quieted down, he asked, "Where am I going, sir?"

"Well, you see, here's the thing, Eli," the sheriff said. "I was going to leave you at your current station since you're doing so well there." The wind went out of everyone's sails, until the sheriff continued. "But then I realized that we had a hole to fill in another division that I think could use your skill set. How does Homicide sound to you?"

The room erupted once more. Everyone knew it was Eli's professional goal to make it to the San Bernardino County Sheriff's Homicide Detail. Speechless, Eli choked back tears.

"That...that sounds great, Sheriff." He cleared his throat. "Thank you."

Seeing the emotion that overcame Detective-select Eli Hockney, the captain picked up the phone handset and passed it to Eli to allow him to talk with the sheriff. There wasn't a dry eye as the captain waved everyone out of the office and closed the door.

The Browers

An easy sea breeze blew cool air across the lawn of the Brower residence on a late evening in June in the Brentwood Hills of Los Angeles, California. These temperatures might have seemed cold to a Southern Californian, but it was laughably warm to a Minnesotan.

Bill Brower sat in his home office wearing a USC Trojans T-shirt and black shorts, clicking away at his desktop computer. Classic rock music softly filled the well-appointed and custom-decorated room. Bill muttered to himself, calling out numbers as he read from his clients' paperwork before entering them into the tax program that he used to prepare his clients for the coming tax season.

His wife, Abby, dressed in a long satin nightshirt, sat at the dinette set in the kitchen, creating personalized spring and Easter cards with her highly organized and abundant craft-stamp collection.

Teddy, their snow-white Maltese who was the Browers' only child, sat comfortably on Abby's lap while she worked diligently personalizing cards for friends and family in the perfect fashion that Abby was known for. She never missed anyone's birthday, special event, holiday, or season.

Her gifts always brought joy to people because they were thoughtful and gorgeously wrapped in perfect form, with custom handmade bows. Her cards and gift presentation were so lovely, most people didn't want to spoil them by opening them.

A certified tax accountant, Bill was quick with numbers and the practical aspects of life. Before meeting Abby, he didn't pay much attention to how he dressed. Jeans and golf shirt had been the extent of his style. Nowadays, however, Bill dressed much more chic-professional. Abby made sure his clothing kept current with the fashions and changed with the seasons. He'd grown accustomed to and really appreciated Abby deciding what he would wear, and even laying out his wardrobe for him for special events.

In their late thirties now, they had grown comfortable in their lives, surrounded by a circle of friends of equal status. They weren't rich by strict definition, but neither they nor their friends had flown coach or driven a used domestic car in a decade.

Having just gotten home from dinner out with friends a short while ago, Abby was surprised by the ringing of the doorbell. Teddy sprang into action, barking and running to the front door, his only real job in his entire spoiled life.

Looking through the side windowpane next to the front door, Abby was surprised but not alarmed by the friend who stood outside on the front porch. She opened the door with a polite smile and let him in.

"Hey there, Abby, sorry it's so late," he said.

"Not to worry. Is everything all right?" Abby asked.

"Yes, it will be. But I really need to speak with you and Bill. He's here, isn't he?"

"In his office."

The two walked together into the study down the hall, where Bill was oblivious to the doorbell, the barking, and the world around him as he studied his client's tax records and receipts.

"Honey, look who's here."

Bill glanced up from his computer and immediately looked horrified. Slightly behind Abby out of her peripheral vision, the man raised a pistol. Abby reacted to Bill's expression by spinning around, only to see the man holding them both at gunpoint.

"What the fuck?" Bill exclaimed.

"It's strictly business."

F.N.G.

Eli's nerves were about to get the best of him. He pulled up to sheriff headquarters in his Mustang at 0745 hours. He was expected at 0800 hours to meet with his new teammates and probably do a bunch of paperwork relative to his new position. The last thing he was going to do was be late. Truth be told, he'd been in the area driving around for the past forty-five minutes. He didn't want to appear too eager, so he waited up the street in a gas station parking lot so as not to draw too much attention to himself sitting in front of sheriff's headquarters an hour early.

Prior to today, he'd only been to headquarters a few times. The first time was when his career was getting started when he met with his background investigator, then later in that same year to submit to a polygraph examination. But the remainder of the tests, medical, physical agility, psychological, and all other appointments, were either at other offices or at the academy several miles away in Devore. The very last time he was at headquarters was with about fifty-five other people of varying ranks and divisions who were all there to receive their new badges and assignments.

The badge ceremony was last week, where he proudly stood before friends and family, shaking the sheriff's hand and being issued the brand-new sheriff's detective badge #212. Eli's mother cried. Eli's sister Emily cried. Eli cried.

Emily was no longer a Hockney, having married Sebastian Falcone, a young musician who had every intention of writing music to be heard by the masses, but in the meantime was working at Best Buy to pay the bills. Thus, Emily Falcone it was. Sebastian's long hair and braided beard made him a standout in the crowd of the conservative law enforcement families. Regardless of whether he developed a real musical career into livable earnings, he treated Emily like a princess, doting on her and making sure she knew she was loved. For that alone, he earned Eli's respect and friendship.

At 7:53 a.m., Eli got out of his car and walked up to the front doors, only to find them locked. Oh, no, now what? Being late on the first day was not the impression he wanted to make. If no one opened the doors before 8:00 a.m., then by the time he got inside and made his way to the homicide detail, he would already be late. Not good. Just then, he heard a muffled voice come through the speaker.

"ID?"

Eli thought a moment, then realized all he had to do was take out his shiny new flat badge and show it to the camera and be let in. It was at that moment he realized he wasn't in uniform anymore and that he might have to "flash his badge" on occasion. He was a real detective now. Wearing a new black wool/poly-blend suit over a white dress shirt and a striped blue tie, Eli looked professional and classy, neither overdressed nor a *GQ* poser. He reached into his right rear pants pocket and took out his badge wallet and opened it to show the ID card to the camera, after which he heard a distinct buzz, his cue to grab the door and pull it open.

He was inside the main lobby, which wasn't yet open to the public. Frosted glass doors and solid-core doors to various parts of the facility surrounded him, some labeled and some not. This was, after all, sheriff's headquarters and generally a secure building. Labeling each door or putting up signs with arrows indicating where certain divisions were located wasn't a safe or smart thing to do. Once beyond the lobby, anyone without a badge and ID would need to be escorted by someone who had one. There was, however, the front counter, where a receptionist or two would sit through shifts during office hours when the building was open. Just as Eli was wondering what he might do next, a young woman walked into the reception window from somewhere inside the back of the building with a thermos in one hand and a pile of papers underneath her arm and a bagel held between her teeth.

"Hi, can you point me toward homicide?" Eli asked. He still had his badge wallet in his hand.

Half dropping her armload of stuff and ripping the bagel from her mouth, leaving the bite inside, she replied while chewing, "Sorry, kids running me late this morning. Didn't get breakfast. I'll pop you through."

Eli stood motionless for a moment. He didn't hear a buzz, click, or anything that indicated which door was the one he was supposed to walk through.

"Oh yeah, that one," the woman replied. She pointed with her coffee thermos that she then took a swig from to a door to Eli's left. It was an unlabeled, nondescript door that, when he pulled on it, opened. Next to it was a black magna-card reader for which he'd eventually get issued a cardkey.

Once he passed through the door into the inner sanctum, he was a bit awestruck that in the center of the building complex was a huge four-sided glass wall structure that led to an outdoor area that was inside the building. A hallway traveled the perimeter of the four walls. If one walked counterclockwise, the glass walls were to one's left and doors leading to various divisions and offices were on the right. Halfway down on each of the four sides was a glass door leading into the outside atrium where employees could sit, smoke if they did, enjoy some sunshine, and be outside within a secure facility.

The atrium had perfectly manicured grass and shrubs, two pairs of matching wooden benches on opposite ends, and solemnly on one side of the atrium stood a large polished black stone memorial for all of the department's fallen officers. Fortunately, yet uncharacteristically for a department this old and this busy, there were only a few badges permanently retired into the stone. It was a testament to the training and departmental philosophy that more officers weren't killed in the line of duty.

The hallway was a stark contrast to the lobby, where Eli had been the sole person. Here in the hallway, it buzzed with people coming in to work, heading in and out of various doors. He was nearly blocking the way when a jacketless detective tried to get by without bumping into him.

"Excuse me. Can you tell me where homicide is?" Eli asked.

"Specialized. Down that hallway and make a right at the end. Doors are marked." The detective continued on his way, having only turned around and walked backward while not quite shouting the directions as he moved. The energy in this hallway alone was already invigorating. Eli's stomach jumped a bit with excitement. Was he really here? Was he really a homicide detective? He took it in for one more moment, then spotted a digital clock at the end of the hall which read 7:59.

His pace quickened as he made the right turn and saw the sign labeled on the glass that read "Specialized Investigations Division" and listed units of homicide, arson-bomb, hi-tech, polygraph, and the sadly necessary crimes against children division. Having arrived, Eli straightened his tie, dried off his sweaty palms by wiping them down the sides of his trousers, then took a deep, cleansing breath and walked in, hoping no one would notice just how nervous he was. He couldn't imagine this being any more nerve-racking than if he'd made it to the big leagues and walked onto the field in Dodger Stadium.

"Hello. I mean good morning, my name is..." The phone was already ringing when Eli tried to introduce himself.

Cheryl Higgins, the receptionist, answered the phone sweetly. "Specialized Investigations, how may I direct your call?" Eli looked at the woman behind the desk, who smiled back at him with her finger in the air, indicating the call wouldn't take long. "Let me transfer you to records, honey. That's where you need to be." She hung up the phone and, while putting on her headset for the first time this morning, finally addressed him.

"I'm sorry, what was it that you needed?"

"Oh, well, I'm Eli Hockney. Detective Hockney, I guess. I'm new here."

"Oh, the FNG, yeah sure. I forgot you were starting today. Do you know where you're going?"

"Nope. Not one bit. FNG?"

"Not to worry, son, you're on John's team. When he's done with you, come on back. I've got some files I need to start on you."

"John?"

"Sgt. Kesling, but I haven't called him that except for once when he got promoted, just to let him know I was proud of him. Known him since he was running around here in diapers. He's down the hall on the right. Go on through here."

A distinct buzzing unlocked the door that led directly into the homicide detail. The room was electric. People were already sitting at their desks working their phones, others coming in, slinging their coats onto their chairs and grabbing their coffee mugs and heading to the filling station, others more relaxed.

As Eli walked past one set of detectives, he thought they looked different somehow, and it took him a moment, then he figured it out. They were tired. Their tie knots were down, the top buttons of their dress shirts were undone, their sleeves were rolled up, their faces hadn't been shaved in a day or two, and their hair was less than perfect. He imagined if he got closer, they probably wouldn't have smelled too good either.

He'd seen that look before from homicide detectives when he was on patrol and was assigned to relieve a crime scene security post on the third- or fourth-shift rotation. The homicide guys had been on the scene the entire time without any relief multiple days in a row. This wasn't television. Crimes didn't get solved in forty-four minutes plus commercials. They took time. That much he knew. He'd seen it. He'd been told about it from patrol sergeants and other members of the brass for whom he'd worked. He'd heard it from his father.

Once Eli learned that one of his bosses had formerly been a homicide detective, he'd bugged the shit out of him for any advice, insight, or scrap of information that would better his chances of earning one of only sixteen coveted positions that existed at any one time in sheriff's homicide.

They were known for being the best of the best. Sometimes arrogant, and prima donnas for sure, but also the hardest-working, most exhausted cops in the department. Eli was now one of them. Or soon would be. He hadn't even met his team yet. Would he be good enough? Yes, he most certainly would. He was a Hockney, the second in a line of deputies selected for this detail. He would complete what his father wasn't given the chance to do.

As Eli approached the office marked with "Sergeant John Kesling" carved in white letters onto a graphite background affixed to the open officer door, he saw his new boss who appeared tense while scanningas he scanned his computer screen and clickeding away at whatever he was working on. Easily fifty years old, Eli guessed by the salt-and-pepper hair, he nevertheless looked to be in good shape with a slender build, not currently athletic, but probably once he'd been a decent scrapper. Dressed professionally in a crisp white shirt and solid navy blue necktie, confidence exuded from him. "Oh, this is fucking bullshit!" Kesling exclaimed without looking up from his computer.

Eli stopped in his tracks as an older man with wild white hair crossed in front of Eli's path and lumbered into Kesling's office. Short and pudgy, wearing a red and blue checker-patterned, short-sleeved dress shirt with a clashing blue and green stripped tie over black pants, the detective looked as if he dressed in the dark. Obviously, he lacked any sense of style, or he just simply didn't seem to care.

"They jacked up the price of the fishing trip this year by like twenty-five percent. What a fucking rip-off!"

Eli stood silently at the office doorway while the detective plopped down in one of the two chairs across from Kesling's desk. "So how much more is this trip going to cost?"

"Seventy-five dollars. Can you believe that?" Kesling leaned back in his chair and threw his hands up.

"Are you kidding me?"

"No! Ridiculous, right?" Kesling swatted the computer mouse away from his hand.

"Seventy-five dollars is nothing. Would you relax, John? With all the overtime we get in this place, that's not even two hours, you fucking cheapskate."

"Okay, let's stop arguing in front of the children," John said with a nod to Eli, who had been standing there taking it all in. "You coming in or just going to stand there?"

"Oh hey, yeah, I'm Eli Hockney," Eli said as he walked in and shook his sergeant's hand.

"I honestly forgot you were coming in this morning. Glad to have you. We've been down a guy for a few months now, so it'll be nice to get back up to full speed. This is Artie Williams, one of your partners," Kesling said with a grin.

"Hey," was all that Artie offered from the chair he was seated in.

"Eli Hockney," Eli replied with an outstretched hand.

Before they could shake hands or another word could be said, Detective Nate Parker, a tall, medium build man with the beginnings of a dad-bod, bounded in with his mobile phone stuck to his face.

"Hey, John," Nate nearly shouted in his quick-paced, excited tone, "Ruth is able to score a serious deal on a trip to Hawaii for my birthday in April. Mind if I take two weeks over the thirteenth?"

"Bring me back a tiki doll," Kesling replied to Nate, then he pointed to Eli to take a seat in the other chair across from his desk.

"Hear that, Ruth? Book it, baby," Nate gushed into the phone, "I love you too. Gotta go!" With that, Nate slipped his mobile phone into his pocket, then extended a hand to Eli. "Hey, buddy, long time no see, huh?"

"You two know each other?" Kesling asked.

"Academy. One-hundredth session," Nate responded. "Eli here wasn't even twenty-one years old when he started. He got his first legal beer during the academy at that dirty little pub up in Devore."

"After hours, of course," Eli interjected as if it weren't obvious. He wanted to make sure it was known he didn't drink on duty.

"Yeah well, of course," Nate joked. "But we haven't ever worked together. You went to the desert, right?"

"Yeah, and you were at...Big Bear?"

"Twin Peaks, actually," Nate corrected.

"Hey, so your birthday is in April? What date?" Eli asked.

"Thirteenth. I'll be thirty-nine," Nate responded with a hint of pride that he was still not forty years old.

"Cool, ten years and ten days," Eli offered. The room went silent as they processed this bit of information.

"Wait, you're only twenty-eight right now?" Artie asked incredulously.

"Yeah."

"Oh, for fuck's sake!" Artie jumped up out of his chair and walked out of Kesling's office. Eli looked back to see Artie grab his coat off his chair, and storm out of the bureau.

"What just happened?" Eli asked with total confusion.

"You're young," Kesling replied.

"Seriously?"

"Yeah," Nate said. "Took him decades to get into the detail."

Eli pondered that for a moment, unsure what to say or do next.

"Bad enough the FNG is young, he's tall too," Kesling added.

"FNG?" Eli asked.

"Fucking New Guy," Nate clarified. "Come on, let me show you around. You okay with that, Sarge?"

"Go. Just bring him by Cheryl's desk before too long so she doesn't chew my ass out."

Something's Not Right

Parked on the driveway of the Browers' residence was a Mercedes SUV occupied by a well-dressed couple, Elaine and Richard McAllister. They got out and walked around the front of the house and peered in the windows on the garage, the front windows, and doors.

"I think we should just use the key. That's what it's for," Elaine said in a hushed voice.

"It's for emergencies," Richard answered back.

"This *is* an emergency! I have never not heard from Bill or Abby for over twenty-four hours, let alone three days. Has Bill ever not returned your phone call in the same day?"

"No, unless he's playing golf."

"Seriously, you think he's been playing golf for three days straight?"

"Okay, okay, use the key. But if we hear from them later today that they've taken a quick trip to Las Vegas, I'm saying it was you who snooped around in their house."

"Fine. I hope I'm wrong."

Elaine used a key she had in her purse to unlock the front door. She walked into the foyer with her husband right on her heels. She called out, "Abby, hon! You here?"

Richard joined in. "Bill! Hey, yo, Bill! You guys home?"

"Where is Teddy?" Elaine asked.

"Well, I'm sure they wouldn't leave him behind, honey. They surely took him with them or kenneled him. They love that little fur ball like he's their child. So far, I'm not seeing anything suspicious. Let's go. This is weird, and I feel really stupid."

"Hang on. Okay, Richard, this *is* totally weird," Elaine said while pointing to the teacup and saucer on the kitchen dinette table. "You know how Abby is."

Elaine pressed the voice mail button on the speaker phone of the base station in the kitchen. The computerized voice told them there were twelve missed calls with five messages. The messages were all from their closest friends asking for Bill or Abby to call them back, worried about missing scheduled meetings for breakfasts and lunches, friends stating they were getting worried. Then one message made their blood turn cold. They heard a recorded voice say, *"Hi there, my name is Jim, Jim Stallworth. I found Teddy out here in Yucaipa by the regional park. I thought, well, seeing how nicely groomed he is and all, I thought you might want to know I found him. But I'm sad to say he isn't alive. I'm leaving him here for now, but I can come back and get him and bring him to my home or something for you to meet me...in case you want to...come get him. So, well, um, my phone number is..."*

The McAllisters were stunned to hear the message.

Rollin' Out Hot

Taking a nap on a good-weather Saturday may have seemed like a waste of a good day, but everyone Eli had met thus far told him to sleep whenever he could when "up" or "first call." The on-call system at Sheriff's Homicide was quite simple, really. There were four homicide teams, each made up of three detectives and their sergeant. There are four weeks per month, so each team was on-call for one week at a time from first to fourth call. After first call was concluded on Monday morning, that team fell to fourth call, meaning fourth priority to get a call, which was highly unlikely. During fourth- and third-call weeks, the team would work the fresh cases they just picked up during first call. But teams would be ready to go out on second call too. It could get very busy in homicide, especially during the hot summer months when tempers tended to match the thermometer.

The call rotation started Monday morning at 08:00 hours and ended the following Monday morning at 07:59 hours. Every call that came in during that week while that team was "first call" or "up" was that team's responsibility to handle, unless they were already on a fresh murder and couldn't handle a new case. When that happened, the first-call team would reluctantly hand off the new case to the second-call team, who had already been "bumped up to first."

However, as ego, pride, and competition hold true to a group of cops as with any other teams, there are bragging rights regarding how many callouts any one team handled in a week, or a year, as well as their solve rate. But if no fresh murders happened during a first-call week, well then, that team "got skunked." For the public to learn that a week went by in San Bernardino County without a murder would be a good thing. And it was. But to a group of homicide detectives, that meant no new case, nothing new to dig their teeth into, no new exciting stories to tell, no suspects to interrogate and coax a confession from, and lastly, no overtime.

That might have even been the worst part. Homicide detectives can earn a twenty-five to thirty percent bump in pay over their regular salary per year on overtime and expenses. New homicide detectives were always told to save their overtime money, to invest it in their 401k or save it somehow, and specifically *not* to buy a hot new car, boat, or RV. Yet every promotional season, some newly minted sergeants leaving homicide or narcotics were found to soon be selling off boats and motorhomes when they realized that their sergeant's pay was nowhere near what their detective pay was with overtime. Also, spending several years commuting in a department-issued unmarked sedan was a huge cost savings with the free gas and maintenance. Overall, being a homicide detective came with prestige, perks, money, and awesome stories.

"Dude, why are you sleeping on a day like this?" Avi asked incredulously as he entered Eli's rented home. He'd been staying with Eli ever since he got kicked out of his former girlfriend's apartment. It's true what they say about police relationships. If the spouse dated a cop, their marriage might last within normal societal parameters. However, if the spouse married a banker-turned-cop, the marriage was almost certainly doomed for failure. It wasn't what the spouse signed on for when they met. The academy, and the job, changes people.

"Yeah, well, I figured since we didn't get a call all week, we're bound to get one soon," Eli replied through blinking eyes. He got up from the couch to follow Avi into the kitchen, having seen that he was carrying several bags of groceries. "What did we get?"

"Stuff for me to eat."

"Just you? What the—"

"Pay up, bro. You haven't done the shopping for the last three rounds, *and* you haven't paid me for half of those trips."

"Aw, come on, you know I'm a little strapped right now. The promotion cost me money for all these suits and stuff."

"You're pathetic. You know that, right?"

As Eli was responding, he could hear his mobile phone vibrating on the counter near him. "Yeah, pretty much," Eli said as he grabbed his phone and turned the screen to Avi, showing him that the caller was Sgt. Kesling.

While scrambling to grab a pad and pen, Eli answered his phone. "Hey, Sarge."

Avi heard Eli complaining that his first two weeks had started slowly because the team was on third call, and then second call, without having been called out. He'd been sitting around reading older cold cases to get a feel for the process, but nothing teaches like experience. Avi was happy for his buddy that there was actually a fresh case coming in for Eli to get to work on. He couldn't wait to hear what the call would be about.

"Yeah okay, I'll shit, shower, and shave and head out. Thanks, Sarge!" Eli realized that thanking his sergeant was actually the wrong response, but it came from the feeling of excitement that he was finally getting to roll out hot to a fresh case.

"Well, what is it?" Avi asked. He'd stopped putting groceries away when he could tell the conversation was coming to an end. He stared at Eli with a smile on his face.

"Some drunk driver brought a knife to a gunfight with our deputy and lost. Dude is being transported to ARMC."

"Who was the deputy?"

"I dunno."

"Is he or she okay?"

"I dunno."

"Do you even know where you're going?"

"Hospital."

"Why?"

"I dunno."

"Dude, you've gotta get better details next time."

"Yeah." Eli stood there a moment, frozen by the realization that he hadn't ask any questions and was just, well, in shock that this was it. It was happening. He was really going to go out there and investigate as a detective.

"Go!"

"Yeah, right, thanks." With that, Eli bolted off toward his bedroom to get ready.

Missing Persons

There was a Los Angeles County Sheriff's Department black-and-white patrol unit parked on the driveway behind the McAllisters' Mercedes. The deputy stood inside the living room of the Browers' home, where the McAllisters were providing the details for a missing persons report.

"So, tell me again how you know your friends are missing and not just on a trip?" the deputy asked.

Elaine was fully prepared to answer this question because it had been rolling around in her head for days now. "I told you, she would never leave the room, let alone the house, for any period of time, especially a trip, with dirty dishes and projects lying around. You don't know Abby! And besides, don't you think it's strange that their dog is dead in another county so far from here?"

"Well, ma'am, actually, I don't. In my world, none of this strange. There's no accounting for what people do that seems suspicious but yet always has a reasonable explanation."

"But I..."

Before Mrs. McAllister could become indignant and start making the demands that wealthy citizens tended to make, which almost universally started with *"I pay lots of taxes"* or *"I pay your salary,"* the deputy continued. "Even so, ma'am, I've placed an agency request to the San Bernardino County Sheriff's Department to have a unit check with the guy who found..." he searched his notes, "...Teddy just in case. But if they were at the park on the way to Arizona or something and their dog ran away, then that's all there is to it, I'm sure."

Richard brought the conversation to an end by standing up and putting his arm out to shake hands. "Thank you, Deputy. I'm sure that's all it is. We thank you for your time on this."

As the deputy walked to the door to leave he said, "Sure thing, my pleasure. Here's my card with the report number. When they call you or come home, please call me and leave a message so I can take them out of the missing persons system."

"Thanks again. Let's go, Elaine."

"Maybe we should clean up..."

"No," Richard said quickly and firmly. "In fact, don't touch anything. Not one thing."

Back-To-Back

Eli sat at his desk with his sleeves rolled up, tie knot down a notch, and the top shirt button undone. There was never a shortage of paperwork to fill out, especially if you were providing witness protection paperwork to a mother and son who'd witnessed an all-out attack on a deputy who defended himself. These witnesses would never be able to go back to their neighborhood again in fear of fatal retribution.

Nate walked into the office at his usual breakneck speed, maybe slightly slower with fatigue really setting in on the team now.

"Hey, Eli, are they still here?"

"Front waiting room. Why?"

"I just wanted to meet them myself. Helluva job getting these witnesses to speak up. But stay away from Artie. He's pissed!"

"Why, because I was right and he was wrong?"

"No, because you embarrassed him in front of Sarge."

"How'd I do that?"

Nate spoke through laughter. "Artie had just finished telling Kesling that those witnesses in particular were never, ever going to help the police with the truth against a banger from the neighborhood. Then you come down with them all cozy under your arm and get them to roll on the bad guy. Classic."

"Am I supposed to follow his incompetent lead?"

"No, of course not. Great job with the wits."

"How am I supposed to get along with that idiot? Just be more subservient?"

"Well, you can stop using words like subservient around him."

"Should I buy him a dictionary?"

"No, but that's funny," Nate said with a quiet chuckle. "Nicely done, by the way, buddy. You definitely have the gift of gab!"

Nate moved swiftly to grab Eli and turn him away from the rear entrance of the homicide detail that led to the parking lot and walk him toward the waiting room to avoid Artie, who was making his presence known. Space and time were the only things that were going to save Eli from being chewed on by Artie or, more to the point, save Eli from saying something back to Artie that would cause an even bigger rift. Artie had the political backing of someone high up the chain of command; otherwise, he never would have made it to homicide on meritocracy.

Eli and Nate walked into the homicide waiting room where Antonio "Tony" Morales and his mother Rose Hernandez were sitting next to each other in chairs in the quiet evening hours of the closed headquarters building. Tony played on his mobile phone while Rose sat on her hands, lightly rocking back and forth to burn off nervous energy.

"Mrs. Hernandez, this is my partner, Nate. He was busy on another part of the investigation and just got finished."

Rose stood up to greet Nate and shake his hand. "Thank you."

"You're welcome, but I haven't done anything, really. Eli here is the one to thank."

"Yes, we know." Rose looked down at her son, who was still seated. "Stand up, mijo."

Her son wasn't being disrespectful. He was young and in training. Without a husband to be a fatherly role model, Rose had been doing her best to bring him up with gentlemanly manners. Working full-time at the hospital and serving tables part-time at a local diner had barely allowed her the time or money to give Tony the kind of upbringing she wished she could give him. Allowing herself to get pregnant at fifteen years old by a boy who had long since been sent to prison for a life sentence had not put her on an easy path, and it was certainly not something she wanted for her son.

"So, listen, here's the paperwork for the witness protection program. I've already called my friend at the district attorney's office, and he has a scanned copy that he's getting taken care of tomorrow morning. He authorized me the emergency funding to get you through until next week when all the paperwork will be finalized," Eli said, trying not to forget any details of the process.

"I can't thank you enough for all you have done to help us," Rose said with tears welling in her eyes.

"Ma'am, if it weren't for you, we'd have a different story being reported that would have made our innocent deputy look bad. If it weren't for you two telling the truth about what really happened, we'd have real trouble with this investigation. It is we who thank the two of you," Nate said.

"Yeah, he's so right. You guys have done a great service for your community," Eli said as he looked at Tony. "You going to be all right moving and changing schools?"

"I don't like the school I'm going to. I really don't have any friends. It's pretty scary there," Tony said.

"My sister in Arizona promises that we can live with her until things are ready, and that the schools don't have the gang problems like here."

"That's awesome. So here's the paperwork you need," Eli said, handing her the copies. "We've already called for a patrol unit to come get you and bring you to your apartment. Just get your clothing and your important things. Leave everything else. The witness protection program will get you all set up with new essentials when you get settled in Arizona."

Nate and Eli walked the pair through the rear hallway to the back parking lot, where a patrol car was waiting to escort them to their apartment and then to a hotel for the evening. After the back doors closed on the patrol unit, Eli turned to Nate and said, "Wow, I'm really hungry."

"Yeah, me too. The Chinese buffet?"

"Freakin' excellent!"

They headed for their desks to gather up their stuff to head out, but as they get closer to Kesling's office, they could see and hear him on the phone. "Yeah, no problem. We'll be out there in just a little while. My team is still all here at the office."

From inside his office, Kesling yelled out, "Nate! Eli! Don't run off yet. We got another callout."

Eli turned to Nate and asked, "What? Now? Really? We can't be up. We aren't even done with this one yet."

Nate explained, "Well, since this isn't an in-custody case, it's no longer a priority, so yeah, we roll out on as many as we can handle."

Between their position and the sergeant's office was a former storage room that had been turned into a mini store. Inside this little room was a full-size refrigerator on one wall near the door, whereas the rest of the walls were lined with shelves from floor to ceiling. On these shelves was every kind of wonderfully awful sugary snack, popcorn, candy, hot cocoa packets, oatmeal packets, and Cup O' Noodle containers of every flavor and variety known to man, or at least known to Walmart, where the "store sergeant" bought the supplies.

Each shelf had vinyl stickers on the edge listing the prices of each item. The profit from "The Store" paid for all holiday food for the Thanksgiving and Christmas division parties, plus all the new birth and bereavement cards that were sent out to an employee's family in Specialized Investigations. It also paid for the division plaques for employees who received the personalized item upon their promotion to the next higher rank.

"So instead of Chinese, you want Snickers or Milky Way?" Nate asked.

With a frown, Eli replied, "Milky Way."

Gravesite Briefing

Parked behind yellow crime scene tape was a marked sheriff's patrol unit and a string of unmarked Ford Taurus detective units belonging to the team. Each of the detectives was sleeping in various positions in the front seats of their cars, except for Eli, who wasn't there at the moment.

A marked white Sheriff's CSI van pulled up to the scene and was waved to the front of the line of cars by the uniformed deputy. As it passed Sgt. Kesling's unit, he woke up and realized it was time to get his team up and get back to work. Gravesites didn't get unearthed in the darkness.

So instead of going home, Kesling decided that getting the initial briefing was more important, along with interviewing Jim Stallworth. Afterward, there wasn't much more that could be done other than get a few hours' shut-eye before dawn, when the real work would begin.

Kesling went to the two other detectives' cars and knocked on the window to wake them.

From out of the driver's seat of the CSI van stepped Debbie Jensen, a comfortably confident woman with vast experience. Debbie had worked more murders than anyone in homicide collectively. The sheriff's crime scene investigators for decades were called forensic specialists until the ridiculous television show came out and everyone changed their division title to "CSI" to continue letting life imitate art.

Nevertheless, Debbie was one of the founding members of what was now an all non-sworn staff of forensic specialists or, now, crime scene investigators, whose job it was to work full-time on collecting evidence at crime scenes and processing evidence back at the lab that did not require further technical inspection, such as DNA or actual chemistry. Historically, the positions were occupied by sworn personnel—full-fledged detectives—who, after a few years of getting training and experience and then doing some excellent work, would earn themselves a promotion and leave the detail to become a sergeant somewhere, taking all their institutional knowledge with them. The process would be repeated every few years with new detectives learning the trade. About the time they became an invaluable resource, they'd promote and leave the unit.

Debbie had been working as a museum curator at the San Bernardino County Museum. Due to her archeology background and master's degree in biology, she was called upon numerous times by the forensic units to assist in crime scene investigations, particularly when they involved buried bodies.

At one point, she casually joked to the homicide captain that the department should just hire her to work in the unit instead of her having to constantly train new detectives. Without her knowing, the captain took the idea to the sheriff and suggested they think about reforming the whole division and hire actual scientists and develop a true crime lab. A month later, Debbie got a phone call asking her when she could start and what she would need in supplies. That was twenty-six years ago.

The group was gathered and stood around Sergeant Kesling's hood, waiting rather impatiently, when Eli came tearing up the path. He got out of his car carrying a coffee thermos. He didn't look half as haggard as the others, youth being on his side. He decided vanity was more important than sleep and went home long enough to get a shower, fresh clothes, a thermos of coffee, and let Ranger, his three-year-old German Shepherd, out to pee. He did have one thing in common with the older members of his team: he liked his caffeine from a natural source like coffee and hated those medicinal-tasting energy drinks.

Kesling barely looked over his shoulder at Eli. "Glad you could make it, rook."

"Sorry, I got lost on my way back from letting Ranger out."

"Nice going, Magellan," Artie tossed out dryly.

Everyone laughed a little. Had it come from Nate, it would have been funny and acceptable. But not from Artie. Not after last night with his botched witness contact and subsequent firestorm that somehow made it Eli's fault that Artie looked bad.

"Okay, gang, we've got an interesting one. Seems there's a missing couple from Los Angeles. Somehow, their dog was found dead out here by some local guy walking his own dog who stumbled upon it and called the house. The people there freaked out, called LASO, who sent out their deputy to take a missing persons report."

"How long have they been missing?" Eli asked.

"Geez, kid, don't interrupt your sergeant," Artie fired across the hood of the car.

Eli had already had enough of Artie's teasing today and was about to blow a gasket when Nate put a hand on Eli's shoulder to settle him down.

Kesling continued with a wry smile. "LASO asked our Yucaipa station to run out and meet the guy who found the dog. Well, when our deputy got out there, he found some blood drops on a trail and thinks there may be a gravesite."

"Bullshit. These people from LA are in a grave in Yucaipa?" Artie asked sarcastically. "What, robbers with unlimited miles on their Hertz account?"

Hockney couldn't stop himself. "Who's interrupting now?"

Kesling replied, "It's actually a good question."

Hockney was pissed, embarrassed, and losing the back-and-forth with Artie.

Kesling continued, "Apparently, the missing couple are well-to-do, rich types who shouldn't be missing. But that's what we're going to figure out. Artie, you're next up—you got scene and case agent. Basically, you're going to be Debbie's bitch today."

Debbie smiled. "Nice! Keep the iced tea a-comin', Artie."

Kesling said, "Nate, take the rookie with you and head out to LA and see what we can learn about these people and get the back story."

Road Trip

Detectives Hockney and Parker rode together in Nate's unmarked unit. Nate used to work in Los Angeles and really knew the area, whereas Eli tended to get lost just about everywhere he went. There was no need to drive two cars in tandem, so they dropped Eli's unit at Nate's house, where Nate was able to get in a quick shower and change of clothes while Eli napped on the driveway in the front seat of the car with the engine running and air-conditioning keeping him chilled in hibernation.

After battling the rush-hour parking lot that is Interstate 10 into Los Angeles, they finally made their way up to La Cañada Flintridge to meet with a Los Angeles Sheriff's deputy who was supposed to be securing the scene and waiting for Eli and Nate to arrive. With good reason to believe there was foul play surrounding the Browers' disappearance instead of them simply being on a road trip, Sgt. Kesling had put in a call to LASO Homicide while Eli and Nate were driving.

When Nate exited the freeway and drove toward the Browers' neighborhood, their world visually and drastically changed. Eli was impressed and said, "This is like being in a whole different state."

"Yeah, there's the Los Angeles of concrete sprawl that most of us visit as tourists or on business, then there's *this* Los Angeles most people don't know about or live in." Nate took a swig from his thermos before continuing, "My wife used to work for a high-end caterer helping make those big friggin' cakes for weddings and corporate shindigs. Every once in a while, I'd help her with deliveries on my time off. Dude, my house can fit in some of these people's foyers."

As they approached the Browers' address, they came upon a black-and-white LASO patrol unit blocking the road in front of yellow crime scene tape strung across the road from a phone pole to a tree across the street. Eli dropped the flip-down red light mounted on the ceiling between the visors and clicked it on to let the deputy know that the car approaching wasn't ignoring the roadblock, but instead was another law enforcement officer.

The LA deputy raised the yellow tape and waved them under. Nate rolled down the window. "Hey, brother, we're with Sheriff's Homicide in San Bernardino County."

"Up around the bend," was all the deputy took time to say.

"Thanks," Nate replied while sending the window up its track. He glanced at Eli, and they both shared a look of disappointed surprise.

"Whatta dick," Eli said to Nate, but turned around to gaze through the rear window at the patrol deputy, who had gone back to playing on his mobile phone.

As they made their turn around the bend, both Eli and Nate were awestruck by the number of marked and unmarked police units lining both sides of the street. More yellow tape was strewn across what must be the actual residence in question. Nate parked behind one of several unmarked units. A crowd of people was gathered at both ends of the street behind yellow tape.

"It's a fucking armada," Nate exclaimed.

"Wish we had these kinds of resources," Eli said as he surveyed the scene around him. The houses all had perfectly manicured lawns, blooming flowers, and designer driveways paved with something other than concrete. Each residence looked like it was straight out of a magazine for the rich and famous.

"Bit of overkill. What do you think?" Nate asked rhetorically.

Both men got out of the car and walked up the street toward the Browers' residence.

Eli said under his breath, "Not much, apparently."

"What's that?"

"I'm so tired of Artie's bullshit. The guy can't find his ass with both hands, yet Sarge thinks he walks on water. What's up with that?"

"It's a loyalty thing. They did patrol way back when you were in diapers. Don't get in the middle of that."

"Seriously? You too?"

"Dude, lighten up or you're going to stroke out."

"Come on, Nate, haven't you noticed that in order to get Sarge to take any of my advice, I have to feed it to you or Artie so that it comes from one of you two?"

"No, but I'm so glad that you're allowing me to take credit for your brilliance."

"That's not what I mean..." Eli couldn't win for losing. He was trying to make the point that he was being overlooked just for being young, but now it seemed he might have even offended his only known ally.

They reached the top of a long driveway where uniformed deputies were eating sandwiches on the hood of a patrol unit.

"Wow, if Sarge ever saw that in one of our crime scenes, huh?" Nate said quietly for only Eli to hear.

Just then, pudgy, gray-haired, LASO Detective lumbered toward Nate and Eli, meeting them outside on the path that led to the front door.

"Hey! You guys must be from Berdoo?"

"Yeah, hey, brother. I'm Nate Parker, and this is Eli Hockney—SBSO Homicide."

"Awesome. I'm Jim Zizlowski, but everyone just calls me Ziz." He gave it a moment as if it was going to take time to register this complex bit of information.

"Come on in and look around. Pretty nice house. Not often one of these types gets whacked," Ziz said as he made his way back up the three brick steps, grabbing the black-painted metal handrail to assist himself up each step. His hands were void of gloves, and his shoes were unprotected.

"Well, we haven't confirmed anything yet," Nate responded.

"I hope you do soon. It'll make my day real short, then."

Nate and Eli exchanged quizzical glances. Ziz walked the two detectives to the front door and went right in. Parker and Hockney froze at the threshold.

"Sorry, didn't think to bring my own booties," Nate said loudly for Ziz to hear as he faded into the house.

Ziz turned around. "Huh?"

"Shoe protectors?" Nate replied condescendingly.

Ziz laughed a little and said, "Don't worry, boys, camera crews can't see all the way up here. You're safe."

"I think my partner means..." Eli added.

Parker took a step just forward ahead of Eli and physically cut him off with a slight shoulder interference bump, and in a hushed tone said, "Just put on some gloves."

The two SBSO detectives reached into their coat pockets and pulled out blue latex gloves and slipped them on before heading indoors, only to receive odd looks from the LASO personnel.

In a disgusting display of unprofessionalism and lack of crime scene integrity, people were sitting on furniture, groups were chatting and drinking from soda cans—*nobody* was wearing gloves or booties. The whole scene was chaotic and disorganized.

"Wow!" Eli exclaimed rather loudly. He didn't get everyone's attention, but damn near.

"What's that?" Ziz looked back at him.

"I mean, not one of you believes in crime scene integrity? This looks like a bad TV cop show in here."

The room quieted a bit. Eli had been unintentionally louder than he meant to be. Nate was discomposed at the professional faux pas his partner just delivered. Eli wasn't wrong, but Nate being the elder and senior detective, it was up to him to patch up any hurt feelings if they were going to work together on what could be a very long and involved, multi-jurisdictional murder case.

"What I think my partner was saying was that we've been beat up some in court over the years over scene contamination issues...you know..."

Blank stares were the order of the day amongst the LA contingent. Parker stammered a moment longer before being interrupted by his young partner. "The OJ thing?"

The room's attention immediately turned to the front door behind the detectives, and everyone stopped talking and stared at the man who had just walked in.

Standing there for a moment without saying a word was Bradley Clark, a thirty-something-year-old television and movie star who was famous for his police and detective TV shows and action movies. He was tall, handsome, and on the cover of every magazine as the current "it" star in Hollywood. Dressed in casual yet high-end clothing, with perfectly styled dark brown hair, tanned skin, and wearing sunglasses, Brad addressed the room. "I'm sorry, folks, I didn't mean to interrupt. I was just wondering how it's going."

Eli and Nate knew exactly who the TV star was but were puzzled at his presence not only at, but *in* the crime scene.

Ziz was overjoyed at the actor's presence and pushed past his fellow employees to be first in line to meet and greet the television star. Nate and Eli hadn't seen Ziz move this quickly yet. "Hello, Mr. Clark."

"Call me Brad."

Ziz turned red-faced from embarrassment and replied, "Sure thing...Brad." Ziz smiled from ear to ear and paused only to breathe and gulp in some air to quell his excitement. "We don't have any confirmed information yet..."

Nate and Eli weren't impressed. They pulled back to talk to each other out of earshot of everyone else.

All Dug Up

Debbie was dirty and sweaty from the archeological dig they'd undertaken back in Yucaipa. Although she handled the forensic side of things, she'd gotten some extra help from other CSI staff to come out and assist with the dirty work. Each shovelful was tossed through a three-foot-by-three-foot square metal mesh grave screen comprised of holes no larger than three-quarters of an inch.

These were homemade by screwing together four individual three-foot lengths of two-by-two lumber into a square frame and then stretching the strong gauge mesh of three-quarter-inch squares across the frame and stapling it with an industrial stapler. A second duplicate frame was then screwed to the first frame, sandwiching the mesh between the two frames. Then to hold up the meshed grave screen at any given angle from zero to eighty-five degrees, two shaft bolts were run through opposite ends of the frame, each connecting to a four-foot piece of two-by-four lumber to make swiveling legs. The grave screen could then be placed on the ground with the legs set at various positions to prop up the screen at the desired angle through which to sift each and every shovelful of soil.

Fabric, bullet fragments, fired cartridge casings, teeth, metacarpals, bone fragments, you name it, could all be lost if the dirt were quickly and carelessly excavated. Unearthing a shallow grave in a homicide is no different from any other archeological dig that may have been televised on the History Channel. It is a slow and painstaking process, made so in order not to destroy evidence that no one but the killer knows exists.

It had been five hours of straight digging and sifting sand from the ravine, which was one of the easier digs Debbie had worked. Visible in a sizable hole were the remains of a Caucasian couple, one male and one female. The male was wearing a USC Trojans T-shirt and shorts. The female wore a silk nightgown. Both were barefoot.

Decomposition had been accelerated by being buried in the hot sands of the Southern California inland desert. Essentially, the bodies had been slow-cooking in the sand oven. Standing up on the roadway looking down into the grave, Kesling dialed his phone.

Back in Los Angeles, Nate's phone vibrated in his pocket. He took it out and showed the screen to Eli, letting him know it was Sarge.

"Hey, boss." Nate listened for a moment. "Wow, okay, yeah. Hang on a second." Nate put up a finger to tell Eli to wait a second, and then he gently navigated his way through the crowd that was gathered around the actor getting selfies and autographs. "Excuse me," Nate said kindly to the crime scene photographer, who was leaning against a sofa table perched next to an ornate white couch. It seemed impossible that the couch had ever been sat on as it almost shone from its perfect cleanliness.

On the sofa table was a picture of a couple Nate presumed to be the Browers. Nate took a picture of the couple and texted it to Kesling. "Should have it in a second, but what you described sure sounds like what I'm seeing here."

Nate walked back to where Eli was trying to hide in the corner of the living room. He nodded and, with low volume intended only for Eli, said, "It's them."

Somehow, through all the noise, Zizlowski had the hearing of a bat. "Is it them? Do you have the Browers out there in San Bernardino?"

The room fell completely silent.

Eli had nowhere to go but the truth. "Looks like it. But we won't be one hundred percent sure until a DNA test, of course, but yeah, it looks like it's them."

Zizlowski was excited by the news. "Okay, everyone, hold on a minute. Lemme call the captain." The entire crew of crime scene personnel shifted gears and began slowly heading toward their duffel bags and briefcases of gear, while Zizlowski walked into the kitchen to make his phone call.

Still on the phone, Nate had drifted farther into a corner for privacy as well.

Brad walked over to Eli. "So, Detective...?"

Eli replied, "Hockney."

"Hockney. Right. So, I don't mean to intrude, but do you have any leads?"

"Not that I can honestly share with you, Mr. Clark."

"Brad, please."

"Well, the thing is, and don't take me as rude, but I'm not really at liberty to say right now."

"Wow, you guys really do talk like that?"

"No, not really, I just thought with all your TV detective time, you've probably said it a thousand times and would know what I meant."

Brad was slightly taken aback, but proceeded cautiously. "Hey, listen, I'm really not trying to cause any problems."

Eli then turned the tables on the actor. "Why are you here anyway? Are you on a ride-along or something?"

"The Browers are very close personal friends of mine. This has nothing to do with my job."

"I'm sorry to hear that. But then how'd you get into the crime scene?"

Brad looked a little sheepish. "No one stopped me. Every cop I walked up to just kept pointing me forward until I got here."

"Wow, okay, seems lessons are never learned in LaLa Land," Eli said mostly under his breath.

Zizlowski bounded back into the living room from the kitchen. "Well, boys, looks like you've got this one! We'll hand over what we've got to you and send a link for the digital photos from the secure site once they're uploaded."

Having heard the announcement, Nate said, "Hold on a second, Sarge." He spun the mic from his face. "Whoa, whoa, whoa! What's happening, Ziz?"

"Since the bodies are in your jurisdiction, the captain said it's your case. He said you guys found blood at your scene outside the grave?"

"Yeah, so?" Nate asked indignantly.

"Well, there's no blood here, so we conclude the murder happened in your jurisdiction."

"Are you kidding me?" Nate spoke into his phone, "You hearing this, Sarge?"

"Well, we've been all through this house and haven't found any signs of foul play. So we conclude that it happened in your jurisdiction."

Eli had had enough. "Conclude? How the hell can you conclude anything at this stage of the game?"

"Years and years of practice, kid. Besides, Captain's orders."

"Un-fucking-believable!" Eli was so angry, he was ready to fight the fat-fuck, has-been detective, but he knew that wouldn't solve anything and would only get him demoted or fired.

With a touch of arrogance that came from years of kissing off calls and getting away with it, Ziz said, "You can keep our patrol units for street security for the duration, though. Just give me a call when you're ready to clear so I can have radio let them loose."

All the LASO employees instantly packed up their gear and prepared to leave. No one seemed bothered by the notion that two people were likely kidnapped from their residence and brought out some seventy-five miles away and buried in a deep grave in a ravine. There might not be obvious signs of any foul play inside their home, but then again, there weren't *no* signs of foul play. Kind of hard to tell when a dozen people trampled around the scene haphazardly and without any seeming care for crime scene integrity.

Eli, Nate, and even Brad Clark were stunned and looked back and forth at one another.

Before leaving, Zizlowski said, "Nice meeting you guys. Hey, Brad, can I get your autograph?"

Brad was stuck between a rock and a hard place now. Give an autograph and the guy goes away—which he couldn't tell if that was a good thing or bad. Don't give the autograph and he would once again be called a prima donna dickhead for not giving someone less than a millimeter of ink scribbled on a scrap of paper. "Um, yeah, sure. Be happy to."

Zizlowski opened the notebook that he'd been using for the so-called investigation and flipped, thankfully, at least, to a blank page, where Clark wrote, *Thanks for all you do! Be safe, Brad Clark,* a phrase he wrote every time a cop asked for a signature.

Exasperated, Eli walked over to Nate and shrugged.

Nate had just hung up his phone. "Sarge said for us to stay here and take over this scene. It's obviously related, regardless of how much they don't want to admit it or work it."

"We don't have the right stuff to do this."

"Yeah, Sarge is sending another forensic team out here. Karen Ann, I fear."

"Fear?"

"It's going to take her twenty years just to get out here, and then another thirty years to work this scene. But she doesn't miss a thing."

"Well, of all the scenes we could be stuck in waiting for forensics, this ain't too shabby."

Eli had to admit that this was a beautiful home to have to hang around in. Unlike the dirty meth lab, desert hovels they mostly worked in when some speed freak offed another meth head, this was a palace of luxury and comfort. "So, we just hang out here?"

"For the moment, I guess," Nate replied, "but we should at least start some sketches and get the lay of the land. Maybe if *we* actually investigate, we might find something."

Clark was politely standing by the front door after the last LASO employee left. "Gentlemen. I promise you I'm not trying to be difficult or a bother..."

Realizing they'd forgotten about him, Nate interjected, "Sorry, Mr. Clark, kinda forgot you were there."

"Oh, it's no problem. Listen, the reason I even came up here is to let you, well, them, but now you, I guess... I wanted to let you know that the closest friends of the Browers are gathering at my house shortly." After offering that bit of information, Brad had the detectives' attention. "It's just up the road a few minutes. They've all been talking, and it seems they think they can collectively build out the last days when our friends were last seen and plans that were in place for meetings and lunches and stuff they missed."

Parker and Hockney looked at each other, reading each other's faces that Brad's idea was honestly a really good one. The two detectives spun around and closed ranks to block the view of their hands and front side from Brad, then played a real quick and concealed game of rock-paper-scissors. Nate won. Eli's head sank down.

"Well, Eli, I've got the scene here, so I'll start on the sketch and stuff. Why don't you run up there with...Brad...and talk to the friends? When you're done there, you can come help me finish up."

Through gritted teeth, Eli said, "Yeah, sure."

Brad was pleased. "Great. Thank you, guys."

The three of them walked to the front door, and Eli turned to Nate. "Hey, I forgot I came in your car. Gimme your keys."

"Shoot, that's right. Now I'm going to be stranded. I was hoping to get a sandwich."

"I'll get us something on the way back," Eli promised.

Then Brad had a better idea. "I can give you a ride. Like I said, it's only a few minutes away, and then we'll get you back here afterward. That way, your partner isn't stranded and without his pastrami on rye."

"Turkey on wheat, but that sounds good too."

The mood lightened slightly. The three men walk out front to a Mercedes G-Class SUV parked in the driveway. Nate watched as Eli walked to the passenger side of the SUV.

"Hop in," Brad said casually, as if everyone had a $175,000 car to drive around.

Eli wore a huge grin on his face beneath wide eyes. If he weren't careful, his last few steps toward the car may have looked suspiciously like skipping. He looked back at Nate, whose face had now turned serious. The raised eyebrow was all that Eli needed see to understand the message from Nate to not screw this up.

Bad News

After Eli's father was murdered, the Hockney family suffered financially through all of Eli's school years. It wasn't until he got into high school that he was able to have new baseball gear again, but that was after his mother got her second job and Eli spent his entire summer and fall working at every team fundraiser possible. The side benefit was that Eli learned a great work ethic, and how to make spaghetti and pancakes.

Now, sixteen years later, Eli's eyes were wide as he looked through the car windows like a child who was pulling up to Disneyland for the very first time. It was magical to be surrounded by all this wealth. Iron gates swung open to allow the luxury car to enter into what could only be described as a palatial Hollywood mansion.

"Holy shit, is this your house?"

Brad smiled and, with a bit of embarrassment, replied, "Yeah. Well, while it lasts, of course."

The driveway led up a short distance between hedges that partially blocked the view from the street. Once past them, it led onto a grand expanse of a gray stone paved area that could only be described as a parking lot. Centered in front of the front door, yet at a distance far enough to allow vehicles to pass between the last step of the front walkway, was a breathtaking Greco-Roman fountain made of marble adorned with hand-carved goddesses, Pegasus, and cupid statues whose incredible detail evoked a wonderful world of play. Centered at the top was a nude goddess whose vase was the source of the flowing water beneath.

Brad parked the G-Wagen in front of the front door. Across the parking area were a half dozen of the newest and top-of-the-line sedans and SUVs currently in production. All German or English, except for the Cadillac Escalade.

"Are all these your cars?" Eli asked.

"No, these are our friends'."

"These are *your* friends, not mine."

Ignoring Eli's off-handed comment, Brad said, "Looks like they're almost all here."

The two walked together into a large living room where several people were mingling. Some were standing, some sitting. All were well-dressed, country club types, but not overdone glamour weirdos. There was a minor food spread with sandwiches and side dishes, along with iced drinks waiting for consumption.

The friends' attention turned to Brad and Eli when they came in. The room, which was only slightly livelier than a wake, hushed.

"Friends, this is Detective..." Brad gestured to Eli to fill in his name.

"Hockney," Eli said.

"No, your first name."

"Eli," he added.

"This is Detective Eli Hockney from the San Bernardino County Homicide Unit," Brad said, finishing his somber introduction.

Everyone in the room instantly knew that Eli's presence wasn't a good sign, and their expressions turned glum. While some remained standing, many of the women sat on the sofas and ottomans but held tightly to their husbands' hands.

Brad continued, "I'm afraid he's got bad news for us."

The near silence of the room made their gasps that much more pronounced. Many hung their heads, other's heads shook with the anticipation of what was going to be said next.

Eli had been totally put on the spot by Brad blurting out what he wasn't actually supposed to know. Were it not for the incompetence of the LASO patrol deputies who let him up into the crime scene, Brad wouldn't have known anything more than his friends gathered in his home. In the end, maybe it was better than pussyfooting around the inevitable truth. Surely these people didn't earn their wealth by being stupid and lacking some common sense. Nevertheless, it was a little unnerving to walk in and address a group of strangers without having verified facts in hand. He was shooting from the hip, but the chance of the two decomposing bodies being anyone other than the missing Browers whose gravesite was guarded by their deceased dog, was about one in several million.

"W-well, um, so there's nothing official yet until we get some lab results completed—which could take several days—but at this point, it would seem that, although it's not certain, we're going to work on the theory only at this point that the bodies being recovered from the desert are likely, or possibly are, Bill and Abby Brower."

No one seemed shocked by this painful mini speech, which was anticipated the moment Eli was introduced.

Eli continued, "Mr. Clark tells me that you guys are all their closest friends, and that you all have had recent contact or new or future plans to see them, which could shed some light on when they were last seen safe and sound."

Everyone's heads were nodding in the affirmative, eyes were welling, sideways hugs were shared, and the distinct sounds of someone sniffling were unmistakable.

"This may take a bit of time, but I will need to speak with each of you, alone, so that I get unfiltered interviews."

The silence and reactions from the group accepted this necessity as making perfect sense, and there would be nothing but cooperation. Sad cooperation.

Eli looked to Brad. "Is there somewhere I can set up shop?"

"What do you need?"

"Just a couple of chairs and a table are all, really."

Body Roll

The bodies were fully unearthed, and a deputy coroner was at the scene now carefully putting them in yellow body bags while Debbie took pictures of their process. Much to the surprise of all new detectives to homicide, who typically spent as many hours as the general public watching television cop shows, detectives and CSI investigators in most states can't touch, move, search, or manipulate a dead body without the direct permission and supervision of a deputy coroner. This is a legal matter that ensures that the county coroner is the only legal authority over decedents. It protects the integrity of all death investigations, whether they are criminal, accidental, or natural.

Therefore, not until the scene investigators are ready to move the body, which comes after countless photographs and scale measurements, will the homicide team call for the coroner. The best way not to disturb any evidence that might be on or near a murder victim is to photograph and collect all the visible evidence and search for latent around the body.

Once that's accomplished, the fear of trampling evidence is quelled. There is no sense in having the coroner's personnel sitting around for hours while the investigators methodically move through the scene before reaching the need to manipulate or remove the corpse.

Only on TV shows do detectives come bursting into the room and get all handsy with the decedent. In the real world of homicide investigations, the process is far less dynamic. Crime scene investigations work is methodical, calculated, and an organized process, ideally involving the least amount of people possible. Fewer people equal less contamination. Period.

Artie stood on a hill above the gravesite, peering at the crew of forensic specialists, the deputy coroner, and the body transport team, while he took notes in his personalized leather padfolio with the sheriff's homicide logo embossed into the leather and his last name embossed across the top. Every homicide detective had one custom-made by the retired deputy sheriff who lived in the mountain community of Lake Arrowhead, where he'd converted his garage into a regular hobby shop of personalized leather goods.

Kesling was on his mobile phone updating the lieutenant, while local news reporters were met by Los Angeles media who'd traveled all the way out to San Bernardino County when they heard that a rich couple from La Cañada Flintridge might have been involved in a torrid affair that led to their murders. The impervious thin plastic yellow tape kept them at bay, but telephoto lenses were hard to deal with, especially when the bodies were in the open desert with nothing to block them from view.

Debbie called up to Artie for his notes. "Tan lines, but no jewelry. Both of them. Him a watch for his left wrist and a ring on the wedding finger. Other hand looks like he doesn't wear other rings, but the decomp is making it kind of hard to tell."

"Her?" Artie called back.

"Pierced ears. Watch tan line too, definitely a wedding ring missing, possible other ring tan lines on other fingers, but hard to say. Can't say for sure, but I'm guessing she did wear other rings off and on, not consistently like the wedding finger."

"Strange..." Debbie noted.

"What?"

"There's a crumpled-up green napkin in the grave with them. No blood on it that I can see."

"And?"

"Well, I don't know. It is just, well, here. No real reason I can see."

"Chemicals on it?"

"I'll can it and have the lab folks check it. But I don't see any stains," Debbie replied. Evidence that investigators want to remain dry is stored in varying sizes of manilla envelopes or paper bags like those from a grocery store, not plastic bags. Clear bags are terrific for television shows so the audience can see the item of evidence, but in the real world, put a piece of metal in one of those, and it will rust before the trial. Worse, the best way to ruin a piece of bloody evidence is to let mildew eat away at it and ruin the chance of getting DNA.

But for potentially gaseous materials, a paint can is just the trick. Airtight as they come, the slick metal can is easy to make notes on with a Sharpie. Pre-signing a label makes a perfect method to seal laterally across the rim to note the closure and maintain a chain of custody. The crime lab was a frugal group that scoffed at buying preprinted evidence labels from one of those lab stores that charge a pretty penny for what is essentially a decorative address label. When a department collects thousands upon thousands of pieces of evidence a year, those little savings start to add up. It was once figured that the average cost of conducting a homicide scene investigation was upwards of fifteen thousand dollars with salaries on overtime and all the material involved in developing and collecting forensic evidence.

Debbie retrieved a fresh paint can from her truck and put the green paper napkin inside, then closed the lid with a rubber mallet. She was sure not to damage the rubber stopper in the center of the lid. The crime lab technicians would insert a needle through the stopper to extract the air so that it could be tested in a gas chromatograph for contaminants, fuel sources, poisons or other toxins.

But for now, the collection of evidence from on and around the bodies would continue for several more hours.

Friendly Interviews

Eli was offered space to work in Brad's home office, a tastefully decorated room with an ornate, masculine wooden desk likely the size of the Resolute desk in the Oval Office. An unoccupied traditional dark red leather, button-tufted wingback chair sat behind the desk. On the shelves were pictures of Brad with too many famous actors, sports stars, and politicians of both political parties to count. On the credenza behind him was an Emmy he'd won for best supporting actor in a drama series for his part in the former police drama television show *South Bay Detectives*.

Eli sat across from a thirty-something blonde female he'd been interviewing for a couple of minutes already. She was saying, "...not last week, but we were supposed to get together, tomorrow." The woman snatched a fresh Kleenex from the box on the desk. "My niece is getting married, and Abby was going to help with decorations..."

Next was the woman's husband. "...golfing buddy. Always pays his bets. Shares in the tab. Very generous; more often than not, picking up the tab. This is awful. I can't think of any reason why anyone would want to hurt them..."

Then another woman: "They were such wonderful people. The nicest, best friends you could ever ask for. Abby was always quick to help. Bill would give you the shirt off his back. There isn't one person that I know of who has ever had a mean word to say about them..."

Then her husband: "It was probably a couple weeks ago that I saw them. I hadn't yet been to their new place. You know they just sold their home and were renting the place up here?"

Eli said, "No, I didn't know that. The house Mr. Clark picked me up from isn't theirs? It's a rental?"

"Yeah, they made a killing on their home they sold down in the valley. They wanted to live up here but couldn't find what they wanted for sale, so they're renting this place until they do. Couldn't tell they only moved in one month ago, could you? Yeah, that's Abby. She could work logistics for the military and teach them a thing or two."

Eli had spent the better part of three hours talking to maybe some of the nicest people he'd ever met. He was truly surprised that with all the money they obviously had, none of them treated him any differently. In fact, they were the most respectful too. Even though every single one of them was several years Eli's senior, they all called him Detective Hockney and none of them tried to use his first name or talk to him like he was a kid. It was refreshing, actually. But maybe one of the most important interviews was saved for last by the group, who had presorted themselves into their own timeline as to who last saw whom and in what order. Very thoughtful and helpful indeed.

Elaine McAllister went to high school with Abby, and they'd been inseparable since their days on the cheer squad. "Oh yes, she is a clean freak. Well, a neat freak, really—not a germaphobe. She's just the most organized person you'd ever meet. And very ritualistic. Loved her nightly tea. That's why I thought it was strange about the teacup."

"What do you mean?"

"So, listen, Abby doesn't even use the dishwasher except during parties. She'd wash the dish you just used with soap and water while still chatting with you, then dry it and put it away in the cupboard. Like I said, not a germaphobe, but she hated, I mean absolutely *hated*, clutter. So, when I saw the teacup on the table with dried-out tea stains, I knew something was wrong right away. Unless the house was on fire, she would never, *ever* leave a single dirty dish out. Let alone a half-completed project on the dining table."

Eli nodded without saying a word to encourage Elaine to continue speaking. These personal habits and traits were invaluable information that could potentially be incredibly important to discovering the time-frame of events that led up to their deaths.

"Everything had its place, and she was an absolute creature of routine. Like she didn't believe in keeping trash in a 'wastepaper basket,' *she* corrected me once. Trash cans are kept outside or in the garage, but what you have under your desk or the bathroom was a wastepaper basket."

"What do you call the kitchen trash?" Eli asked with a bit of amusement.

"Well, I think that was still a trash can, but she treated them the same way."

"How's that?"

"No overnight trash. So, if she was sitting at her desk doing the bills or clipping coupons—as wealthy as they were, she totally believed in saving money and used coupons—the mail and coupon trash would be emptied at the end of her task. The same with the kitchen trash. When she cooked, which wasn't that often, although she could cook a Martha Stewart meal at the drop of a hat, at the end of dinner, she would empty the kitchen trash. No overnight trash was ever left in the house."

Even though at times the information overload was exhausting, it was vital not to interrupt. It was in these seemingly innocuous sidebar discussions where the investigation's missing puzzle might be revealed.

Her husband, Richard, was a nice guy and was far more succinct. "Yeah, I found it strange too that he didn't call me back after a couple of days. Not like him at all. But I wasn't really worried. Didn't want to go in the house. Felt stupid, but Elaine was right. Don't tell her I said that. But I hadn't heard Bill say anything about any threats or worries he was having. In fact, looking back, I still can't think of anything I find suspicious or unusual in his or Abby's behavior. I mean, they'd just moved, but that wasn't itself unusual."

Last but not least was who the group believed was the last person to see the Browers alive, well, except for the suspects, of course. Marcus

Wright. "Yeah, so I think we were the last people out with them. Friday night, we had plans for dinner. We go out at least once a month, sometimes more. Bill picked us up in his new Jeep Cherokee—did you find that, by the way?"

"No, but we have a BOLO out for it."

"A what?"

"A broadcast on the car. Be On the Look Out is what BOLO stands for. The license plate and VIN are in the system in case any cops stop it anywhere in the United States. Please continue."

Richard said, "Ah, okay. Well, I told Bill that we had to go to dinner earlier than normal because I needed to be home by nine that night. I was catching an early flight out the next morning for a sales meeting in Dallas. Well, after dinner, he got us back home exactly at 9:00 p.m. on the dot."

"How do you know exactly?"

"Because when we pulled into my driveway, the clock on his dash read 8:59 p.m. and Bill pointed to it and made a cheesy joke about needing a big chauffeur tip for getting me back a minute early."

Marcus started with a little laugh about how silly the joke seemed, then his face changed as he remembered that he wouldn't be hearing corny jokes from his friend anymore. He took a moment's pause and then wiped the corner of his eye and across the bottom of his nose. "As far as I know from talking with everyone out there, I think Amy and I were the last to be with them. Eight fifty-nine Friday..."

"How far is your house from theirs?"

"Three minutes if you catch the light green, five if you don't."

"Can you describe what they were wearing?"

"No, I don't remember. Nothing unusual. This time of year, he'd be wearing pants and a polo shirt or casual collared shirt, but I don't remember what it was. Better ask Mrs. Wright. She'll probably know where Abby bought it too."

Amy Wright was now seated silently in front of Eli, having gotten a big hug from her husband when he called her to come to take his place. She sat down, grabbed a tissue from the box, and started crying right away. Just the thought of talking about their friends in the past tense was almost too much to bear.

Eli asked gingerly, "Whenever you're able, I was wondering if you could recall what Bill or Abby might have been wearing when you and Marcus went to dinner last Friday."

"A blue striped button-down. In fact, if you look in the washing machine, and if it is true that we were the last people to see them, then those clothes will still be there. She didn't have a hamper or clothes bin. Clothes were either in the closet, on your body, or in the washing machine or dryer. Except for dry cleaning, which went into a bag behind the door of the closet."

"How do you—"

"Also, if you want to know if they ever left the next morning, then check the dresser in their master bedroom. Abby always undressed and prepared for bed after the last guests left. In this case, she would have changed immediately into a silk sleep shirt, removed all her jewelry, and put them in the crystal dish on the dresser. That was her routine every night."

"Okay, so how—"

"We stayed with them for almost two weeks when our house was being renovated. She insisted that we not stay in a hotel and board Lillie, our Dachshund. She and Teddy got along famously. By the way, do you know where Teddy is?"

"I'm afraid I have some more bad news."

The Plunge

Eli stood in the palatial backyard with a beautiful view of the valley below. He was by the pool talking on his mobile phone with Nate when Clark walked outside toward him. The water was perfectly still and crystal clear. There wasn't a single leaf out of place in this professionally maintained garden backyard. Eli had, of course, swum in plenty of friends' backyards, but they were nothing like what he was witnessing.

Beyond the pool, the greenest grass he had ever seen stretched out beyond Eli's view. There wasn't one single weed or dead spot. Beds of bright-colored flowers lined each side of the gravel trail that led between various shrubs and squared hedges to a gazebo raised up three steps above the ground. This was no simple swing set gazebo. There was a full eight-seat round dining table in the middle protected by a solid roof that covered the dining area, cooled by the two ceiling fans.

"Yeah, see if it's in the washer or dryer, or behind the master closet door in a dry-cleaning cinch bag."

Brad motioned and said quietly, "That's the last of them, I think."

Eli spun his phone up to keep listening, but directed the mic from his mouth. "Nice place you got here."

Brad smiled and said, "Thanks."

"Nice folks too. I was expecting a group of pretentious snobs, but they were actually all very nice to this blue-collar guy." Just then, he rotated his phone back down and spoke into it. "Okay, well then, everything checks out on that too. I'll be up shortly."

"You know the difference between people isn't usually money as much as attitude," Brad said kindly yet matter-of-factly. He wasn't lecturing Eli, but he was giving him some insight into the human condition.

Eli smirked and replied, "Right. Well, that's what people with money tend to say."

Just then, an adorable little brown-and-gray Yorkshire Terrier ran out from the house from a door down by the other end of the pool. Eli knelt to pet him. "Hey, little one, what's your name?"

"Buddy," Brad informed him.

"Hey there, Buddy." Eli was enjoying giving Buddy a belly rub when a large Labrador retriever who didn't want to miss out on getting attention himself ran up full sprint from behind Eli. Before Eli knew there was another dog in the mix, he heard Brad shout, "No, Buster!"

Eli looked up to see where Brad was looking. He turned just in time to see Buster running full speed directly at him. Buster's face was pure joy. and Eli knew he wasn't in danger of being attacked, but as he tried to stand up and before he could get his balance, Buster bowled right into him, causing him to fall backward. Eli tried to regain his balance by stepping back to settle his weight only to find nothing there. His left foot was over the pool, as was more than fifty percent of his body at this point.

A million thoughts went through his brain before he hit the water. He hoped the water wasn't freezing cold. Then, and this was going to be a problem, his mobile phone was going to take the worst hit. The department was still using older models that weren't waterproof. In his short time in the detail, he'd already lost one mobile phone by leaving it on the trunk of his unit and scattering its remains on the Southbound I-15 when returning from a murder-suicide call in Baker. Sarge wasn't going to be happy that he'd killed another iPhone.

What was he going to do about clothes? A drenched suit wasn't going to dry quickly, and it would also likely be ruined. Essentially a brand-new suit that he was still paying off on his credit card. As he was a terrific swimmer, drowning wasn't a problem. But this was going to be another set of stories for everyone to talk shit about back at the office. But there was nothing else he could do other than take a quick breath and be ready for the plunge.

From underneath the water the brief moment he was there, he heard Brad yell at Buster, who must have thought it was a further call to action. Eli effortlessly emerged from the quick dunk, treading water in what had to be the perfect temperature.

"Are you all right?" Brad asked with a look of sheer terror on his face. Buster was at the side of the pool with his tongue hanging out. After a couple of playful barks, Buster decided that diving into the pool was the game of the day. He easily cleared Eli's head and was enjoying himself immensely as he swam around in no particular direction.

Eli made his way to the edge where he'd fallen in and, with one athletic movement, extracted himself from the pool to a standing position once again. He just stood there dripping a gallon of water onto the deck and then looked at Brad, who was visibly stunned and clearly worried.

"Mia!" Brad yelled out toward the house. But after a second of staring silently at each other, watching Eli drip, they both burst out laughing.

"I'm really sorry about Buster. He's barely two years old and is still such a puppy, but a big strong one."

"Yeah, well, I could tell he just wanted to play, but it was way too late."

A beautiful young woman in her early twenties came running from the door leading to the kitchen. She appeared frantic, and it didn't take long for Eli to figure out she was the inadvertent culprit of Buster's escape.

She was wearing mini cut-off jean shorts and a halter top over braless breasts. Her blouse didn't cover her trim and well-defined abs. Her long black hair flowed down in loose curls around her heart-shaped face, accentuated by her emerald eyes. Adding to her striking looks were her long tan, toned legs that had her moving gracefully as she snatched up the dogs. Eli stood motionless with his mouth open.

"I'm sorry, Brad, I thought the doggie door was locked," Mia cried out. "Oh my God, I am so, so sorry." Seeing Eli dripping wet, his shirt clinging to his body exposing his chest, Mia stopped a moment and asked, "Are you okay?"

"Yeah, just a little wet is all," Eli replied without taking his eyes off her.

Brad interrupted the exchange. "Yeah, let's get you dried off and into some fresh clothes. Looks like we're about the same size. Come on."

Brad walked Eli through a set of double doors into a large master bathroom from the poolside. Shiny marble floor lay before a huge shower with multiple showerheads and enough room for several people, adjacent to a full jacuzzi tub sunken into the floor. It wasn't quite as large as the one outside, but it would still hold a small crowd.

"Here's a towel. You can change out of your stuff and lay it over there. I'll have it taken care of."

While Eli emptied out his pockets and took off his badge, gun, and handcuffs, Brad went into his master closet to get some clothes for Eli to wear home. From what he could see through the open door, the closet looked bigger than his whole master bedroom back home.

Wearing only pants and underwear, having stripped off his sopping wet clothes and shoes, Eli was surprised to see that Brad had brought out an entire wardrobe. He could tell just by the way the suit hung on the wooden hanger that this wasn't something you could get at JCPenney, where Eli had purchased his suits for his promotion to detective. He'd tried Men's Warehouse, only to be shocked at the prices. There were some nice suits there, but he could neither afford them nor justify maxing out another credit card.

So far, the promotion had cost him around fifteen hundred dollars in clothing and other equipment he would need if he were going to wear a gun on duty underneath a suit. The department issued all personnel their safety gear for patrol and did, in fact, issue an "off-duty" weapon holster, but it was big and bulky and didn't do much for concealment. Typically, Eli used a waistband holster to carry in his off-duty clothing, which was nearly always jeans and boots and an untucked button-down shirt. He wore his weapon tucked by his right kidney, covered by the shirt.

But to wear a weapon comfortably and securely under a suit jacket all day required the purchase of a different duty holster. There were a dozen to choose from, including the once-ubiquitous shoulder holster that now only the old-timers wore. But he gave it some serious thought for a moment. It was very practical to have your weapon and two extra magazines with all the weight distributed across the shoulders and back, rather than having just the weapon on one hip. The leather holster looped through a thin dress belt pulled at your pants all day. But if he got a shoulder holster like those former homicide guys who were mostly retired now, he'd look out of place in the bureau when he took his jacket off. Looks and acceptance were all too important for Eli.

Brad held up the suit and asked Eli to turn around so he could put the suit against his back to see if the shoulders of the suit were large enough. "Looks like it should fit. Forty long in the jacket, and thirty-two, thirty-two pants?"

"Thirty-one waist," Eli said proudly with a grin.

"Hmm." Brad held a pair of shoes in his left hand and asked, "Elevens?"

"Yeah, perfect, thanks. But listen, I don't need all that. Just some sweats and sneakers would get the job done."

"Nonsense. It's the least I can do. Besides, I've got plenty of clothes, trust me. It's getting to be a thing, actually. I might need therapy. Though I think it's required in my business," Brad quipped with a sigh.

Eli wasn't sure what to say to all that. It was a really uncomfortable situation to be half-dressed in front of a strange man holding clothes for him to wear. Strange, but also familiar at the same time, because Brad Clark was famous around the world. But here was Eli, a schmo cop from the desert of San Bernardino County, standing inside the man's house, about to try on his exclusive clothing.

The dark blue suit was a Davin Harris, according to the label. Eli had never heard of that suit maker, but just the way it hung on the special wooden hanger told Eli the quality was beyond what he could ever afford. The crisp white shirt was made of a fabric he hadn't ever felt before. It was a thick yet soft cotton blend of material that felt wonderful to the touch. More impressive was that it was actually opaque and didn't require an undershirt, something that had always bothered Eli with the shirts he bought. There was definitely a time to show off all the work put in at the gym, and Eli never missed an opportunity to go shirtless, but displaying mini pepperonis through a white dress shirt wasn't the preferred method.

Hung around the shirt hanger was a gold floral spot Turnbull & Asser silk necktie that looked brand-new as it had not one wrinkle from being worn. The feel of the silk and the fact he hadn't heard the name before told him it too was expensive. Probably worth more money than he would spend in a fancy restaurant, whereas Eli tried to get his ties on sale for less than twenty dollars.

"Here are some socks, but uh..."

Eli knew exactly what was going through Brad's mind. Borrowing socks was one thing, but underwear? Um, not so much. The problem was solved very quickly. "Yeah, I'll just go commando."

"Okay, yeah, well, good. Listen, use anything you need to get ready. There's the shower, a hair dryer, and all kinds of products of, well, every kind, really, on the counter over there, perks of being a spokesman. So, I'll leave you to it, then. Just leave your suit, and I'll getting it cleaned or replaced if it's too far gone."

"No, no, don't worry about it."

"Detective, seriously, it's no trouble, and I really need to take care of that for you. I feel awful about all this."

"Fine, yeah, okay."

"Great. Out that door and down the hall leads back to the main living room and kitchen when you're done. Take your time."

After Brad left the room, Eli finished the last of his undressing, tossing the wet clothes with the others onto the tile. He thought a moment about the shower and then decided he might as well get the chlorine out of his hair, so a rinse-off shower wouldn't be intrusive. Brad did offer, after all. He stood inside the glass-encased shower that put his body on display in the center of the massive bathroom. Not a single tattoo obscured the view of his muscular frame, nor was there a tan line at his arms or midsection due to time spent tanning in the nude in his backyard or the tanning booths.

He spent only enough time to quickly wash his hair with some shampoo he'd never heard of. Once he was done and rinsed off, he got out and grabbed a fresh towel out of a rack of rolled towels from a crisscross shelving unit and tossed it over his head to rub his hair dry.

He didn't see that Mia had come into the room. She was pleased to get a few moments to examine his body while he remained oblivious under the towel. She was impressed by his square shoulders and perfectly formed pecs that hovered over a tight eight-pack of abdomen muscles which farther down led to his fully exposed manhood that, even postshower, was impressive.

Eli pulled the towel down off his head, but he still had his head bowed forward toward the ground while he grabbed the short ends of the towel to run the length of it back and forth across his back. It was another moment before he looked up to see he was being spied on. When he did, he was caught completely off guard by seeing Mia standing there, staring at him. Caught dripping once again, this time in the nude, he rushed the towel to his front to cover his groin.

"Um, hey?"

"Every time I see you, you're wet," Mia said with a cute little grin. Eli just stood there with his mouth open while Mia continued, "Brad asked me to get your wet clothes so we can get them off to the cleaners."

Showing no embarrassment that she was present in front of a nude male bearing only a towel, she walked extremely close to him, nearly brushing up against him, and then over to the pile of wet clothes and picked them up. Eli's embarrassment continued as he felt himself thickening a little with excitement at having been the subject of some voyeurism.

"These must be they."

Speechless, Eli just watched himself being watched by the beautiful young woman who made sure to check out his backside in the mirror before walking out of the room.

Eli muttered to himself, "Fucking Hollywood..."

Packing Up

Boxes were packed and taped; large paper evidence bags were folded over at the top and sealed. Bill Brower's laptop sat on top of the stack of boxes. Nate and backup Forensic Specialist Becky LaFever were wrapping things up at the Browers'. It had been over an hour since Nate had heard from Eli, who said he'd be coming back over soon. He wasn't expecting the sandwich at this point anymore. He got that taken care of with a phone call to Becky on her way into Los Angeles. Turned out that a pastrami on rye was a good choice after all.

"Why isn't he answering his phone?" Nate asked out loud and then ripped the phone from his face.

Just then, Eli walked in the front door.

"Hey, Nate, hey, Karen Ann!"

"Dude, I've been calling. What the hell?"

"Hey, Eli," Karen Ann called out from behind a stack of boxes.

"I fell in the pool. Well, got pushed into the pool by Buster. My mobile phone is dead from the swim. He just dropped me off."

"You don't look wet."

"Not my suit. Borrowed it."

"From Clark?"

"Yeah, Brad and I are apparently the same size. And man, this is a nice suit, huh? Never heard of the maker, but who cares, this is nice, huh? Feel this," Eli said as he put out his arm for Nate to feel the sleeve.

Nate wryly asked, "Brad?"

"Yeah. He's actually pretty cool. So, I had just hung up with you when his little Yorkshire Terrier came out for a meet and greet."

"You got knocked into the pool by a Yorkshire Terrier?" Karen asked.

"No, no, hang on, so I'm petting the little dog when his big dog, Buster, just fucking bowled me over into the pool. Which killed another mobile phone. How pissed do you think Sarge is going to be?"

Nate said, "Um, yeah, pretty pissed. So, he just gave you the suit?"

"Well, no, I borrowed it. I dunno, I didn't ask specifically, but I'm sure it's just a loan. I told him I'd be cool with sweats and some sneakers just to get me home, but he insisted. Dude, his closet is the size of my bedroom, and his bedroom and bathroom combined are like, almost as big as my whole house. Totally crazy. I could live like that."

"Not on this pay, you aren't. We're basically ready to go. Help me with this stuff, will ya?" Nate said.

"As long as I don't mess up this suit."

"They're fucking boxes, bro," Nate said, shaking his head.

Eli is Home

It was dark, and since it was summer in California, that meant it was really late when Eli pulled his Taurus into the driveway and clicked the garage door opener to reveal his 1970 Mustang.

The car was an inheritance from his father, passed down to his mother, who drove it a few times before just letting it partially rot in the apartment parking lot and later on the side of the home they rented in the High Desert. Although it was worth enough money even in fair condition and it would have really helped them out financially, Eli's mother kept her promise to her husband. He'd pleaded with her that if something ever happened to him, she would never sell it. He wanted it handed down to their son.

Eli got the car on his sixteenth birthday and spent three months saving up for the parts he needed. He worked on it with his friends, who knew even less than Eli did about how an internal combustion engine functioned. Once the car was running, though, Eli drove the hell out of it to every Friday night football game, the after-parties, and, of course, to every high school and college baseball game he ever played in.

Before he got promoted to detective and was issued a detective unit, he drove the Mustang to the academy, then after graduation, he drove across the county to West Valley Detention Center, where he spent his first years working in the jail, then later to his patrol station in the High Desert. But for the past couple of months, the car had been sitting quietly in the garage. No more wear and tear, but no time to do all the upgrades and refurbishment that he longed to do, now that he could actually afford to buy parts without having to sell bad spaghetti.

Eli walked through the garage and clicked the closer before opening the interior garage door, where Ranger was waiting for him. She bounced with joy at her master's presence. Ever since Avi patched things up with his girlfriend, Ranger had been lonely by herself. She had plenty of toys, so thankfully she didn't chew up the house, and there was a doggy door that led to the backyard for her to take care of her business. But she wasn't able to get her own water or fill her own food dish.

"Hey, girl! I'm sorry I've been gone so long. You hungry?" He looked down into her bowl and saw that her food was half full and so was the water. On the counter was a note from his neighbor: *Hey, buddy, I noticed that you haven't been home. Figured you're out on a case. I took care of Ranger for you. I'm looking forward to a story and a beer. P.S. I took one in trade for my labor.*

"Great idea, Fred," Eli said out loud to himself as he grabbed a beer and headed to his master bedroom. Usually, he needed a shower after a long day of investigation, but since he'd had one just a couple of hours ago at Brad Clark's house, a surreal moment in so many ways, he didn't need one this night.

There was one empty suit hanger, the one left behind from Eli's suit that was more than likely ruined. After sliding the pants onto the middle bar, he then clasped the wooden bar into the wire holder as he had done many times before. But this time, he added a step he learned earlier. When he went to take the fresh pants off the hanger in Brad Clark's bathroom, he noticed that simply unlatching the wooden bar didn't release the pants to slide off like they did at home. Instead, one pant leg had been put up through the triangular opening, thus splitting the pant legs on either side of the metal and guaranteeing the pants did not slip through and fall off in the closet. A simple yet ingenious extra step he'd never himself considered.

He walked over to the bed where the jacket lay, but instead of picking it up, he grabbed the remote control from the nightstand and turned on the TV. He searched the cable system for Brad Clark, found one of his TV shows in progress, and turned it on. He listened to it while he continued to hang up the suit, shirt, and tie.

After putting on some gym shorts, he made Ranger move over from hogging the entire middle of the bed so he could sit down with his back up against the pillows propped against the wall. He snatched up his beer from the nightstand and patted his left thigh to signal Ranger to come over and take up her movie-watching position with her head resting on his thigh and her body stretched out across the rest of the bed.

He finished the beer in a few large swigs and then settled down a little lower to watch the rest of the show, which he'd only heard of but never seen. It was a pretty typical cop show, which meant it was pretty bad. Over-the-top story lines with flat characters who lacked drive, ambition, or any abilities whatsoever, except for, of course, Brad's character. The star of the show was the only one with talent among a cadre of clowns. But long before he could render a full judgment upon the conclusion of the show, Eli was fast asleep, exhaustion having taken hold of him.

Morning Coffee

There was lots of hustle and bustle as the detectives and secretaries came into work and crowded around the coffeemaker to get a fresh cup. "Good mornings" were passed all around. Eli came in wearing Brad's suit from the night before, dropped his notebook off at his desk, grabbed his black porcelain mug emblazoned with the sheriff's badge on one side and the homicide detail logo on the other, and headed straight for the coffeemaker, where he ran into his partner, Nate.

"You know that shit'll kill you, right?" Eli said matter-of-factly as he watched Nate dose his coffee with three artificial sweeteners.

"Gotta die of something." Nate poured in enough creamer to turn his coffee a color that could only be called dark milk. "Hey, you wearing the actor's suit?"

Hockney was slightly red-faced. "Um, yeah. Nice suit. Only wore it for a couple of hours. Seemed a shame to let it go to waste without getting a full day out of it, right?"

"You planning on keeping it?"

"No, but this is a nice suit. Besides, my best suit is the one that I went swimming with, so..."

Nate interrupted. "I couldn't really care less. Listen, we collected a bunch of stuff from the Browers' home office," Nate started as the two of them walked to their desks in the bullpen after Eli poured his coffee into the mug without doctoring it. "Most of that shit is his tax files, but one of the interesting things was a will that was recently dated. Gives all

81

their assets to a Shelly Weller. Is that one of the names you interviewed up the house?"

"I don't think so. Doesn't sound familiar." Eli didn't recall the name, but he did interview around a dozen people, most of them not totally relevant, so he grabbed his notebook and flipped through the pages, "Nope. Not one of mine."

Artie came waltzing in. "You guys got something on my case?"

"Wow, *your* case?"

"Yeah."

The role of "case agent" rotates naturally from detective to detective in order of turn. Being case agent doesn't make the detective in charge, it just means that one detective is the repository of all the reports that are completed and signed off by the sergeant. The case agent will build the murder book, which is a three-ringed binder whose ring size is based upon how large the case is with regard to reports. A simple murder where the fact pattern is conclusive and without any mystery might fit into a one-inch binder, whereas other cases can consume multiple three-inch binders. It is the team, not the case agent, that solves the case.

"As a matter of fact—" Nate tried to tell Artie about the Browers' will, but before he could continue, Artie's desk phone rang loudly.

"Homicide, Williams," Artie said into his phone, ignoring his two partners.

Nate and Eli never ceased to be amazed at what a dick Artie could be.

"That was Mark at the morgue. He said he could get the Brower autopsies in later today, but I gotta head to court on the Mason prelim right now. I'll head over after." Gathering up his jacket, binder, and reading glasses, Artie called out toward Sgt. Kesling's office, "John, you hear that?"

"Yep. Bye," Kesling replied. Without looking up from his computer screen, he said, "We getting that computer over to high-tech?"

"Yeah, I was heading over soon," Nate replied.

Kesling asked, "What's Eli doing?"

"Ya know I'm standing right next to him, right?" Eli shot back.

Now Kesling looked up over the reading glasses perched on his nose. "Okay, smart-ass, what are you doing?"

Eli took a breath to start to speak, but was interrupted, or maybe saved, by Nate.

"Boss, Eli is heading out to LA to talk with the parole officer."

"Parole officer?"

"Yeah, that's what I was getting to earlier. That Shelly I was telling you about, she's an LA County parole officer and the executor of the victims' will."

"What the hell?" Eli was stunned at this information.

"When I saw her name on the will, I remembered seeing her name in the tax files. Her occupation as of last year was listed as a parole officer assigned to LA County. I called on my way in to the office and found out which unit she's working in."

"What if she isn't in?"

"She's expecting you. Well, me, really, but now you." With this information, Nate took Eli aside and back toward their desks. "Listen, I need to be home tonight if I can... Family stuff. Please? Do me this favor?"

"Aw, come on. I won't get out of that crazy-ass LA traffic and get home until late."

"Thanks, brother," Nate said before Eli could protest. "I'm going to read through all this crap that I know you hate doing, so there's that."

"Fine, but you owe me."

"Yeah, yeah, I'll make it up to you."

Parole Visit

After hours of plodding along the I-10 to Los Angeles, and also getting lost three times, Eli finally made his way to the California State Department of Corrections and Rehabilitation—South Central Office. He found parking easily enough and pulled open the swinging glass front door of the very drab old building. Early 1980s desk furniture adorned the cramped, broken-down reception area. A counter separated the public from the parole agents' work area.

The lobby was full of parolees, kids running around in the way, and the place was just dingy. A frustrated woman who spent too much time dealing with liars, cheats, thieves, wife-beaters, and sexual predators sat at the front desk behind a thick glass partition. "When he gets here, he gets here! Don't give me any lip, mister. I'm not the one throwing my life away sucking down drugs like they're soda, and God knows what else. Next!"

The fact the parolee was dressed in his gang attire didn't help his cause. "Fuckin' bitch!"

Eli stood in line behind several people, waiting his turn at the window. Coming from the speaker in the clerk's window, he heard, "Officer! You can come forward. These people can wait!"

After a couple of head swivels back and forth to survey the room, he noticed that everyone was staring at him. Apparently, Eli was the only person in the room who didn't think everyone else instantly knew he was a cop.

"Yeah, you. Come on up to the front."

Eli walked through the sea of people, nearly getting tripped up by a toddler, the mother of whom threw Eli a nasty look as if it weren't her fault the kid was running wild and nearly got trampled.

"Hey, I'm looking for Agent Weller," Eli stated as he showed his badge through the window.

Briefly acknowledging him, the receptionist buzzed the electronic lock to the nondescript door to Eli's right, "Yeah, through that door. She's back 'bout halfway down on the right."

She then continued to deal with the parole gangster still standing there as he had been. "Just sit down and wait. You ain't got no job, you ain't in no hurry."

Eli looked back momentarily at the three-ring circus going on in the lobby before heading to his destination. Before too long, he'd made his way down the hall to find "Agent Weller" engraved on red plastic affixed to a carpeted gray cubicle, inside of which sat a Bohemian styled woman amid an avalanche of paper stacks and three-ringed binders. The bangs of her long, red hair were held back at the top of her head by her thick black-framed reading glasses. A Minnie Mouse frame held a picture of Shelly with her arms around a man in front of Cinderella's Castle at Disneyland. She couldn't be much over forty-five years old, but it was the miles, not the years, that had worn her down.

"You Agent Weller?"

"Yup. Whatcha need?"

"I'm Eli Hockney from San Bernardino Sheriff's Homicide."

"Oh yeah. Wow, that is *not* the name I remember you telling me on the phone. Wasn't it Frank?

"No, yeah, Nate, not Frank."

"So now it's Eli?" Shelly asked and slumped back in her chair.

"That was my partner who called, Nate Parker. I'm Eli Hockney."

"Okay, so I'm not going crazy. Whatever. What's up?"

"I needed to talk to you about the Browers. Weren't they friends of yours?"

"Right, right. You know, sad about them. I'm sorry, I've just gotten in night before last, and the jet lag is killing me." Weller took a big swig from a purple stainless steel coffee thermos before she continued. "I don't think this has all settled in yet. Got a call from Elaine...McAllister..."

"Yeah, we met."

"But I haven't seen anybody 'cause vacation is over. I needed to get back to work."

"Sure, yeah. I understand. Where'd you go, by the way?"

"Disney World."

"Florida?"

"Yeah, Disneyland—Anaheim. Disney World—Orlando."

"No, no, I know, but with living here, I never thought to go across the country for the same thing."

"First, it's not the same thing. Second, the trip was paid for by my boyfriend's work. Think I could afford that kind of trip? He works for ol' Walt here in Anaheim, but one of the perks is free entry to any park, anywhere. Well, anyway. I was out of town when everything happened."

"When did you leave, or how long were you gone?"

"Left on Wednesday, got back in Sunday afternoon. By the time I got home, there a dozen voice mail messages on my home phone."

"Not your cell?"

"They don't have my cell. Bill and Abby do, did, but not those other people."

"Thought you guys were all friends?"

"We were friends when we all went to high school, but I went to work, and they, well, they married well and I married a cop. We were all young once. You'll see, it happens quick."

"You don't keep up with them socially, I'm guessing."

"I got married when I was a new agent, but we divorced a couple of years after our daughter was born."

Not really a response to his question, but he let it go. Eli left a moment of pause for Shelly to continue, but she didn't fill the silent void as he hoped. "Hmm. Okay, well, I was wondering if you could tell me about their will and how you got to be executor."

Shelly seemed a bit taken aback for just a hint of a moment, as if she wasn't expecting Eli to know she was named executor. She shuffled some papers as a cover and checked her watch. "Hmm, oh yeah, that. I guess Bill and Abby thought I was the most trustworthy with having this job and all. But I don't know where their assets are or how I'm going to make any disbursements."

"Really? I kinda thought that was the whole point."

"Yeah, but that was before the move and all the lawsuits."

"Lawsuits?"

"Shit, the Browers have been sued by everyone except Santa Clause," Shelly said as a matter of obvious fact. "Wait, you mean no one told you about that stuff? I thought you talked to the gang up at douchebag's house."

"By douchebag, I'm guessing you mean Brad?"

"His movies are stupid, don't you think? And he always tried to 'talk shop' with me the few times we met at some birthday party or something. No one really knows what it's like, right?"

"Yeah, totally," Eli replied, pretending to agree. He was confused now. Who was holding out on him and why? "So, who was suing them? And what for?"

"Bill allegedly embezzled a bunch of money, like millions over several years, when he was Davin Harris's accountant."

"Davin Harris?"

"The big clothing designer. Hollywood muckety-muck. Harris Clothing. It's a big deal if you're part of the rich and shameless crowd."

"No shit, that Davin Harris? Never heard of him," Eli replied with a grin, realizing he *had* heard of Davin Harris clothing, very recently, as it turned out. As a matter of fact, he was wearing one of his custom suits.

"He's dressed first ladies, most of the big stars going to the Oscars, and other Hollywood shit shows. Nothing he makes starts under ten grand."

"What happened with the lawsuit, then?"

"I don't really know. I guess they were still battling it out. But now I guess I'll have to pay out from the estate, since the bodies were found."

Now that caught Eli's attention. "What do you mean, 'found'?"

"Well, at first they were missing for a few days. The talk was that Bill and Abby skipped town to avoid paying back what they owed. I mean, had they left town, they'd have avoided the lawsuits for a while. But since they died, I guess the estate has to take care of it. And I guess that's me."

Eli wasn't sure if he should progress down this path. He actually didn't know enough to ask any more questions after that bombshell she'd just dropped. She hadn't mentioned talking to everyone earlier, but now she corroborated the working theories of the friends and family. Something wasn't adding up. In order to not tip his hand that he'd caught the comment, he rounded back to the previous topic. "So, I take it you don't like the Hollywood elite crowd that Brad and the rest of them belong to?"

"Look, Abby was my friend from school. All the girls were. And yeah, we still are, I guess. I'm just the only one making my own money the old-fashioned way. I work for it. Don't get me wrong, I don't hate them for marrying wealthy fellas. I just don't get into their designer labels and society club stuff."

"What's going to happen now?" Eli asked.

"What do you mean?"

"With the will? Do you have everything you need?"

"Nope. Not even the will. I never thought I'd need to execute it...was supposed to be only temporary...never figured I even needed a copy."

"I can get you a copy from evidence if you don't have one."

"Um, sure, yeah, that'd be great. Listen, I don't mean to be rude, but I gotta go check on a parolee who's been dodging me for a month now. I just learned he's shacked up at some chick's house in Chinatown."

"Yeah, sure. Don't let me keep you from all the fun. Wait, how, I mean, do you speak Chinese?"

"Are you kidding? No. I wish though. Wouldn't that be cool? But that's not my area, but my P.A.L. – parolee at large – loves Chinese girls. Always seems to be getting into trouble because of them."

"Ah, well, sure, makes sense. I'm going to head back," Eli said as he shook hands with Shelly, who didn't bother to get up, but did offer a very firm return handshake.

"Oh, hey, you wouldn't happen to know who the Browers' lawyer was, would you?"

"No, why would I know that?"

"Just thought...never mind. I'm sure it's in some of the boxes of paperwork we got from their house."

"Boxes?"

"Yeah, we took every piece of paper we could find plus his computer. Nate and I will be going through that until we go blind. Somewhere in there must be a trail to the suspect," Eli said while subtly looking for a reaction, but getting none. "Not as exciting as chasing down parolees in Chinatown, but it's a living."

"Well, we've all got our crosses to bear."

"Yeah, well, thanks so much for your time," Eli said as he made a quick exit. He was concerned he was treading toward something he couldn't quite figure out. It was a strange conversation, to be sure. Something about it seemed honest yet also crooked at the same time. He would have to do more digging before it would make sense.

It's a great trait for a homicide detective to be suspicious of people in general, to watch everything they do with their bodies and faces, to listen to every syllable spoken and judge every inflection, tone, and word choice made. The problem was, sometimes in quick meetings, without a baseline to establish the person's norms, it was difficult to discern whether the person was being deceitful in their presentation, or if they were a genuinely uncomfortable and shy soul who gave off weird vibes in the most comfortable of settings. Either way, there was indeed something off about Shelly.

Call Back to HQ

Eli got back in his car and immediately dialed up Nate. "Hey, so check it out. I just had an interesting meeting with Shelly."

"Oh yeah?" Nate replied.

"Yeah, for being friends, she sure seemed disinterested in talking with me much, and she wasn't the least bit broken up about them, but maybe that's because she was at work and didn't want to show emotion or something."

"Well, yeah, that could be it," ?" Nate agreed. "You headed home? Wiat a sec, John is walking by. Hey, Sarge, I got Eli on the line. He just left Shelly's."

"Put him on speaker," Eli heard Kesling say in the background.

"Yeah, hang on, Eli, you're going on speaker with Sarge and me," Nate said into his phone while selecting speaker mode. "Try that again, bud."

"Well, Shelly isn't what I was expecting. She comes off innocent enough, but by her handshake, I think she may be tougher than some of the deputies I've worked with. She's fully capable of taking out the Browers. She has a gun and the familiarity to take these people by surprise. She knows how to secure people, how to avoid police activity, how we think and investigate. But the problem is, she might have a physical alibi."

"What's the alibi?"

"She was in Disney World."

"Land," said Kesling.

"No, World. She claims she was in Florida at the big mouse house. Her boyfriend works for Disney here at Burbank headquarters and gets all the free perks. Said she was gone from Thursday before the Friday we think they were abducted, and just got back in late Sunday night."

"She said she was gone during the kidnap period?" Nate asked.

"No, I'm saying that. She just said she was gone from Thursday until Sunday. That covers the time period. But get this, she also told me Bill worked for some clothing designer here in the garment district. Supposed to be some famous rich guy who did all kinds of exclusive stuff. Anyway, apparently Bill embezzled almost two million dollars. Sounds like reason to kill someone, doesn't it?"

"Aw, man, you're kidding. Someone like that probably has a team of lawyers," Kesling said. "But hey, it's worth a shot. Call over there and see if he'll talk to you. Just do a lockdown interview for now. Don't press him."

When detectives want to talk to a potential suspect early but don't have enough information to actually interrogate, they will do an early interview to set the stage. Getting to a suspect early is tricky business. Sometimes it causes the case to go upside down and crazy; other times, it works out very well.

By locking down a suspect to an early statement, while the fresh excitement of the event is still simmering in their minds and they haven't yet calmed down to think through all their possible defense stories, the first scenario they provide during an early interview is usually pretty stupid. But that's exactly why detectives will do a lockdown interview early.

When the detectives gain more evidence and come back for a second interview with the intention of settling into a nice long interrogation, the suspect can't deviate from his first story without having to explain all the irregularities and why his story differs. Locking him down to his first statement ultimately allows the question, "Were you lying then or are you lying now?" It's a damned if you do, damned if you don't proposition that only works on guilty people. Honest people's stories don't change.

"Okay, Sarge, I'll call over. Who the hell knows if he's even in town or what. But I'll call you guys back either way and let you know."

Enter Davin Harris

Eli pulled up in front of a ten-story building with the name "Harris" labeled across the top in a brass signature like Steve Wynn did with his Wynn Las Vegas Hotel and Casino. Based on the age of the building, Steve might have actually copied Davin.

Without any parking available, Eli parked in the red zone right in front of the building and slung his radio microphone up and over the rearview mirror to let beat cops know he was on the job and not to ticket his unit.

The lobby showed the age of the building. It had once been the nicest of its time, but, guessing by the decor and the wear and tear, it hadn't been updated since it was built in the 1970s. Clean and functional, but not at all an ornate or high-end design.

Eli took the far elevator, which was an express to the tenth floor where Davin Harris's offices were located per the lobby signage. When the soft *ding* announced his arrival, the elevator doors opened into a beautiful expanse. Glass walls and doors allowed viewing throughout most of the floor. People wearing high fashion walked about or sat in their offices or in the grand meeting room that occupied the center of the floor.

A sleek and shiny white reception desk was stationed a few steps across from the elevator. Behind the desk sat a gorgeous woman in her early thirties. Hair and makeup were perfectly applied, not overdone as he saw in so many of the women in headquarters and on calls for service to citizens' homes.

The receptionist wore a sleeveless black dress that clung to her body to show off her well-maintained curves, but wasn't at all revealing or sleazy. "Hello, welcome to Harris Fashions," the woman said with a friendly smile that showed off perfect teeth and glistening sapphires for eyes.

"Hi, I'm looking for Davin Harris. I called ahead..."

"Oh, are you Detective Hockney? You spoke with me on the phone. I'm Ellie," she said, continuing with a friendly smile, almost flirtatiously. "Davin is expecting you. Go right in."

Eli replied, "Thanks so much." But when he turned in the direction Ellie indicated, he wasn't sure where he was supposed to go. There was a large stone wall with the brass *Harris Fashions* logo set diagonally across it, next to it was a glass-front office with another young woman inside, and then from there, the corner of a glass wall that surrounded the large interior conference room started the hallway that led down the rest of the floor.

"Head toward the stone wall, Detective. The doors will open," she said with a hint of fun in her voice. As Eli walked toward the stone wall, hidden sensors detected his approach and started the opening process. The wall that seemed cast from one large stone was actually split vertically, and opened silently and effortlessly to allow Eli to pass through. He couldn't help but touch the surface to see whether it was real stone. It was real, but his musing over how in the hell those large stones got up to the tenth floor was interrupted by a voice from inside.

"Hello, Detective," Davin said with an outstretched hand adorned in multiple gold rings on fingers with perfectly manicured nails. The index-finger ring was an oversized piece carrying a 100 Hungarian Forint coin encircled by diamonds banded in a filigree pattern. His pinkie finger was decorated with a three-carat heart-shaped diamond traced by emeralds in a gold setting with a band made of alternating X and O letters interlocking one another. A thick gold rope bracelet dangled loosely from his wrist.

Davin's thinning light blond hair was combed back exposing a large forehead above his steely blue eyes. Wearing black from head to toe, he still bought his T-shirt in the size he wore when he was a starving and fledgling designer. Now it clung tightly to him, showing off what would kindly be called a dad bod if he were the kind of man who might father children. Even with his black jeans and black high-gloss three-quarter Prada dress boots, he stood all of five foot five inches.

One of the walls was covered in cork paneling from corner to corner. An adjacent wall had a large butcher paper roll suspended on an industrial roller. Davin's desk was a very basic drawing table, not an ornate executive desk. He truly was the designer and wasn't simply a figurehead with minions who did the designs for which he took full credit. Sure, there was collaboration, but Davin really was the heart and soul of his business.

On his desk was a cheap plastic bucket, almost like the kind you might get for your children to play with in the sand. The bucket was filled with sharpened number two pencils. Another matching bucket sat on a shelf under the hanging butcher roll, but within arm's reach of the cork wall. When Davin got an idea, he pulled down a length of paper and tore it from the holder, pinned it to the wall, and started drawing. When the pencil he was drawing with got dull, he just reached in and got a new one, like a professional drummer who broke a stick in concert. The audience never heard a missed beat when the drummer launched the broken stick to the side and retrieved another one in a highly practiced motion.

"Hello, Mr. Harris. Thanks for seeing me on such short notice," Eli said.

For the handshake, Davin offered only his fingers and partial palm facing down. When their hands met, Eli found it beyond strange to receive an overly feminine handshake. Not even his female friends and other women whom he'd met on- or off-duty ever offered such a dainty handshake.

"Please call me Davin," he said as he reached with his left hand and clasped over both of Eli's in a grandmotherly pat. "Wait. Is that one of mine?" Davin paused a moment, switching grips, and took Eli's right hand with his left, then took his right hand and placed it palm open on Eli's right breast area and felt the fabric. Eli wanted to pull back from a seriously awkward moment of near groping, but he knew the man was weirdly nonthreatening. Had he gone for the groin, that would have gotten a punch to Davin's face, but at the moment, he was a fashionista examining what Eli knew for a fact was a suit he'd tailor-made for one of his most famous clients.

Davin continued his forensic examination. Without lifting his hand, he ran it over to the lapel and rubbed it between his thumb and forefinger. "Mm-hmm." He continued to rub down the jacket to the front opening and lifted the right side to examine the button. "Yes, definitely one of mine. But it is definitely not yours. That is, of course, unless I don't remember tailoring this for you, and by the looks of you, I would remember."

"It's borrowed. My suit took a dive into a swimming pool while I was in it, and so my, um, friend let me borrow one of his. Thankfully, we're the same size...ish."

"Nice friend..."

"Indeed. So, Mr. Harris..."

"Davin."

"Davin, obviously I'm here to talk to you about the murders of the Browers—"

"*What?* Bill is dead?" Davin clutched his chest with both hands and walked backward in shock in a manner that Eli would have normally attributed to being overdramatic, but in this case, it might have been a genuine reaction. Davin continued until his rear end hit the back of one of the two high-back black leather guest chairs that sat across from his desk. He turned and sat in one and put his head in his hands. Elis sat down next him in the other chair.

"I'm afraid so. So is Abby."

"What? Oh, dear lord! How?"

"I'm sorry to break the news so abruptly. You know, I honestly just thought you would know. It's been on the news and, well, I just assumed. I'm sorry to drop that on you like that." Eli wasn't sorry in the least. Although he didn't know for sure whether or not Davin knew they were dead from being involved in the murders himself or just simply from being informed through friends, it was good to see what kind of reaction he'd receive if Davin genuinely hadn't yet known. But, come to think of it, Eli hadn't stated he was from homicide on the phone to Davin's receptionist, nor had he said he was from San Bernardino County.

"So, tell me, Davin, why did you think I wanted to talk to you?"

"I just assumed it was about the embezzlement case."

"Yeah, I'd like to know more about that. Please tell me about what happened."

"What happened? What happened was I trusted someone like a brother. I thought Bill was loyal to me. I certainly was to him. But I guess that's how the conman does it. The devil never shows up wearing horns and a cape, right?"

"Right." Eli was leaning in to show his interest. Although he was always interested to hear what people had to say, he'd learned a great technique from his partner Nate for really drawing people in.

Nate would lean forward in his chair and put both forearms across his thighs nearly at the knees and push his head forward with wide eyes like the person talking was telling the most compelling story Nate had ever heard. After seeing Nate do it countless times, Eli tried it a couple of times himself and found that it led to great success.

People want to be listened to. Even when they're lying, then they want to be heard and believed, if at all possible. For Eli, this was the perfect opportunity to hone his skills with Davin, who already did everything for effect and attention. Leaning in on his arms gave Eli the posture of an entranced member of the king's court. Davin was obviously delirious with joy at the audience he was receiving, especially from such a handsome young man.

"Bill worked for me for about, I'd say, right up till five years ago. He was a master at the gray area of taxes. I never paid so little, and never once was there an audit. He helped me with some cash issues, and everything was moving smoothly, or so I thought."

"So, what happened?" Eli asked with the tone of a friend who'd learned there was a terrible tragedy.

"Simple, really. Kind of innocent how it happened too. I was looking for my season passes to come in for the Hollywood Bowl. Now, I haven't even seen the mailbox since Bill started, but on this day, I really wanted to see if my tickets had arrived, so I checked Bill's desk and found some bank statements to a bank we don't use, or at least I didn't know we used.

"I called Bill to ask him if he'd seen my tickets or if he could confirm he purchased them like I asked him to. He said he'd bought them, but as far as he knew, they hadn't come in yet. Then at the last second before we hung up, I asked him about this other bank. That's when he totally freaked out. Said he'd be right in to explain. I wasn't even that curious, really, but his reaction was sure something, I'll tell you."

"Wow, so then what happened?" Eli asked.

"He came in like twenty minutes later and accused me of searching his office. First, I reminded him it was *my* office, and second, I really wasn't searching it or curious until his tirade. That's when I called for a forensic accountant to come in."

"And?"

"One point eight million dollars. That we know of."

"That you know of?" Eli asked incredulously.

"Yes, well, some of my clients like to deal in cash, so who knows what percentage of the income was actually making it to the bank? Took more than a month for a team of forensic accountants to figure it all out. Not sure that we actually did in total."

"So, then what happened?" Eli repeated. The most powerful method of getting people to tell a story from their perspective was to not ask questions with any of the assumed answers in the question. Instead, asking the person what happened next, and repeating that phrase throughout the interview, was a prompt that kept people flowing in their story. Liars have difficulty reciting a story with rich detail point after made-up point.

"I'm not really sure, to tell you the truth. When Bill came back to clean out his personal effects, I stayed in my office per the advice of counsel." Then Davin play-acted the way he did on that day when he yelled, "But I did shout out so he could hear, 'You can't trust anybody these days!' He got the point." Davin reached over to his desk and grabbed a tissue to wipe his nose. "But I never meant for anything like this to happen."

"I'm sorry."

"For the past two years, I've wished nothing but bad luck for him. Even wished him dead for betraying me. But I never meant it." Davin cried into his tissue.

"But with regard to the embezzlement..."

"I sued him!"

"Why didn't you call the police?"

"No offense, Detective, but do you really think the police would be able to handle such a large and unique case as this?"

"Um, yeah. That's what we do."

"Well, not in my experience. Most of the cops around here couldn't catch a fish in a five-gallon bucket of water."

"Well, anyway..."

"This lawsuit has dragged on for a couple of years now. Mine and Maggie's."

"Maggie?"

"My personal assistant. Bill convinced her to go in on a land development deal in Georgia. She gave him all two hundred fifty thousand dollars she and her husband had saved together over the past many years. It was their retirement investment. Bill promised Maggie that her investment would double in eighteen months. They just needed the money to buy the land and get all the permits, then they'd be off to the races selling McMansions in Duluth, Georgia, I believe."

"How did that all come about?"

"I'm not entirely sure, but as I recall, the developer was a contractor from here in LA County somewhere and used Bill for his taxes. They got to talking about how much land there was in Georgia—why Georgia in particular, I don't know—but regardless, they said the area was ripe for upscale homes on acre lots."

"So you let Maggie invest?"

"I didn't *let her* do anything! She's a grown, married woman. But I did tell her I thought it was a shady deal and the reason Bill came to her was because I turned him down."

"Why did you?"

"Did I what?"

"Turn him down. What gave you the clue that it was a bad deal? Or wait, I'm making an assumption. Was it a bad deal? Was it a real deal at all, or just straight theft?"

"No, no, the idea and the land and the contractor were all real. The question I'd asked was what kind of experience with other developments did he have. Turns out this was going to be his first attempt at developing an entire project. What it boiled down to was that he was a good foreman on many multi-residential developments, but never was he the leader behind the scenes. He was just the primary builder.

"I know that although I've got tremendous, maybe even the best, seamstresses in the world working for me, it doesn't mean they can design a dress. Sew it perfectly? Yes. Design it? No. I wasn't about to give them money to play with. And I told Maggie not to either, but she didn't listen."

"So what happened with the project?"

"It went belly up. I don't recall why, but politics, logistics, implementation, some or all of it, I really don't know the details. But I do know this. Money gone."

"Wow," was all that Eli could muster. His head was spinning.

"What about your money?"

"I didn't invest."

"No, I mean the embezzlement monies."

"Well, we were moving ever so slowly through the court process. There were some discussions about a settlement, but I didn't quite hear the details. I thought Bill was going to offer me something that would have covered Maggie's losses and some sort of return of money to me. I probably would have accepted it at that point, just to make it all go away."

"So, no details, but you did hear something? From whom?"

"Bill."

"Isn't that unusual? Wouldn't it normally come from his attorney? I mean, at this point, why would you even speak with Bill without the lawyers being involved?"

"It was indeed unusual, but he called, I answered. I don't know. Habit. Curiosity. Sentimentality. I honestly don't know."

"Do you mind if I speak with your attorney? Would you give him permission to speak with me?"

"I'll ask him if he thinks that's a good idea or not. Give me your card, and I promise someone will call you."

Eli stood up and reached into his badge wallet to retrieve a business card and handed it to Davin, who also stood up and accepted the card, this time without groping Eli in any way. "Thank you, Davin. You've been a great help. Thanks for your time."

"You're very welcome. It was certainly my pleasure to meet you. Come back any time. I'd love to measure you...for a personalized suit."

"I probably couldn't afford it."

"I'm sure we could work something out." Davin wasn't being very coy at all with his comment.

Ignoring the comment and staying professional, Eli asked, "Hey, by any chance, do you know the name of Bill's lawyer?"

"Of course I do. Met him several times over the years. Harold King. He used to be an LA County DA, as I understood it from Bill. They met through their friend Shelly..." Davin tried to recall the last name.

"Weller?"

"Yes, that's it. Shelly Weller. They met when he was trying cases as a junior prosecutor many years ago before Harold went private. That's when her husband and she were still married, as I recall. Before the poor sergeant learned she was catching for the other team."

"Sergeant?" Eli was blown away with that little tidbit that Shelly forgot to mention.

"Yes, I believe it was sergeant. I think that's what Bill said about him. Maybe it was captain? I don't know all those rank names and how you guys keep all that straight in your heads."

"Well, you get used to it. Do you know where he works? With which agency?"

"Now, that I'm not sure of. I just recall that he was a police sergeant. Maybe he's a detective now too."

"Well, sergeants outrank detectives, but...never mind. So, if I got this straight, Shelly was married to a law enforcement officer while she was..." Eli started a search for words or phraseology that was appropriate.

Davin came to his rescue. "Still in the closet, as we say. Yes, they have a daughter together. She must be in her teens now, I'd think. Boy, time does fly."

"And you know all this how?"

"Bill worked in that very office"—Davin pointed through the window into the neighboring office where a young lady now occupied the space—"for five years and spent half that time talking with me when I wasn't inspired to draw. I think Shelly was his best friend outside of his wife. He trusted Shelly and taught her how to invest her own money and flip houses."

"Flip houses?"

"Yes, it's a term referring..."

"I know what it means. I just didn't think that Shelly... Well, now I honestly don't know what all to think."

"Well, Detective, when you get a chance to speak to Harold, I'm sure he'll give you all that you need to know on Shelly."

Stunned and speechless and almost overwhelmed by the scrambling of ideas going through his brain, Eli finally replied, "Yeah, right, okay, thanks. I have to go. Can I come back if I have more questions?"

"I would love it." Davin took a couple of steps toward Eli, but Eli didn't want to find out what he had in mind, hoping it wasn't a hug or some European male-to-male kiss-on-the-cheek kind of thing. He'd had enough surprises and touchy-feely stuff for one day. Thus, Eli half waved and made a quick exit through the open wall of stone.

Gotta Call This In

With the afternoon upon him, making it back to the office was absolutely not going to happen. The best he might hope for with this LA traffic was to get something to eat and head east before the primary rush-hour traffic started.

Although he grew up in Southern California, Eli had never had a famous Pink's hot dog. Since he was on company gas and time, he made the best of it and indulged himself in what he had been told for years was the best hot dog on the West Coast. Famous for celebrity patrons and being on the corner of Melrose and North La Brea Avenue in the heart of Hollywood, Pink's was just down the street from Paramount Pictures. Nice little sightseeing trip on the county's dime.

Eli stood outside taking in the sun and had his mobile phone pressed to his cheek. "Nate, these people have screwed over and been sued by everybody under the sun. The list of suspects just got a mile longer. You want to go to Georgia?"

"Hold on, Eli, let me put you on speaker phone in Sarge's office," Nate said as he fumbled with the buttons and made his way across the bureau into Sergeant Kesling's office. He set his phone down on Kesling's desk and said, "It's Eli."

Kesling's voice came across into Eli's ear. "What's up, kid?" Eli rolled his eyes since no one in the office could see him. He hated being called kid.

"So it seems our victims were hated as much as they were loved."

"How so?" Kesling asked.

"Apparently, Bill screwed his former-client-slash-boss Davin Harris out of a few million dollars, some marketing chick that works for Davin for a quarter mil on some out-of-state land deal that went bankrupt, and there are supposedly more issues or lawsuits that Shelly told me Bill's lawyer would be able to tell us about."

"Are you kidding me?"

"Nope. Can't make this shit up. And get this strangeness. Shelly tells me she doesn't know much about anything, can't tell me who Bill and Abby's lawyer is, but when I'm talking with Davin, who is himself a story for another time, he told me Shelly was the one who introduced the lawyer to the Browers."

"Wait, so did she or she did *not* know about the lawsuits?" Nate asked.

"Well, that's the thing. She seemed to know something, then backed off like she didn't, then told me she doesn't know who the lawyer is, but according to Davin, Bill and Shelly were like best friends."

"Hanky-panky maybe?" asked Kesling.

"Not a chance. Shelly is not the trophy girlfriend type. Oh, and get this! Her ex-husband? Wait for it, is a sergeant with law enforcement somewhere out here."

"Bullshit!" Kesling shouted over the speaker.

"I'm not kidding. Like I said, can't make this shit up. Question is where he works and whether or not we should talk to him yet or wait it out some more," Eli said.

Nate added his thoughts. "Well, I'm really liking Shelly right now. I mean, with her having their will, she has control of all their assets. And in light of finding the car in a parolee neighborhood, this is looking really promising."

"Wait, what car?" Eli asked excitedly.

"Oh shit, yeah, you've been out of the loop. LAPD called, and they found the Browers' missing SUV in Chinatown in a gang-infested neighborhood where I'd guess half the population is on parole," Nate told him.

"Chinatown? Really, well, that is interesting. Shelly wanted to cut our meeting short because she had to go find a parolee-at-large she said was eluding her in Chinatown. Man, she must have let that slip in her nervousness."

"Interesting," Kesling said. "I sent our surveillance guys to go sit on the Browers' car, and we'll see what happens."

"LAPD didn't do the recovery or tow it?"

"Surprisingly, we got a couple of officers with their heads screwed on right and tight. They ran the plate, got the thrity-five-frank for our one-eighty-seven, saw that it was unoccupied, left it alone, and set up on it down the block. Didn't fuck with it at all, so we're not burned yet. Our guys should be out there in a couple of hours. They'll call me with updates with anything that happens since we can't connect that far on radio."

The worker at the window at Pink's called out, "Eli! Your order is ready!"

Eli walked over and picked up his food, pinching the phone between his shoulder and cheek. "Thank you."

"Rebecca! Your order is up," was clearly heard over the phone and transmitted over the speaker in Kesling's office.

"Where are you?" Nate asked.

"Pink's," Eli replied smugly. "Always wanted to try one of these."

"Look at you, going all Hollywood on us," Nate joked.

"Not a chance. This place is a strange mess," Eli said.

Kesling interrupted. "Well, enjoy your tube of mystery meat and then get your ass back home. We're going up on Shelly tomorrow morning. Let's meet out there at oh-five-thirty. I'll text you the briefing location when we get that figured out back here. Get on home."

Going up meant they'd be setting up surveillance. Eli hung up, pocketed his phone, and took a big bite of his hot dog. A squirt of mustard hit the suit jacket, shirt, and tie that he'd borrowed from Brad Clark. "Shit!"

Autopsy

Artie was dressed in a paper gown over his shirt and tie, wearing a hairnet over his shaved head, shoe booties, and latex gloves. Dr. Frank Kellogg, chief medical examiner, a sixty-year-old Irish-born, thick-accented, renowned expert forensic pathologist, was tending to the autopsies of the Browers and their dog, Teddy.

Dr. Kellogg had Bill up on the examination table. The decomposing body was already in late stage two or early stage three of decomposition due to the advanced skin slippage present. There were large spots over sixty percent of the body that looked similar to third-degree burns where the underlying skin was exposed with the top layers rolling back on themselves.

Because the bodies had been buried in the sand beneath the hot desert sun, it caused decomposition to run through stage one rather quickly and advance to other stages at an accelerated rate. Thankfully, the bodies were void of any insect or animal activity. In those cases where bodies are dumped in the open or in a very shallow grave, the animal and insect activity can distort and even sometimes ruin the evidence that points to the cause of death.

Insects and animals, like most creatures, will choose the path of least resistance. Bullet and knife holes in bodies make it easier for creatures to tear open and eat flesh than if they had to create a new hole. Therefore, sometimes the death-causing injuries are eaten away by nature. But not in this case.

After being disrobed of his clothing, which consisted of blue boxer briefs, black running shorts, and a USC Trojans T-shirt, Bill was carefully examined from head to toe for external injuries. In light of the fact that blood was found on the trail leading to the burial site, one or both of the bodies should have had some sort of wound that would have caused the blood droplets. Unless, of course, the bodies were transported dead already and the blood belonged to the suspect, who injured him or herself during the commission of the crime. They wouldn't know that until a DNA test was performed on the blood collected at the scene and compared with that of the Browers. The hope was that it wasn't their blood and in fact did belong to a suspect, making it impossible for him to claim he wasn't there.

When it came to dead bodies, unlike surgeons for the living who try to do the least amount of damage, forensic pathologists don't fret themselves with their patient's healing. The Y-incision started at the waistline up the center of the torso to just north of the nipple line, where the scalpel made a turn toward the shoulder to form one half of a Y.

A second cut was started at the divergent line and ran to the opposite shoulder, forming the whole Y. The decedent's flesh was then peeled back, exposing the entire torso's muscular and skeletal system. The muscles were examined for any subdural hematoma or other abnormalities. After their absence or presence was documented, the next stage was the removal of the entire front chest area rib cage.

First-time viewers were always surprised that the ribs were cut out with large pruning shears. The entire hood of the car was removed to check out the engine and its parts. No scoping through a small hole. The entire organ system was revealed and plain to see. Primary organs were removed, examined, weighed, and biopsied for future reference.

In the case of Bill, there were no unnatural injuries noted in the torso. There was, however, a puncture wound at the base of the neck. "Hmm," mumbled Dr. Kellogg.

"Whaddya got, Doc?" Artie asked.

"Well, I can't really say for certain...but I think the cause of death is going to be strangulation. But due to the advanced stages of decomposition, I cannot say for sure. My supposition is that it will be ligature, not manual. Not enough gross damage." Dr. Kellogg continued his examination for another moment, then continued, "But the decay can also be indicating the same kind of markings that I would attribute to a ligature mark. Nevertheless, the injury to his neck at the base of his skull is superficial and not at all the cause of death. Due to the decay, I can't say for sure, but it may even be a postmortem injury."

"Stabbed after death?"

"That'd be my guess."

"So, cause of death?"

"Unless tox comes back with some sort of poison, I'm going with strangulation. There are no other injuries antemortem that caused either one of these people to die."

"And the pup?"

"No sign of trauma for a cause of death. Although he did have a contusion to his right eye. I think he died of exposure and dehydration. Dr. Barnes, a local vet, will come over and conclude the necropsy, but I don't expect her to find anything different."

Brad Calls

Eli's mobile phone rang, disrupting the classic rock station that had been playing some Pink Floyd. It was an unknown Los Angeles number. He pushed the HandsFree button on his steering wheel and answered, "Hockney!"

A familiar voice that he couldn't quite put a finger on responded, "Detective Hockney? Good, I'm glad I got you. Do you have a minute?"

Then it hit him. "Mr. Clark?"

"You really gotta stop calling me that. Brad is just fine."

"Okay, you just surprised me is all. Wasn't expecting a call from you."

"Is this a bad time?"

"No, perfect time, really. I'm just moving slowly in your Los Angeles traffic. What's up?"

"You're in LA? Wow, that's perfect. I hate to ask this, but since you're here, I'd rather speak face-to-face. Any chance you can come up?"

Eli was northbound on the Glendale Freeway a few minutes shy of the 210. Taking that east would connect him with the I-15 Northbound and get him home to the High Desert. At the moment, he was a few minutes ahead of the main rush hour, and speeds on the freeway were surprisingly fast at forty-five mph. If everyone would keep their eyes on the road and off their mobile phones, then maybe no one would run into the back of another car and screw up the entire freeway. Each minute that passed, thousands of cars were entering the freeway headed east, where living was far cheaper than in Los Angeles proper. If he didn't get on the 210 Eastbound in the next few minutes, the hour-long drive ahead of him might turn into two-plus hours later.

He really did *not* want to go up to La Cañada at this hour, but this was a murder investigation, so no time like the present. Plus, the drive home would be after-hours and overtime, so there was that.

"Sure, what's up?" Eli asked.

"Just got a weird call from Shelly. Haven't talked to her for months, maybe better part of a year, then out of the blue, she calls. I'd like to go over this in detail with you. Plus, there's something else I'd like to run by you. How far away are you?"

"About thirty minutes, I'd guess," Eli said quickly, but then he realized he was still wearing Brad's suit. He couldn't show up there wearing the suit like some poser. How embarrassing that would be. Before Brad could reply, Eli looked down at the mustard stains and said, "But, uh, I've got to make a stop first. How about an hour instead?"

"That's perfect. Still remember where the house is?"

"No, but Siri will help me."

"All right, when you get to the gate, just push pound fifty-one fifty, and it'll open for you."

"Fifty-one fifty? You a Van Halen fan?"

"No, yeah, but no, this is the police code for the crazy people, right?"

"Yeah, it is." Eli laughed. "Okay see you up there in like an hour." Hockney clicked the End button on the steering wheel then let out a screaming, "*Shit!*"

New Suit

Fortunately for Eli, there was a JCPenney in Glendale two exits ahead of him and on the way to Brad's. He found the men's department and frantically searched through racks of suits in order to find one that fit and wasn't too expensive. Suit, shirt...tie...belt, oh man, and shoes too! This just got expensive.

He found a charcoal-gray suit, a color he didn't currently own. He was waiting impatiently in line behind a chatty woman who was talking to the clerk about her grandchildren.

"That's so sweet. You have to bring them in next time you sit for your daughter. I'd love to meet them both," said the cashier.

The female shopper had gotten her merchandise bagged up and the cashier put the receipt in the bag, but the old woman was content and staying for a chat. Eli looked around and couldn't see another open cashier, and besides, he was next in line and could have been out of there in just five more minutes if the old bat would just hurry the fuck up and leave.

"I will. How's your hubby?" asked the woman.

Eli couldn't wait any longer, so he walked up and placed his pile of clothes on the counter before the old woman had taken her bags. He interrupted and ended the conversation with "I'm sure he's fine." Although he didn't touch the shopper, his presence and verbal tone was like a hip check to the woman, who left in a speechless huff.

"Hi, thanks," Eli said, almost out of breath, to the cashier.

"My, a whole new wardrobe," said the cashier, who seemed to be moving at sloth-like speed as retribution for Eli's impatience and rudeness. She checked every label and refolded the clothes to make them fit nicely in the bag.

"Hey, listen, I'm kind of in a huge rush. I'm going to change into this right away, so I don't need a bag or anything."

"But you're wearing a suit already," she pointed out.

"Yup," Eli replied shortly as he stared at her with a stone face, which didn't take a veteran behavioral analyst to read as *just do your thing and stop talking to me.*

"That'll be four hundred eighty-eight dollars and seventy-two cents. Do you have a rewards card with us?"

Hockney had his credit card in his hand already. "No, I don't. Here ya go."

"You could save a bunch of money on this if you just took ten minutes and filled out..."

"I'm really trying not to be rude, but I don't have a week's worth of my homicide investigation to explain to you why I'm in such a hurry. Can we just—"

"I'm sorry, sir, this card is declined."

"Really? Shit. Oh, um..." Eli looked in his wallet and at the only other form of payment he had, which was his debit card. He honestly didn't know if there was enough in his checking account to cover the bill. If there was, it was the last of his money until next Thursday when he got paid again.

"Let's try this instead," Eli said and handed over his life savings.

The waiting to see if his card cleared felt like an eternity. If it didn't clear, maybe he could just leave off the shirt and tie. He'd wear the new suit without a tie since he was only going one more place, then home.

"Okay," she said, "there we go. Want to keep the hangers?"

"No, no, in fact, I'll just take it like this," he said as he grabbed up the clothing in his arms and reached out with a couple of fingers to grab the receipt from the cashier before speed walking out of the store and to his car.

Standing outside his Ford Taurus, he had both passenger-side doors open. The front passenger door held the new suit. The new shoes and dress shirt in the package were on the roof. Having not worn a T-shirt because he had on Brad's shirt, which didn't require one, he'd purchased a medium-dark-blue shirt so his skin wouldn't show through the cheap material.

He emptied the pockets of the suit he was wearing and put it all on the roof. He tossed the jacket into the back seat and ripped open the tie packaging while he kicked the shoes into the right rear floorboard. He unbuttoned the cuffs of the sleeves and the top four buttons, then pulled off the dress shirt like it was a T-shirt and tossed it into the back seat as well.

Standing there shirtless, he was about to remove his pants when he noticed a pair of female shoppers who were walking past with strollers. They stopped and stared at him, smiling. It would only have been indecent exposure if he had dropped his pants without wearing underwear. But since he was wearing them, who would really complain if they saw his boxer briefs? They weren't smaller than the swim trunks he wore at the beach. But after some quick consideration about diving into the car to finish dressing, he decided that switching pants wouldn't take but two seconds. He doubted the women minded at all.

Dinner at Brad's

Eli pulled up to the front of Brad Clark's house and parked in the circle at the front door. He stepped out of his car wearing the new clothes he'd just bought. When he reached the front door, it opened to Mia holding it for him.

"Hey, Detective. Good to see you again."

"Dry and fully clothed this time," Eli replied.

"Shame," she tossed over her shoulder as she led him down the hall. Mia stopped in front of him and eyed him up and down, blocking his path before letting Eli into the study, where Brad sat behind his desk. After she walked off, she looked back once more over her shoulder before disappearing down the hall.

"Hey, buddy!" Brad said excitedly.

"Hi."

"Glad you could come by so quickly. Want a beer?"

"Yeah, thanks but no thanks. On duty," Eli said. Needing to know something for his own sake, he asked, "So Mia... She is...?"

"My assistant." Brad smiled and looked at Eli. "She isn't my girl-friend."

"Oh, okay, I was just..."

"And never has been.

"Ah."

"She doesn't have a boyfriend is the answer to the question you were never going to ask."

Eli's face turned a little red, and Brad smiled even bigger.

"So, Shelly?" Eli asked to change the subject.

"Oh, yeah, right. Well, listen, Shelly called me," Brad said as he pointed to one of a couple of leather sitting chairs. "Please." Eli sat down and had his notebook in his hands, ready to write if necessary. Brad continued, "Which is unusual in and of itself. I can't think of the last time we've spoken on the phone, if ever. I just normally see her at Bill and Abby's...or used to, I guess that is."

Brad paused a moment, seeming to realize how that sounded and that he would be using the past tense from now on with regard to Bill and Abby. "Anyway, she was all nutted up about you coming to see her and ask questions about the will."

"Really?"

"Yup, and you know what else?" Brad leaned in for effect as if doling out a secret. "I think she may know more than she's saying. I just get this feeling. Now, I know you think I'm some doofus actor who plays a cop on TV and I'm sticking my Hollywood nose where it doesn't belong..."

"Well, um..."

"See, yeah, I thought so! But listen, I'm not trying to be a pain in the ass or get special privileges. Truth be told, I admire you as the real deal. I jump at the opportunity of playing these roles, even the cheesy one I'm in now, because it's as close to being a real cop as I could ever get."

"Good to know you know it's awful."

"Hey, I said cheesy, not awful. You think it's awful?"

Eli realized he might have crossed the line of being rude and thus hurt case relations. But just as he was becoming concerned, Brad burst out laughing, causing Eli to laugh, and the tension was released.

"Yeah, it's pretty fuckin' awful."

"Yeah, I know. I really do. But holy shit, does it pay well."

"I noticed," Eli said. He then stood, preparing to leave. Obviously, Brad didn't have any details to pass on. His assumptions might be accurate, but they weren't documentable evidence.

"Hey, listen, before you go, I actually wanted to talk to you about something else."

"Oh yeah?"

"For a few weeks now, I've been in conversations with the network about a different kind of police show. A truer-to-life type of show that would be shot in a way that might make you think you were watching *COPS* more than a fictional TV show, a hidden-camera style with a real great ensemble cast and not this solo-hero crap they've had me doing. It's garnered some serious interest, and with my name attached, it's getting legs."

"Okay," Eli said, wondering why Brad was telling him this.

"I was wondering if you might have some time to sit down with me and some studio folks to hash some things out. Do some consulting for us on the project. I'd even pay you for your time and expenses."

Eli was caught off guard for the second time in as many days at Brad's house. He was intrigued, though, and wondered why he was being asked. Surely Brad had countless contacts in the police world, especially here in Los Angeles. "Well, I don't know how that'd work with my job and all."

"Lots of cops moonlight, don't they? I know we use some LAPD guys for the uniform and equipment stuff, but this would be more of a producer role for you."

"What the hell do I know about producing?"

"It's not what you think. You're probably thinking director and the other people who actually make the TV shows. Producer is more a generic role for someone with ideas or a basic story, either fact or fiction, or someone who can give input into the people who make the stuff happen on camera."

"Well, I don't know. This is all crazy talk. I'm just a cop from San Bernardino County—"

"You're more than that," Brad interrupted. "You have some insight and something special that no one else in my business around me has."

"What's that?"

"Real experience," Brad said and let it hang in the air for a moment before continuing, "I'm meeting some folks tonight, in about an hour, as a matter of fact. Can you make it?"

"Aw, not tonight. I gotta head back home now because I have to be back out here super early tomorrow morning for a surveillance on Shelly." The moment the words left his mouth, he knew he'd blown it.

"Really?" Brad asked with a glint in his eye.

"Uh, yeah, see I wasn't really supposed to say that. Don't repeat that to anyone."

"Secret's safe with me."

"I mean it. Not a word to anyone. It could really blow things."

Brad raised his right hand in corny fashion as if he were being sworn in as a new officer. "I promise. Listen, the Browers were my friends. I need you to catch the killers and put them away. I won't screw that up by blabbing."

Eli was contemplating his words and read his face to be genuine, but he was dealing with a professional actor after all. He'd have to just trust his gut at this point.

"Wait a minute. You're heading home now to San Bernardino, then coming right back out tomorrow?"

"Yeah, that's the job."

"Well, hang on, now. I've got an idea. Listen, why don't you go to dinner with us tonight? Let me introduce you to some of these people, and afterward, you can stay here. I mean, I've got like five extra unoccupied bedrooms in this place."

"I don't know. Kinda weird."

"What's weird? You'll have complete privacy, and you can head out in the morning without dealing with all the traffic. The commute alone will save you hours."

Eli considered how it might be perceived, him staying the night at a material witness's house. But he wasn't a suspect, and it wasn't like it was some female's tiny apartment. Brad's house was practically a small hotel. What could the harm be in taking him up on the offer? If he called Sarge and asked him, he'd definitely say it was a bad idea. But Sarge rarely liked Eli's ideas and seemed to think him impetuous. So what if Eli had an uninvolved friend who lived in the Los Angeles area and he chose to stay the night? Would anyone care? Nope. Well, Brad was becoming a friend, and he surely wasn't the suspect, so why not? Better not call Sarge, though. Couldn't unring that bell.

"Besides, you'd be really helping me out, buddy. I need someone like you to help me convince them to stop writing these over-the-top ridiculous clown scenes."

Eli's wheels were spinning. It was really nice to have someone of importance value his opinion for once. It was refreshing and, honestly, kind of exciting. Who wouldn't want to be part of making a television show? Hanging out with Brad was all right too. He was down-to-earth, even with all his fame, awards, and fortune.

"Trust me. You're going to be a big hit with them. Whaddya say?"

"Um..." Eli said. Without having said he'd decided, it was obvious that he wasn't saying no either.

"Come on, let's get you something else to wear that's more casual yet has a little more star quality."

"Huh?"

"Trust me. Man, I wish you'd worn the suit I gave you. Could have just lost the tie and you'd been all set."

"Yeah...wait, *gave me*? I thought that was a loaner to get me back to the office?"

"No way, brother, that is yours to keep. We aren't getting your suit cleaned either. I'm getting you another one, and I don't want to hear a word out of you about it," Brad said as he reached over and put his arm around Eli's shoulder in a best-friend style and escorted him the first few steps toward his bedroom closet once again.

Malibu

Nate balanced a set of multiple copies and folders as he walked from the copy room to his desk halfway across the bureau. He heard his desk phone ringing and quickened his pace to a jog to get to his phone. After hours, he only got three rings before it went to voicemail.

He sprinted the last few steps, which created enough momentum that he couldn't stop the files he was carrying from sliding off one another and spilling onto the top of his desk, chair and the floor. "Shit!"

Nate snatched up the desk phone handle only to hear a dial tone. "Dammit!" he growled as he slammed down the receiver. Just as he bent down to start picking up the files, his mobile phone started ringing. He reached for his pocket only to realize it wasn't in his pants, but instead was now buried under a pile of paper somewhere on his desk. He found his phone after making an even bigger mess.

Seeing that it was his partner calling, he breathed out a heavy and exasperated breath. "Hey, Eli!"

"Yo, dude, you all right?"

Nate examined the mess before him in the darkened homicide detail. Everyone else had already gone home, in particular Artie, who, after calling from the morgue with an update in the midafternoon, was never heard from again. He somehow regularly disappeared into what Nate and Eli had come to call "Artieville." It was a place of unknown origin where Artie disappeared to avoid work. The bosses didn't seem to notice, and if they did, they just didn't seem to care.

"Yeah, I'm good, I was just...yeah. What's up?"

Eli was standing in the front parking area of Brad's house, having moved his Taurus from the visiting circle and parked it farther across from the house. He had changed into some of Brad's clothes once again.

Instead of the wool/poly blend suit he'd bought earlier in the day, Eli now wore tan Hugo Boss cotton-blend twill pants over brown leather Berluti oxfords, topped off by a James Perse white linen button-down shirt with blue pinstripes, with the top three buttons undone at Brad's suggestion. The navy-blue Caruso cashmere blazer felt wonderful to the touch and to wear. The final touch was a white cotton pocket square to complete the ensemble.

Eli had never heard of any of these labels before. While changing into the clothing, he simultaneously searched Google on his cell phone. He couldn't believe the prices were real, but then again, it was why he looked like he just came off of a photoshoot for *GQ* magazine.

"Traffic's a nightmare. Brad Clark didn't have anything to add other than that Shelly was all weird with him on the phone. The call itself was unusual, he said, but she didn't tell him anything incriminating. He feels she's hiding something."

"Well, don't we all? He may actually be right. We've been tracking some big cash deposits to her account. Probably from the Browers. But we can't be sure yet. This has gotten really interesting. Sarge said he's taking our team down from rotation and letting us work just this one straight for the time being."

"That's awesome. Taking on a bunch of other murders right now would be killer. Pun intended."

"Cute."

"Hey, let the boss know I'm headed straight home and then I'll 87 with you guys at oh-five-thirty?"

"Sure. Hey, you sound weird. You okay?" Nate asked.

Eli felt bad for lying to his partner and friend. But strange things were happening in Eli's favor that he couldn't ignore. "Yeah, totally. I'm just tired. Hate this fucking LA traffic. Who'd want to live out here, huh?" Eli stared out over the valley as the setting sun was beginning a red descent into the smog layer. It was truly beautiful and a completely different Los Angeles than he'd ever known.

"Yeah, no shit. Thanks for taking one for the team."

"I didn't do it for the team, just you, buddy. See ya."

Nate hung up, then stared at the mess and dove into picking it up.

Eli was about to walk back inside the house when he heard the distinct engine noise of a high-performance car. He looked in the direction of the sound to see Brad coming around from the side of the house driving a red Ferrari Portofino. Eli just watched as Brad drove around the circle and pulled up next to him.

"You ready to go?"

"Holy shit, is this your car?"

"No, it was just sitting on the side of the house. No one was using it, so...of course it's my car! Jump in!"

Eli was grinning from ear to ear when he slid into the leather seats of the most beautiful car he'd ever seen.

"Ever been in one of these before?" Brad asked.

"Never even pulled one over."

Brad laughed. "Well, do you think you can get us out of a ticket if we get pulled over?"

Eli reached into his breast pocket and pulled out his flat badge and flipped it open television style. "I've got my get-out-of-jail card right here."

"Outstanding! Let's go meet some people."

They roared off in the Ferrari with both men enjoying themselves as they ripped down the street.

Simultaneously, Nate was loading up boxes of papers into the back of his police unit before he fell into the driver's seat. He sat there a moment and inhaled deeply, held it for a count of three, then exhaled it quickly. Nate had learned this process of calming himself when he was a child, but he'd never used it as much as he had since being selected for the homicide detail.

Brad drove his Ferrari through traffic on the LA streets and up a freeway on-ramp at breakneck speed. Eli was still grinning from ear to ear.

Nate walked away from a grocery store in his neighborhood, carry-ing a couple of bags of groceries and a gallon of milk all in his left hand. The right hand remained free in the unlikely event he needed to draw his concealed firearm. Nate chirped the alarm to unlock his unit and put the groceries on the front passenger floorboard. He looked at his watch to see that it was already past eight. The nights had been getting long on this case already.

The sun was still not completely set as the Ferrari drove north along the Westbound 134 toward Beverly Hills. Eli was no longer grinning. Instead, he had taken up a settled look of acceptance that he was in a two-hundred-thousand-dollar car with clothes that cost two months of his current salary. He could get used to this. Why not him? Why not work with these Hollywood people and teach them a thing or two about authentic police work and make a profitable living as a consultant? He'd given his life to public service and had survived thus far. It wouldn't be wrong to make some money, to live less in insecurity and a little more in luxury. Why did this lifestyle have to be for "other" people? Why couldn't he be "other" people? The Ferrari turned south on Coldwater Canyon Avenue and sped through the curves. Brad really knew how to drive this car.

Nate pulled up into the driveway of his home, but had to stop short on the driveway to move his child's tricycle before he could pull all the way up and park. He clicked the garage door opener to lift the roll-up door. The interior of the garage was no place for a car. There were far too many children's toys and boxes accumulated over years of marriage, from their recent move to the new house. Between two little ones and his long hours, they hadn't yet had time to unpack everything. It was going to take a while by the looks of the garage.

As Brad and Eli continued their journey, they were cruising through streets and neighborhoods unlike anything Eli had ever seen. The homes grew larger with each mile they drove. These were some of the largest mansions he had ever seen that weren't on television.

Nate tried sneaking into the house carrying the overloaded box of files, plus the gallon of milk and groceries hanging from one finger. But his toddlers were expecting their daddy and were lying in wait for him to hit the threshold. "Attack!" shouted Nate's two boys, ages three and five. Nate put down the box, groceries, and his coat on the ground and fell to the floor to be wrestled with by his boys.

Brad and Eli pulled up to a sprawling, multistory mansion. A valet got into the car and drove it off to be parked somewhere else on the property. The pair walked up the steps to the front door and entered inside.

Nate's kids each grabbed a grocery bag and the gallon of milk and ran into the kitchen. Nate picked up his box and followed. "Hey hon," Nate called out as he quickly kissed his wife of nine years.

"Hey, babe," Helen Parker said. "Did you get the French bread?"

"Sure did, and the parmesan cheese too," he said with a smile. Helen took the grocery bag and used the items to finish dinner. Their children were running, then sliding on the wooden floor, trying to outdo each other, making the family beagle, Buttons, a nervous wreck. The television was on showing a children's program that no one was watching. To an outsider, this would appear to be pure chaos, but neither Nate nor Helen were fazed in the least. Stepping over and around his two "knuckleheads," as he loved to call them, Nate grabbed a beer from the fridge and plopped down on a kitchen chair next to his cardboard box of files.

"What's for dinner, hon?" Nate asked.

"Chicken and pasta. Or leftover meatloaf, depending on how this turns out." Helen reached into the oven to check on the food, but misjudged the distance and touched her forearm on the oven opening. "Ouch!"

There were dozens of people in this grand house at the end of Lania Lane in the Hollywood Hills. Everyone was dressed casually elegant. Eli was stunned to see the number of famous movie and TV stars, athletes and prominent business leaders holding champagne glasses or crystal drink tumblers with whatever drink they preferred, custom-made by one of the many bartenders at the various stations throughout the house and backyard.

Eli stood shoulder to shoulder with Brad and leaned in to make sure no one heard him rhetorically ask, "This is dinner with some friends?"

Brad turned his head to face Eli, winked, and said with a mischievous grin, "This is dinner with some friends."

Once the guests saw Brad, he was greeted by everyone he passed with "Brad!" or "Great to see you!" or "Love the show!"

What surprised Eli was how Brad didn't ditch him and run off into the sea of people vying for his attention. Instead, he kept Eli with him and introduced him to everyone as people came up to him, or those people whom he thought Eli should meet. Brad introduced him as "a real-life homicide detective."

Everyone was impressed and seemed genuinely interested in meeting Eli. Most had big smiles and asked him the routine questions all cops get at non-cop parties. *Have you shot anyone? What is the craziest or scariest thing you have seen? What is it like to be Tased? Ever been in a fight with a suspect? Do cops really eat donuts all the time?*

At the Parker dinner table, the family bowed their heads to start their blessing, but one of the boys got his hand smacked for being rude and trying to snatch up food during prayers. After the amen, Helen dished out food and passed the bowls of salad and veggies that were supposed to go with chicken, but they'd do just fine with reheated meatloaf.

Eli held a mixed drink in his left hand, shaking hands with superstars with his right. He held court with a few people, regaling them with real police stories. Brad looked across at Eli and gave him an approving look for relaxing and getting into the atmosphere. There was a quick look between them, with Brad's body language communicating, *You're doing good.* Eli's expression replied with, *This is cool, thanks!*

Nate wore sweat shorts and a T-shirt while he sat on the couch drinking from a beer bottle and reading the paperwork he'd brought home from the office. Next to him was his notebook in which he wrote feverishly. His wife sat next to him folding laundry and watching TV. The kids were long in bed.

Eli was eating in the backyard from the grand buffet of food set up there. He saw Mia from across the crowd. She came over to him, grabbed him by the hand, and dragged him to where people were dancing, and they joined in. The song was slow enough that they could dance very closely together. Neither uttered a word, but what they said with their eyes spoke volumes.

Helen Parker was already asleep on her side of the bed wearing a long T-shirt. Nate got into bed, kissed her gently, then rolled over and saw the clock as it turned to 12:10 a.m. He set the alarm for 3:30 a.m., then clicked off the light.

The Ride Home

Brad and Eli stood together in the front of the grand home with a small group of elderly men whose trophy wives hung from their arms. They were all waiting for the valet to bring up their cars.

A man with white hair, one of the few people wearing jeans at the party, handed Eli a card and said, "I mean it, give me a call next week when I get back. I'd love to talk about this further." He then turned to Brad. "See you later, Brad. Good find," the man said with a head-point toward Eli, then got into his Mercedes G550 SUV.

"Was that for real?" Eli asked Brad.

The red Ferrari made its appearance at their feet, and the valet held open the driver's door.

"Yeah, it was. You know what else is for real? I've had a few too many. I swore a long time ago that I'd stop doing that. How about you?"

"I actually only had one in the front end. Got to talking too much to have much more."

"Good. You drive."

"Are you serious?"

"Sure, buddy. In the end, it's just a car. You can drive a stick, right?"

"Hell yes!"

Brad got into the passenger seat while Eli ran around the car as if to get in before Brad changed his mind. As they got to the end of the driveway...

Brad gently reminded Eli, "But it's an expensive car."

Eli dropped the clutch at the end of the driveway and left quite the trail down the street. Brad held on tight, but, seeing Eli had control, leaned back and smiled.

Eli enjoyed the power of the race car. The sound of a Ferrari's engine is distinctive and just makes you want to drive fast. That's what the car was built for. It was made to handle the speed in and out of turns. Initially, Eli wasn't too aggressive, especially in the mountain curves of Coldwater Canyon Avenue, but after a few miles, the speed increased little by little until Eli could feel the car employing the adaptive steering to assist in maintaining control and friction with the roadway surface. Before too long, Eli was driving the car twice as fast as he would have in his detective unit.

Once on the freeway, Eli asked Brad, "Mind if I open her up a little?"

"Sure, go ahead."

Eli gladly stepped on the gas pedal and felt the car spring forward without hesitation. The extra momentum pushed him deeper in the leather contoured seats, which hugged him slightly to keep him in place during tight curves. The roaring of the Ferrari engine was music to Eli's ears.

As Eli drove the car eastbound on the Hollywood Freeway at a little after midnight, the sparse traffic allowed for some room to run. Reaching one hundred miles per hour is easy to do these days in most cars, but going from sixty-five miles per hour from when he merged onto the freeway to hitting one hundred twenty in a couple of seconds without straining the engine gave Eli a rush of power that he'd never felt before, and he liked it.

Driving this car was exhilarating and created heightened sensations in Eli that were very much like the adrenaline rush of searching for an armed suspect in a dark warehouse. It was like being in the most perfect amusement ride ever. But this was reality, not a roller coaster at Magic Mountain. Why couldn't he own a fine car like this? Was there anything wrong with making money instead of slogging it out in civil service? Sure, everyone liked cops (mostly) and there was the pride and prestige that came with being a homicide detective in one of the premier agencies in the country, but it didn't pay the kind of money that would afford Eli this sort of lifestyle that he was quickly becoming accustomed to.

Although he was watching for other drivers to ensure no one was going to change lanes in front of them, he wasn't particularly watching what kind of cars were occupying the lanes that Eli was treating like Le Mans. It wasn't surprising, then, that he didn't see the CHP unit that came on during the merge with the Ventura Freeway.

Flashing red and blue lights behind the Ferrari were unmistakable, and Eli slowed down to seventy miles per hour and merged over one lane, hoping the unit was needed elsewhere and would pass right on by. But it didn't. It merged with Eli. "Oops," Eli let out.

"Well, this should be interesting," remarked Brad with a grin.

Not wanting to put the officer and other drivers at risk for a freeway traffic stop, Eli took the Cahuenga Boulevard exit followed by the CHP unit. Eli knew that the CHP officer was wondering if this was going to be the start of a wild street chase. Most people don't know how dangerous a freeway stop can be and wouldn't exit the freeway as pure courtesy. Most often, drivers who didn't pull over right away and instead exited were contemplating running or had already planned to run. But Eli kept the speeds low and used turn signals to indicate his intentions and then pulled over at the curb in front of the Toluca Lake Florist.

"Let's help him out with the view inside," Brad said as he flipped a lever on the center console. "I may not be a real cop, but I understand cops don't want to walk up to a gun in their face."

The comment hit close to home, and Eli snapped his head around to look at Brad, but was then mesmerized as the automated mechanism lifted the rear half section of the roof and moved it forward and stacked it on top of the main roof to make room for the rear trunk lid to open. Then both stacked roof sections slid backward and tucked themselves into the trunk.

"Here we go," Eli said as he peered into the rearview mirror and saw the officer get out of his unit. With both the driver's side and passenger side spotlights focused into the mirrors on either side of the Ferrari and the takedown lights flooding the cockpit with their blinding LED lights, the night was turned into day.

The officer walked around the rear of his car to step up onto the curb and make a passenger's-side approach. It was an officer safety method with two positive outcomes. First, it kept the officer from standing in traffic lanes and prevented him or her from being struck by other drivers. The most problematic at this hour would be drunk drivers who, in a moth-to-flame effect, were attracted to the strobing police lights and often ran right into the police car or sideswiped the officer standing at the driver's door of the subject vehicle.

The second and equally important reason for engaging on the passenger's side was that most drivers were expecting a driver's-side approach and therefore, if they had any evil intentions, they were focused on the wrong side. Something Eli's father hadn't considered the night he was killed by the driver of what Deputy Ernie Hockney thought was a routine traffic stop.

"Good evening. My name is Officer Patterson with the California Highway Patrol. The reason I pulled you over is for going over one hundred miles per hour on the freeway. Any legal reason for going that fast?"

"First let me say, that was an excellent five-step traffic stop introduction. My name is Detective Eli Hockney, Sheriff's Homicide, San Bernardino County," Eli said politely as he handed over his badge wallet for inspection.

"And I'm—"

"Brad Clark, yes, I know, sir. I ran the plate and also recognize you, of course. Has he taken you hostage, or is he your private security?"

"Neither, Officer. This is my friend Eli, and he's driving my car because I've had too much to drink and he hasn't," Brad said with a confident smile. "He's never driven this car before, so I let him throttle up a little. It's my fault. I'm sorry."

"Well, sir, you weren't driving, and even though you say you gave permission, you can't actually authorize him to speed, and the detective here knows that. But since you guys are friends and there's no harm done, I'll put forth a little professional courtesy to you both. *If* the detective here promises he has the speed demon inside him under control."

"Yes, Officer, I do. Sorry about that, and I appreciate your professionalism."

Officer Patterson handed back Eli's badge wallet and gave a little wave as he walked back to his unit. Within a couple of seconds, the police lighting was turned off and it was nighttime again.

"Thanks for helping me out there, Robin," Eli said with a smirk.

"Um, yeah, no way I am Robin. *You* are Robin, and I am Batman in this little play," Brad replied.

"Oh, yeah? Hold on!" Eli roared the engine and dropped the clutch to leave a trail of tire smoke and spun the car around one hundred-eighty degrees to point toward the freeway once more. Then without missing a beat or a gear, the Ferrari rocketed forward under Eli's complete control toward the freeway on-ramp.

"Holy, shit! Okay, okay, okay! You're Batman!" Brad shouted and laughed.

Pool Party

Back in La Cañada, the men came bursting in the front door of Brad's house, animated and excited by the drive and the camaraderie.

"That badge of yours actually works!"

"I think you being you had more to do with it."

"Well, maybe. But did you see his face when you pulled that badge out from the driver's seat of a Ferrari?"

As the two crossed the foyer through the living room, Mia and an equally beautiful friend passed through in bathrobes. Brad and Eli kept walking and talking through the main room into the backyard.

"But he knew it wasn't mine when he ran the plate and saw you."

"Bet he's wondering how you and I became friends."

Eli was surprised at the use of the word. "Friends?"

A little steam left Brad's sails when he said, "Yeah, I thought so. Do you think I'm using you somehow?"

"No, well, I just...I mean—"

"What, we can't be friends because you're a real cop and I'm a Hollywood douchebag?"

The two had made their way to the outside patio area. Where some people might have a mini fridge to keep a few cold drinks, Brad had a full-size kitchen outside for cooking and grilling.

"Beer?"

"No, thanks. Wait, yes, please. Forgot I don't have to drive home."

"Listen, for like the first time in, I don't know, five years or more, I'm hanging out with someone who isn't trying to get into one of my movies or TV shows, and isn't handing me some god-awful script they pulled out of their ass," Brad said with a bit of release from getting that off his chest. "You, on the other hand, I'm *trying* to convince to help out with this stuff, and you're reluctant as hell. That's actually refreshing."

Eli was stunned at the comment. He just realized that Brad might not have any true friends, or at least none around him he could consistently trust. Those who were usually around him all wanted something from the Hollywood star, not from Brad, the guy who liked to hike, hunt, and fish like he used to when he grew up in Oregon.

Before Brad made his move to Los Angeles to become a professional actor, something he fell in love with during high school theater classes, he had normal friends who told him the truth, got mad at him when he was being sour, or just plain liked him with nothing to gain but camaraderie. But now things were different. Life had irrevocably changed.

Brad took out two bottles of beer and removed both caps with the opener affixed to one of the legs of the bar stand, then handed Eli his beer. Eli took a big swig.

"You might be the only real person I've talked to in quite a while who doesn't want something from me. And your shit is way more exciting than my faking it in front of a camera," Brad said before he took his own long pull off the bottle.

Before they could see them, the guys could hear one of the girls call out, "You boys coming in?"

Brad and Eli turned their heads in the direction of the voice and saw that Mia and her friend were walking toward the pool barefoot, covered by their robes. Mia's long black hair was pulled into a ponytail, as was her blonde friend's.

When they got near the edge of the pool, they stopped a moment and stared at the men, slowly untied their robe sashes, then let them slip off their shoulders and dropped them on the chaise lounges. They stood there in the nude as if it were a normal activity for a weeknight.

The pool lighting was something special. The lighting features themselves were hidden in the design, and there wasn't one square inch of the pool that wasn't brightly lit and perfectly visible. The water was absolutely still as the lights in and around the pool put on a beautiful display of ambiance and elegance.

By the looks of them, it appeared that both women spent considerable time in the gym maintaining physiques of toned muscles that accentuated their natural curves. Having created all the enticement they could pre-swim, the girls walked casually into the pool and broke up the glass-like water.

Brad was smiling and Eli was wide-eyed and speechless, the beer bottle stuck to his lips. Brad put down his beer and kicked off his shoes. He looked at Eli and laughed a little as he nearly tore off his shirt. Brad had developed and maintained a muscular chest for the many times he had to go shirtless in his movies and TV shows. He wasn't currently in production, so he wasn't as defined as Eli, nor quite as muscular, but he liked his nude body and so did the women.

Brad dropped his pants and underwear together and started toward the pool, hopping as he removed first one, then the other sock, throwing them over his shoulder. He dove headfirst between the girls with a proper swimmer's dive, making hardly a splash.

Eli was stunned and frozen, gaping as he watched with nervous excitement at the scene unfolding before him.

"Come on, Detective!" Mia shouted. "You got nothing to be ashamed of." Then with a little giggle, she added, "Trust me, I know."

"Get in here, buddy. Water's perfect...in more ways than one," Brad said.

Eli's gaze was broken by his decision. With a hidden smile and in a hushed tone one octave higher than normal, he muttered to himself, "Fucking Hollywood!"

He took a huge drink from the bottle, nearly finishing it before he put it down. He kicked off his shoes and stripped as he walked toward the pool, leaving a trail of clothes that led up to the pool's edge. He too jumped into the pool completely nude. The water was slightly warmer than the air, but not too hot. It was absolutely perfect. Not a bit of wind to chill the wet skin.

***

Mia crawled up the bed and chose the side that she was going to sleep on, pulled back the sheets, and then patted the mattress for Eli to join her. He lay on his back, and she put her head up on his shoulder and stroked his chest with her hand.

Eli looked at the clock on the nightstand. 3:10 a.m. He knew he'd have to get up and retrieve his phone from the patio and set his alarm for 4:30 if he wanted a shower and a shave before meeting his team to start the day, but he was still catching his breath and cooling down after the best sex of his life. He would lie there for just another moment. Two minutes later, they were both asleep.

The Morning After

Nate's hand crashed down on the alarm, turning it off. It was still dark in his bedroom at 3:45 a.m. His wife stirred a moment. She could sleep through a tornado, but if one of their children coughed or sneezed, she awakened ready for battle.

Nate pulled himself out of bed groaning and stumble-walked to the bathroom, where he shut the door and turned on the light. The shower came on a moment later. A hot shower did not relax Nate. Instead, he felt that it invigorated him. The body needed to deal with the heat by moving blood around, causing his heart rate to kick up a notch and help wake him up. Shaving in the shower was a must. The steam on his face and wet whiskers made for easy and cut-free work with a multiblade razor.

Afterward, when his body was fully heated front and back, getting out into the cool air of the bathroom and walk-in closet along with the rest of the house also helped energize him and make him feel awake. The killer part of the early morning was going to be the long drive to Los Angeles after breakfast.

Dawn had not yet broken when Nate, Artie, and Sergeant Kesling got back into their respective cars and drove off from the Denny's in Rancho Cucamonga where they met for breakfast together. There should have been a fourth car driven by their teammate Eli, but he had promised to meet them at the rendezvous location at 5:30 a.m. instead.

Nate was worried for his partner. These rare meals together were the perfect time to get to know one another a little more and break down any barriers.

Nate decided he should make sure everything was good with Eli. The night before when Nate called him to tell him about breakfast, Eli seemed distracted and was a bit standoffish. He said he was with some friends and wasn't going to be able to make breakfast, but promised he'd make the meeting at the Ralph's grocery store on West Victoria Boulevard in Burbank as directed.

"Call Eli," Nate said out loud after pushing the hands-free button on his steering wheel.

"Calling Eli Hockney, mobile," SIRI replied.

When Nate heard Eli's voicemail prompt come across the radio speakers, he hung up in frustration.

***

The sun was starting to brighten the bedroom. Eli stirred a little and looked around. After less than two hours' sleep, he wasn't even sure where he was. He examined the other side of the bed to discover he was by himself. He thought for another moment and sat up, fighting through the fog of his exhausted brain. His thoughts became clearer as he recognized his surroundings. He was in Brad Clark's spare master suite. He remembered the blissful pool party, the after-party in this very bedroom, and then he smiled. He started to lie back when he awakened fully to the realization that he was LATE!

"Aw, shit!" Eli shouted as he bolted out of bed. He was still naked from the pleasures of the night before when he ran into the attached bathroom and gargled some mouthwash before spitting it out. He splashed water on his face and ran water through his hair and tried to comb through and tame his bedhead. It didn't work. He got into the shower and washed and rinsed his hair before the water even warmed up completely. The first cold shower he'd taken in quite some time.

Thankfully, the new suit he'd bought the day before was hung up in the closet and was still fresh since he'd only worn it for about an hour.

He was just wondering where Mia had gone off to when she came back into the bedroom carrying a glass of water and Eli's mobile phone.

"I got thirsty and heard this ringing out back when I went to the kitchen," Mia said as she eyed Eli's body once more before he put on his shirt. He buttoned as hastily as he could, but made sure he wasn't misaligned like a six-year-old who dressed himself for church. He didn't want to take the time to go back out to the patio to get his underwear, so he'd go commando one more time. He shoved the shirttails into the pants and zipped up.

"I brought you one too. I figured you'd be dehydrated after all the sweat you lost last night. Well, just a couple of hours ago, really," Mia said with a grin.

Enjoying the memories as he chugged down the whole glass of water, he'd only gotten his pants and shirt on before his mobile phone started buzzing and Mia handed it to him. It was Nate, and the time was 5:15 a.m.

Eli answered, "Hey, Nate!"

Nate, Kesling, and Artie were standing by their cars at the far end of the Ralph's parking lot. With them were other unmarked cars and trucks with some bearded narcotics detectives who were going to help with surveillance detail.

When Eli answered the phone, Nate walked away from the group. With a hushed and angry tone, he growled, "Dude, where the fuck are you and why the hell haven't you been answering your phone?"

Eli put the phone on the nightstand on speaker while still dressing himself. "I just woke up. My phone wasn't—"

"Just woke up? Shit! You're *way* behind the traffic eight ball, and you're so fucking late now!"

"I'll be there in a few minutes. I'm not that far away, maybe fifteen minutes." Eli looked to Mia for confirmation, and she nodded, which really reassured him.

"Not that far? You said you just woke up," Nate said while processing the information. "Wait, did you get a room out here or something?"

Eli yanked socks onto his feet and slammed them into shoes. "Something like that. Look, I'll explain later. Tell Sarge I had some trouble, I had to get gas or something, and that I'm stuck in traffic and only a few minutes late. Deploy without me. and I'll meet up and get my assignment."

Eli punched the red End Call button, then looked at Mia, who took off her top, exposing her perfect breasts as she climbed back under the covers.

"Hey, yeah, so, sorry to run out on you. I gotta go to work and..."

"Go. I get it."

Eli was headed out the bedroom door with his tie under his collar but not yet tied, but then he turned to run back and give her a decent kiss. Afterward, he looked into her eyes, contemplating tearing off his clothes and climbing back into bed and ravaging her once more, but duty called, and instead, he turned and bolted out the door.

Surveillance

Eli pulled up to meet with Kesling and the remaining units who were all standing outside their cars with portable radios on their hoods and roofs. Eli parked his unit, got out, and walked up to the group.

"Sorry, I'm late, boss," Eli said sheepishly and slightly out of breath. His necktie was tied and looked pretty good for a car-drive knotting. But his hair was nowhere the perfection it normally was.

"I take it you found Ranger," Kesling stated with a hidden smile.

"Huh?"

"Your dog, knucklehead. You guys better get your fuckin' stories straight," Kesling said with some irritation. "Did she eat your razor too?" he added, noticing that Eli had a decent amount of stubble on his face.

Eli was so wound up, he wasn't even hurt by the comment. Besides, he knew Sarge was right and Nate had lied to cover for him being late without a great excuse. Truth be told, it was a fantastic excuse considering the excellent time he'd had with Brad and his friends, and especially the special time he spent with Mia. Sleep is for rich people, he'd once heard. Well, Eli wasn't rich yet, so sleep was optional if he wanted to live the life he was getting himself into.

"Where do you need me, Sarge?" Eli asked respectfully.

"Here for now. Shelly's still home. Once she goes mobile, so will we. You've got fourth turn."

Artie announced over the multiple handheld radio units, nicknamed "HT" for the former archaic name of "handie-talkie," stating, "Okay, heads up, here we go. Garage opening, she's going mobile."

Shelly's state-issued sedan backed out of the garage and onto Pepper Street, then drove at a normal rate of speed. She looked like any other commuter, sipping coffee from a thermos and listening to NPR on the radio.

"Subject is southbound on Pepper and set up for an eastbound turn onto Jeffries," Artie said across the radio. "If she makes the turn onto N. Hollywood Way, let's have another unit take lead."

"62-David-9, I'll take the turn," said the narcotics detective wearing a T-shirt and jeans, a goatee on his face, and a Dodgers baseball cap on his head. He was driving a stock half-ton white Chevrolet Silverado truck.

There was nothing special about the surveillance vehicles that would ever announce their presence as police vehicles. All standard detective units were used four-door sedans, purchased from rental companies like Hertz and Enterprise. However, for the surveillance teams, the department purchased a variety of sizes, makes, and models to have them blend into traffic like everyone else.

A string of Ford Taurus sedans with special little trunk antennas with a bunch of guys wearing suits stuck out like a bad FBI movie. Instead, the surveillance teams drove foreign and domestic subcompacts, hatchbacks, medium-sized cars, pickup trucks, and all-around normal cars. These weren't for high-speed chases or police actions. They were for blending into the freeway and neighborhood streets. They didn't have one bit of police equipment in them. All communication was either through the HTs or by mobile phone merged calls. One of the best surveillance teams that never, ever got noticed was the male-and-female detective team dressed in normal clothes who followed suspects to every place they went from a department-owned, silver minivan.

Eli had taken up the primary follow detail a couple of car lengths behind Shelly driving west on I-10 toward Santa Monica. He blended in just fine with all the other sedans driven by men in business suits traveling on the freeway.

When Shelly headed toward the Mateo Street exit, Eli followed her down the off ramp, leaving only one car between them. He couldn't afford to be too far behind her and get caught by a red light. He surely couldn't use his police lights and siren to break traffic and keep up That'd be a dead giveaway.

"62-Nora-7 to all units, the freeway just stopped due to a TC—we're caught behind."

"Sixty Sam one, copy that. Nora-7, Artie and I will exit back here and try surface streets to catch up," Kesling said over the radio, "Henry-3, you keep primary until we can catch back up to you."

"Henry-3, 10-4, traffic is slow on surface streets," Eli replied into his unit radio.

Eli's phone rang, displaying Brad Clark's name and the selfie picture they took together at the dinner party.

"Hey, Brad!"

"Hey, buddy! You all right? Heard you got a late start this morning. Hope you didn't get into any trouble."

"No, not real trouble. But I gotta go."

"Listen, really quick, what time are you getting off tonight?"

"Why? What's up?"

"Need to get you fitted for this Sunday."

"Fitted for what? What's Sunday?"

"You need a new tuxedo if you're going with me to the Emmy Awards! I finagled two more tickets, figured you'd want Mia to go with?"

"Are you serious?"

"Yeah, buddy, dead serious. The studio guys wanted to talk some more, and this is the perfect time when they'll all be together, drinking and wanting to spend money. Especially if I win! But anyway, it's going to be a total blast."

While he was talking with Brad, Shelly blinked and made a left-hand turn onto East Olympic Boulevard. Eli was so engrossed in conversation, he missed seeing the turn and kept driving straight.

"Are you sure there aren't other people who are going to jam you up for taking me instead of them?"

"Not people whose opinions I really care about. Don't you want to go? I mean, do you have better plans?"

"No, no, it's not that. I think it'd be very cool to go. Totally awesome, actually. Something I'll never get a chance to ever do again."

Brad's laughter came over the speaker. "Hell, if the ratings drop, I won't be going again either."

Eli looked around frantically, realizing he didn't see Shelly's car anymore.

"Shit!" Eli shouted in anger.

"What?"

"Fuck me!"

"What? You all right?"

"No. Gotta go."

"Come by tonight?"

"Yeah, maybe. I don't know. I'll call you back later."

Eli hung up then reluctantly, after a moment's consideration, picked up the radio microphone.

Before keying up the mic, he let out one more frustrated exclamation to clear his mind and release some adrenaline. "Fuuuuuuck!"

Kesling had turned on his emergency lights and was driving down the side of the freeway, passing the blocked traffic, trying to get himself back in the surveillance position. He heard Eli's voice come across his radio in a unit-to-unit transmission. "60-Sam, 60-Henry-3."

"Go ahead, Henry-3," Kesling said into the mic as he slowly maneuvered past the blocked traffic and avoided getting hit by those drivers who didn't realize he was a police unit and not some jerk trying to cut in front of everyone.

"I lost the target in traffic."

"10-9?" Kesling requested Eli repeat his last message, but his tone was unmistakable. Sarge didn't misunderstand what was said, he just couldn't believe it was being said in the first place.

"I got cut off by a lane-changing truck that stopped short for a yellow, and she got too far off and I lost sight."

Inside Eli's car, he pulled the microphone from his face after his last transmission and winced as if expecting to be slapped on the back of the head like a child mouthing off to his father. There was a long, scary silence while Eli pulled into the parking lot of a strip mall to wait for the next set of orders.

The next thing he heard coming across his radio was the exasperated voice of his sergeant. "Henry-1, go straight to her office and wait there to see if and when she shows up there."

One of the narcotics detectives, who was a primary department surveillance team member, spoke up on his radio.

Eli listened from inside his unit. "60-Sam, Nora-7..."

"Go ahead, Nora-7."

"Listen, why don't you let us go set up on her. If she's at her job, we can set up on her and get better obs. The rest of our crew is only thirty minutes out, so we'll have a full contingent to take her mobile anywhere she goes. Your team can gather up or head back to the office, and we'll follow and report anything significant via twenty-one to you."

"Yeah, that's affirm. Break. Henry-1, when you're relieved, head back nineteen and get caught up on those other bank warrants."

Artie replied with a somewhat saddened "10-4." He was going to have to "go nineteen," which is short code for "ten-nineteen." which means return to office/base/headquarters. The sadness came from Artie being requested to do some actual work preparing search warrants. Not a difficult task overall, but Artie would much rather spend his entire day and into the night on overtime, sitting in his car smoking cigarettes and watching a parked car go nowhere.

Inside Eli's car, Eli feared the slap to the back of his head was coming when he heard Kesling call out to him, "Henry-3, Sam-1, you and Henry-2 need to interview the lawyer?"

Eli replied, "Affirmative."

"Take care of that, then give me a twenty-one when you're clear, and we'll see where we're all at then."

Eli was relieved his sergeant didn't ask him to meet him somewhere door-to-door, which would have been an ass-chewing for sure. Instead, he was given an assignment relative to the case and not scutwork. For all their bluster about Eli being young and impetuous, they did recognize he had the gift of gab and was already becoming one of homicide's best interrogators.

Enter the Lawyer

Nate and Eli walked into the upscale law offices of Harold King & Associates, hoping he might be able to shed some light on the Browers' background and maybe even point them in the direction of a suspect or suspects who were so upset that they would brutally kill a couple who, by all appearances, were upstanding citizens.

"Hello, gentlemen," the receptionist said from behind a sleek black desk. Everything in the office was upscale. The waiting room looked like a smaller version of the Ritz-Carlton.

Nate politely said, "Hi. We're from the sheriff's department out in San Bernardino, and we called ahead to speak with Harold King."

"Yes, indeed. Mr. King is expecting you. Go right in. He's in the corner office past the conference room."

"Thanks," replied Eli. As they walked away, Eli took a quick look back to see that the receptionist was watching them. She smiled at being caught staring.

King's office was well-appointed, with warm, rich wood paneling that covered the ceiling and three of the walls. The fourth wall was all glass, providing an extensive view over the Los Angeles skyline. Harold sat behind his large glass top desk.

Eli expected a private attorney's desk to be piled with papers, but instead, it was completely devoid of clutter. The only papers on the desk were what Harold was reading and making notes on when the detectives entered. He didn't lift his head from what he was doing when they walked in.

Judging by the manner in which his desk was decorated with memorabilia and autographed pictures of Harold and famous public figures wearing fishing gear and holding their prizes, it was obvious Harold was a well-known and highly paid Los Angeles lawyer.

It would seem to be standard practice for a secretary to alert her boss that an appointment had arrived and was headed back to his office. She said the detectives were expected, so why was he still scribbling notes on a file? Was this intended to impress the detectives that he was a busy and important man? Wouldn't it seem more practical that a person as highly organized as it appeared Harold was would have finished his notes before allowing the receptionist to send them back? Then he could have been prepared to meet them professionally.

Instead, Harold made them wait a moment before he acknowledged their presence while he made one final note, closed the file, and put it away in a desk drawer, then screwed closed his Montblanc pen and finally looked up.

Eli reached out a hand. "Mr. King?"

Harold stood up and said with a perfectly warm smile, "Call me Harold." He offered a firm handshake in return.

"Harold, I'm Eli Hockney, and this is my partner, Nate Parker. We're hoping you might be able to shed some light on the affairs of the Browers."

Nate added, "We understand you were maybe handling a couple of pieces of litigation for them?"

"A couple? More like six. The Browers were very busy people, both socially and legally," Harold said as he offered the men each a comfortable chair in the seating area away from his desk. There were two matching leather rolled-arm, tufted-button couches opposite each other, with a pair of matching high-back leather chairs on one end forming a giant three-sided rectangle of seating space.

In the middle of the square, on top of an oversized Tabriz, hand-knotted wool area rug, was a hand-crafted wooden table polished to shine like glass. Centered on the table was an ornate silver tray upon which sat crystal tumblers and a decanter filled halfway.

Harold, a slender man with slicked-back receding silver hair accentuating his widow's peak, took up his coffee cup and saucer from his desk and brought it with him as he sat on one of the end chairs, making himself the head of the seating group. "Would either of you like something to eat or drink? It's a little early in the day for Dalmore, but if you are so inclined."

"Dalmore?" Eli asked and looked over to Nate who shrugged his shoulders.

"Eighteen-year-old, single malt scotch whiskey," Harold said. "It is over two-hundred per bottle, but I can't keep enough of it around once people get a taste."

Eli was actually starving and thirsty. He hadn't had much to eat at the grand buffet at the Hollywood producer's home because Mia had claimed him as her dance partner. The rest of the night he spent spinning tales from his police career of pursuits, bar fights, and recent homicide investigations, sans the Brower case, of course. The last thing he had to drink was a swig of water earlier that morning before rushing out to meet his team.

"If it isn't too much trouble, I'd really love a cup of coffee," Eli said. He then looked at Nate, who was in a bit of disbelief at the audacity of his request to have a witness fetch him coffee.

Usually when police officers were the guests of their victims or witnesses, they don't request nor do they accept an offer of refreshment. It extended the time spent with a witness beyond the short time officers had on calls. And besides, you never knew how clean people were or what their intentions were with the drink being offered. It wouldn't be beyond some folks to put something untoward in an officer's drink as retribution for not having been there to prevent the crime from happening in the first place.

Unfazed, however, Harold simply clicked on a small speaker box, which alerted his secretary to answer.

"Yes, Mr. King?" came the secretary's voice over the speaker.

"Would you please bring our detectives some coffee?"

Nate interrupted. "None, for me, thanks. I had breakfast." He gave a glance to Eli that, without saying another word, let him know Nate wasn't pleased with Eli for having missed breakfast and causing further delay.

"Just one, then, for our young Master Eli," Harold quipped.

"Master?" Eli asked with a bit of attitude.

"Well, Detective, I didn't see a wedding ring on your finger, so I presumed you weren't married, hence the master title."

"Is that why Alfred calls Batman Master Bruce?"

"Yes, indeed."

"Cool. Learn something new every day in this job," Eli said with a little amusement. "Nate, I think I'd like you to call me Master—"

"Yeah, not a snowball's chance in hell that's happening," Nate shot back.

The men all got a kick out of the old-school education they received from Harold. Turned out he might be an all right guy—for a lawyer, that was. The rhythm of the interview hadn't really gotten going yet, but whenever the coffee came, it would momentarily change the dynamic. Whenever possible, interviews should never be interrupted. But with this little exchange, Nate was no longer as upset at Eli as he was a couple of minutes ago.

Eli prompted Harold. "Well, Harold, please tell us about the Browers' lawsuits. Maybe something will fit into the reason they were killed."

"You think it was someone suing them that killed them?"

"Um, yeah, well, we don't really know yet, but we're not excluding any possible lead until we've looked into it thoroughly."

"Fascinating," Harold said.

Eli turned to meet Nate's quizzical look and added, "Yeah, not so much. Pretty routine method of operating, really."

"Maybe for you, Detective Hockney, but for we laymen, this is all so intriguing."

Nate couldn't help himself. "Didn't I understand you used to work with the district attorney's office some time ago?"

Not caught off guard, but almost pleased that the detectives hadn't come into the interview completely cold, Harold grinned and replied with a dismissive tone, "Oh, well, yes, that's true. Very thorough, Detective. Very thorough. Right out of law school. After an internship. I was there for maybe a year and a half before I realized it wasn't where I wanted to spend my time." After a short pause to sip from his coffee, he explained, "No money in it, you see."

As if on cue, there was a knock on the door, and in walked the secretary with a tray containing three cups and saucers, silver spoons, a small porcelain creamer pitcher, sugar bowl, sweeteners in a box, and a ceramic coffeepot. The whole setup was first class. Eli took to it like a duck to water.

Nate watched Eli, who seemed at ease with these refinements when normally a mug or Styrofoam cup would have done the trick. "What kind of cases did you work at the DA's office?" Nate asked Harold.

"Mostly assaults, drunks, low-grade misdemeanors, and arraignment calendar, etcetera. Baby DAs don't get to handle any real cases for several years while they cut their teeth on the smaller stuff and work their way up. Whereas in private practice," Harold sat back a moment and waved his arms to his surroundings, "there are no limitations to one's abilities or successes."

With that, Harold opened a wooden box on the table next to him and pulled out a large cigar. "Do you mind?"

Nate replied, "Your office."

"True, but it's the polite thing to do."

Harold pointed back and forth with the cigar box, offering one to either detective. Eli glanced up, and Nate looked at Eli with wide eyes that told Eli he'd better not accept. Eli replied back with body language that said, *Relax, I wasn't going to.*

"So just how successful are you?" Eli asked.

"Eli, what kind of question is that?" Nate said with some shock in his voice.

Talking through the process of lighting his cigar with a big puff and a flame, Harold motioned to Nate and said, "No, no, it's perfectly all right, Detective. Our young friend is justifiably curious."

Responding now to Eli's question, Harold answered, "I probably earn your annual salary every few weeks or so. If that answers your question."

"Wow, yeah, it does, thanks," Eli replied with a fake smile.

Nate had just opened his mouth to speak when Eli jumped back in with both feet. "So, with all your success and the big clients, why were you handling this one couple so much and so often?"

"Well, that's just it, Detective. They *were* one of my big clients. They were being sued by several people and businesses both across the United States and internationally."

"Really?" both Nate and Eli said simultaneously.

Harold leaned forward and said, "Okay, you both ready for this?" He mock-whispered to drive home the point: "Your victims weren't the good guys."

Eli responded with incredulity, "But you defended them?"

"That's what lawyers do. Remember, everyone has their Sixth Amendment right to counsel, even the murderers who did this terrible thing." Hearing himself and how that may have sounded so callous, Harold added, "Listen, I'm not suggesting they deserved to die for their misdeeds, but just so you understand, most of their friends and family had no idea what they were into and how many people they tried to swindle over the years."

Nate leaned forward, very interested in where Harold was going with this conversation. "Enlighten us, please."

"Okay, well, not in order, necessarily, but Abby tried to screw her half brother, Gary, out of the inheritance after their father died. Abby got Daddy to rewrite the new will when he may not have been of sound mind and body so that she was the only one in the will upon his death. Not even his second wife, who is the mother of the half brother, got any money. Sad, really."

Eli asked even though he knew the answer: "Did Abby and Bill prevail?"

Harold responded arrogantly, "Of course they did. I was their lawyer."

"So, you think this Gary is a viable suspect?" Eli asked.

"As viable as any of the others."

"Others?" Nate asked.

"Well, you know about Harris the fashionista and that saga. I mean, that's why you're here right? But do you know about the Russian?"

Both detectives looked at each other and then at Harold, who sat there with a cat-that-ate-the-canary grin.

"Yes, well, Bill met a man named Dimitri Goncharov, a Russian-Jew whose parents fled from their homeland at the end of World War II, but before the wall went up. Interesting family, really. He got an engineering degree in West Germany and eventually made his way to America and to California, where he still lives. He has a massive company."

King sat back in his chair and sipped from his coffee and puffed on his cigar before continuing, "Well, Dimitri invented some tools that revolutionized some part of the farming industry. He sold his patent and rights to Stanley Black and Decker for big money and residuals that last in perpetuity. He doesn't ever have to work again, but he loves creating new things, so he's still at it."

Another puff of the cigar. "Bill was his accountant too."

Eli had been leaning forward, but now sank into the couch. "You gotta be kidding me! He embezzled from him too?"

"No, no. Well, not that I'm aware of. But that still remains to be seen, I guess."

Nate looked confused and asked, "So...then what?"

"Ah, yes. Then what? Well, after the Berlin Wall fell back in the 1990s, German state-owned factories were being sold off for next to nothing. One could get a factory for virtually free if you agreed to continue with the manufacturing and keep the legacy employees, provide them with wages and private health care...all the stuff that transitioning into the new world from communism would require."

Nate and Eli looked at each other with wide eyes, wondering where all this was going, but curious to see just how much more detailed and problematic this case was about to get.

"A few years ago, Dimitri reunited with an old childhood friend whose parents had acquired one of these factories years ago. They were looking to expand their production into American markets."

Once again puffing from his cigar for grander effect from a grand-standing lawyer, Harold said, "So Dimitri, in the meantime, had made a name for himself in the farming industry and had been asked to develop a better spindle for cotton-picking machines."

Nate and Eli both asked simultaneously, "Spindles?"

Eli said, "Yeah, what the hell is a spindle?"

"I have to be honest and say that I didn't know either before this lawsuit. But suffice to say they're an integral part of the cotton-picking machine. These machines are huge, and each machine has hundreds of these spinning spindles that reach out and snag the cotton from the plants. It's how it's done in the modern day. Not by hand anymore."

Eli's expression of *Yeah, no shit* wasn't missed by anyone.

"Well, these spindles," Harold continued, "like any other part, have to be precisely machined in order to work properly. Dimitri used his friend in Germany who has this factory full of cheap labor begging for some business. He got the spindles made there at a terrific price and was able to undercut the American-made spindles by around sixty percent. He was making an absolute killing.

"Dimitri and Bill worked on this deal together, and I did the legal portion. I created an indemnity clause that stated that by purchasing these spindles from Germany, that company was solely responsible for any and all claims of damage caused directly or indirectly from their us-age. Dimitri and Bill were completely indemnified."

Eli asked, "Sure sounds great, but what does completely indemnified mean?"

"It means they were judgment proof if something went wrong."

"And did something go wrong?" Nate asked.

Harold and Eli simultaneously exclaimed, "Of course it did!"

Nate looked at his partner, but Eli was laser focused on Harold's statement.

Harold explained, "The spindles were mis-engineered and completely destroyed the machines in which they were installed. Thousands of farming machines across the southern United States and from around the world basically chewed themselves up. On top of that, if you don't pick cotton in a timely fashion, it blows off in the wind and the entire year's crop is wasted. Which was exactly what happened."

"So, what happened after that?" Nate asked.

Harold took a long drag off his cigar, blew it out, and said, "The insurance companies from the farmers came to collect, and I gave them a copy of the indemnification contract with the German firm and told them to try to collect from them."

Nate and Eli were silent, waiting for Harold to continue as they knew he would if not interrupted, but not before he downed the last bit of his coffee. "Ever try to sue an overseas firm? Almost can't be done. No way to enforce anything and get them to pony up what they owe. In the meantime, Dimitri and Bill split a cool couple mil, the German firm made more money than they ever thought possible, I got a nice paycheck for my efforts, while the farmers' insurance companies took the brunt of the loss."

"And you're okay with that?" Nate asked.

"Sure. That's business in the real world, my friends. Insurance companies are betting on your success, you're actually betting on the disaster...remember that."

"What's that now?" Eli asked.

"Listen, insurance companies are hoping you pay them monthly and never have an accident or need a payout. Therefore, they're betting on you living long, not crashing, your house not burning down, etcetera, etcetera. Whereas you fear that something bad *is* going to happen, so you buy insurance to help you recover financially. Thus, you are betting on catastrophe occurring, but the insurance company is hoping nothing bad ever happens to you," Harold explained.

"So, what you're saying is that you knew ahead of time the spindles were bad?" Nate asked.

Eli answered for Harold by saying, "Of course not, Nate. If the counselor, or any of the parties, knew that the spindles were mis-engineered and knowingly put them out to market, then they'd be guilty of conspiracy to commit international fraud." Eli looked directly at the lawyer. "Right, Harold?"

Eli caught the only perceptible nervous tic in an unplanned nostril flare and head tilt. Then to cover the moment, Harold smiled brightly and said, "Sometimes disasters do strike, and it's best to have insurance is all I'm saying."

Eli continued the questioning, not allowing his eyes to leave Harold's head and body. Not staring hard as if they were two bullies preparing to fight, but searching continuously for deceptive body language. "You said the insurance companies bore the brunt?"

"Yes."

"Any farmers not have insurance or not get properly compensated by their insurance companies?"

"Sure, there were some farmers who carried no insurance, and others used some cut-rate companies who refused to pay them until they first could recover from the German firm." He took another puff of the cigar. "Which isn't ever happening. So yeah, some farmers didn't get any recovery. Lost everything and went bankrupt. Again, that's business."

"If you say so," Nate said with a disgusted tone.

Eli blew right past the remark. "How many and where?"

"Two in Florida, one in Georgia, four in Arkansas, three in Louisiana, and two in Texas, if I recall correctly. There may be others."

"Can we see the files?" Eli asked.

"Sorry, no. Attorney-client privilege."

"Seriously? This is a murder investigation, and you're withholding vital information that could be crucial to us solving the case, and you're claiming attorney-client privilege? Besides, your clients are dead, so doesn't their claim die with them?"

"No, it doesn't. It remains in effect with their estate, executors of estate, and, if any, heirs. There are no heirs, but there is their executor, Shelly. Secondly, I'm not withholding information. I've been quite forthcoming with more than I probably ought to tell you, so don't get testy with me."

Nate tried to calm the situation, which had gotten quickly and unexpectedly heated. "I'm sorry about that. Eli didn't get much sleep last night and had some problems with his dog... We really appreciate your help on this." He took a breath and continued, "But we should probably get going now. We've taken up enough of your time, I think."

On cue, both detectives closed their notebooks and stood in preparation to say their goodbyes and leave.

"Not at all. But don't you want to hear about the other lawsuits?"

The detectives looked at each other in disbelief.

Nate and Eli simultaneously said, "There's more?"

After they sat down again, Nate leaned toward Eli and said quietly, "We gotta stop doing that."

"Yes, there's the sale of their condo in San Diego for breach of contract, and the sale of their house here in the Hills that the new owners claim was rat infested. And a few other minor skirmishes along the way."

"Those don't sound so ominous as to be reasons for murder, but sure, let's hear about those," Nate said.

"You're right, even without the experience that you two gentlemen have dealing with murders every day, I'd presume those are the least likely two situations that might cause someone to kill my clients. But the Georgia land deal? That's a whole other matter entirely," Harold said. "More coffee, Detective?"

"Yes, please," Eli said enthusiastically. "It's really good, by the way. What brand is it?"

"Kopi Luwak Gold," Harold said with a grin. "It's from southwestern Sumatra, Indonesia. Ever heard of civet coffee?"

Nate replied, "No, sir, but if this is going to be as long a story as the others, I think I just might get myself a cup too, if you don't mind."

"Not at all," Harold said. He was sure that neither of the detectives knew that a wild, catlike creature in Indonesia had first selected the coffee beans for their own consumption, then afterward passed the bean whole through their digestive system before the bean was then carefully selected by specially trained farmers to source the ripest and best beans.

The digestive mechanisms of the civets enhanced the flavor of the ingested whole coffee beans, resulting in an orange, winey flavor with a hint of roasted truffles. It was considered a luxury coffee for only the most discerning of coffee drinkers, but since it was all that Harold drank in his office, Nate and Eli were getting a chance to experience coffee that cost thirty-three dollars per ounce, whereas your typical ground coffee purchased from a grocery store is around twenty-six cents per ounce.

"A man named Kurt Miller," Harold began, "was one of Bill's tax clients. Although Bill made the majority of his earnings working for Davin and Dimitri, legally or illegally at this point doesn't matter, Bill still maintained his private tax practice. One of those was Kurt, who was a longtime client who grew up in the construction business. He'd done well for himself as a general contractor and spent the majority of his later life working on some major construction projects as one of a few general contractors who carried out the subcontract work. Follow me?"

"Sort of," Eli said, sipping from his second cup of coffee.

"When you think of general contractor, you think of a guy you hire to get a whole thing done for you. Kitchen restoration, add-on to your home, something like that. He might use subcontractors for things he doesn't personally do well himself, like tile or roofing. But you as a consumer hire one guy, and he makes it all happen. Well, in large-scale projects like building a bridge or pipeline, several general contractors may be hired for different phases of the project and the entire thing is run under a project manager. The project manager is responsible for everything that has to happen, from permits to city issues, tax abatements, etcetera. Loads of work, but this person won't swing a hammer. It's all logistics."

"Okay?" Nate said, trying to get Harold to come to his point.

"Well, Kurt has worked for years for lots of project managers, but has never been one. His first attempt was to try to develop a huge parcel of land he found out in Georgia. The area was ripe for developing into a large-scale upper-income community neighborhood. Multiple custom homes on multi-acre lots, several private community pools, clubhouses, shopping centers all surrounding a huge natural lakefront property."

"Sounds nice so far. What's the rub?" Eli asked.

"Well, the *rub* is that Kurt didn't know how to manage a large-scale project. He had great vision, no doubt, but he didn't bring on local talent and got himself lost in the backwoods county politics. They didn't want some out-of-towner coming in and Californicating their little slice of heaven. But these country folks aren't gangsters who threaten or kill. They're far more devious. They went behind Kurt's and Bill's backs and ran off all the possible support they'd garnered in Georgia. Then they created new laws, rules, and taxes and levied the property so high that it wasn't worth trying to salvage.

"Kurt got one house built. I saw pictures. He can definitely build a beautiful home, no doubt about it. But that's all he got done. I think he had to sell off all the land to pay for the taxes and fees, and all that he has left from thousands of acres is a five-acre parcel with the one house. Couldn't even get the road finished.

"Five-million-dollar initial investment from multiple investors disappeared in six months. Tragic." Harold sat up straight. "Listen, boys, if I were tasked with your duty, and thank goodness I'm not, I think I'd start with the Georgia land deal. There are lots of people who trusted Bill and gave him their life savings who now have nothing. Surely one of them had real motive to kidnap and kill Bill and Abby."

Nate and Eli looked at each other and then stood up one final time. Harold rose to meet them and reached out to shake Nate's then Eli's hand.

"Good luck, gentlemen. If there's anything I can do to help, short of giving you the files, of course, please let me know."

"Thanks again, Harold," Nate said.

"Yeah, thanks. Oh, and thanks also for the coffee. Really good stuff," Eli remarked as they walked out of the office.

The two detectives walk out the front glass doors of the building onto the sidewalk.

"Holy shit, this is worse than I thought," Eli said as he stretched his lower back by bending forward at the waist to touch his toes. He stood up quickly, then did a few back-and-forth torso twists, making popping sounds as he adjusted his spine.

"Holy shit, what did you just do?"

"What?"

"You sound like a popcorn machine went off inside your body."

"Oh, that. Yeah, it's a gift. I can do most of my back adjustments myself, but I still love going to the chiropractor to get my neck done in particular. Really resets the body."

"No way is one of those guys torquing on my neck. People get paralyzed from that shit."

"No, they don't. That's all myth, internet crap."

"Well, anyway, *Master Eli*," Nate said with an English accent like Michael Cane, "Pandora's box just blew up, huh? We've got some seriously pissed-off people who have good reason for wanting the Browers dead. I just never thought it'd be so many."

"Yeah, but that's the thing, right?"

"What?"

"Well, they weren't dead."

"I don't follow."

"Something Shelly said yesterday made me think. She said, 'Now that they've been found,' or words to that effect."

"I still don't follow."

"If someone is pissed off and wants to get their pound of flesh, they bust in and kill them in their own kitchen, right? If they're seeking retribution for losing all their money or whatnot, just kick in the door, shotgun blasts to each one, and then leave. They don't go through all this effort to kidnap them and haul them some seventy miles across Southern California, then bury them so deep, they would have never been found. If it weren't for the bad guys screwing up with the dog. I'm really not sure what happened there. Had they killed it instead and stuck it in the grave, would anyone be investigating this?"

"Hmm." Nate was listening and processing intently.

"Listen, LAPD was prompted to take the missing person's report because the friends heard that message from our guy who found the dog. What if there was no dog to find? No phone call on the machine. Sure, the friends still go inside and look around, but it would have appeared like Bill and Abby took off for an impromptu vacation or maybe with some less suspicious circumstances, the friends learn about their legal issues..."

Nate interrupted, "From Shelly, no doubt."

"Right, from Shelly, who takes control of the house and tells everyone she'll be working with Harold over here to take care of everything."

"So, we have to think, who benefited from their disappearance, not their death, right?"

"Right," Eli said.

"Damn, Eli, this is good. This is really fucking good."

Eli beamed with pride. His opinion was often considered to have some value by Nate, even if Artie and Sarge mostly discounted what he had to say. But this? This they would have to listen to Eli about. Nothing else made sense.

"Follow the money," Eli said. "This is all about greed, not sex, drugs, and rock n' roll like normal."

"Yeah, makes sense. You know what else makes sense?" Nate looked to Eli for the obvious response, but didn't get it. "Food. Let's eat."

"I would, but I can't tonight. I gotta do something," Eli said as he turned away from Nate. He'd been so proud of his work on the interview and the case theory he'd developed, but he hated to lie to Nate again.

"Something?"

"Yeah, it's no big deal. I just can't tonight."

"You sure you're all right? You seem..."

"Yeah, brother I'm fine. Just a lot on my mind, plus this case has got me kind of bugged."

Eli saw that Nate was staring at him with mild concern.

"Dude, don't worry. It's really not anything to worry...okay, okay, jeez, I may have met a girl."

"May have? You're not yet sure of the gender?"

"Yeah, no. I mean, I met her, but I don't know. She's so awesome. I've never felt this way about a woman, and so quickly. It's all so fast. Kind of cool fast, but I haven't a clue what I'm doing."

"Ahh. Yes well, I've been married nine years and I still don't know what the hell *I'm* doing, so if you figure it all out, you let me know."

"Right. Yeah, see you tomorrow. Here in LA or at headquarters?"

"Haven't got a clue—which is not good in our line of work. Sarge will call or text us for sure. Want me to call him, or do you want to?"

"You call him. He'll be sure to listen to what you have to say."

"Give it time, Eli. Stop rushing things. Everything you want will happen in due time. Stop trying to force it."

After giving Eli that unsolicited advice, Nate thought he should lighten the moment. "So, can I take credit for the case theory?"

"Fuck you," Eli replied with a smile and a small laugh.

"I didn't think so."

Tuxedo Fitting

Eli pulled up to the front of Brad's house. He'd since been given a personal gate code of 1097, a play on the police ten codes in which 10-97 meant "arrived on scene." Eli had to chuckle when he dialed the digits and hit the pound key. The code was something he might himself have chosen were he fortunate enough to have a house requiring a security gate. Once the gate swung up, Eli pulled up to the front of the house and parked the Taurus next to a navy-blue convertible Rolls Royce.

Eli hoped Mia would still be at the house. She lived in a bungalow out back in what might otherwise be called the maid's quarters. However, Mia wasn't the maid. She might have prepped the house prior to the maid service arrival, but she'd made sure to let Eli know she was indeed not the maid.

It was early evening by the time Eli walked through the front door into the living room to find Davin Harris kneeling at the feet of Mia, who was standing on a stool so that Davin could make marks and pins hems on a beautiful ball gown. Eli was taken aback at the sight of Davin in Brad's house. Davin was clearly still a suspect and Brad was a material witness. Hanging out with Brad was bad enough for appearance's sake, even though he wasn't a suspect. But now to have Davin here made things a little complicated. Eli thought it did make sense, though. He knew Brad got at least some of his suits from Davin, and this was the kind of client Davin would of course be dressing for the Emmy awards show.

"Yes, yes. Lovely, my dear." Davin gushed over his own work being modeled by the stunning young woman.

Brad was watching Davin work his masterpiece when he noticed Eli walking in. "Eli! Glad you could make it in time."

Davin looked up and said, "I thought I recognized that suit. But I didn't put two and two together that you and Brad were friends. Now it makes sense when he said to bring a tuxedo in his size ready for fitting. How interesting."

Brad's head moved back and forth between Davin and Eli like he was watching a tennis match. "Wait, you guys know each other?"

"Just met recently," Eli said with a grin to hide a bit of embarrassment.

"Yes indeed. The detective came by to see if I were the Browers' killer."

Eli wasn't sure what to say to that. It was an entirely accurate statement.

"Really? I didn't know you two had met. Man, this is getting weird," Brad said as he crossed his arms in fascination.

"Yeah, a little. But I'm starting to get used to it, I think," Eli said to Brad and Davin, who had gone back to pinning the hem on the dress. "LA is a different animal to be sure," he said. Mia smiled down at him from her perch.

"Is this going to be too weird for you two?" Brad asked.

Eli took off his suit jacket, which exposed his badge and gun, and hung it up on the portable clothing rack that had been rolled in for the fitting, "Not unless he sticks me with a pin."

With pins at station ready in his mouth, Davin shot back, "Believe me, Detective, a pin is the last thing I'd like to stick you with."

Brad exclaimed, "Davin!"

"Can't blame a guy for trying," Davin said with a twinkle in his eye as he winked at Mia.

Eli rolled his eyes and shook his head in partial disbelief of what was said, but moreover for letting himself be taken down that whole path. "Hi, Mia," Eli said, finally acknowledging her with a smile.

Mia smiled at Eli. "How do I look?"

"Like a princess," he replied.

"Will you be my knight?" Mia asked playfully.

The comeback embarrassed Eli, who still took himself too seriously. The play on words that sparked the B-movie dialogue made him feel a bit uneasy and on display with Brad and Davin anticipating his response. Mia smiled at Eli. She clearly enjoyed getting a reaction out of him.

"I think I'm going to just go change," Eli said with a reddened face. He grabbed the tuxedo hanging from the rack. "This one, I'm guessing?"

"Yes. Please put on those shoes too," Davin said.

Eli came back a few minutes later wearing the tuxedo jacket, shirt, pants, and shoes. He didn't bother with the tie or cummerbund. With the stubble on his face and the shirt open two buttons at the top, Eli looked like James Bond after he'd been at it all day.

"You look great, buddy," Brad said when he spotted Eli walking toward the group.

Mia dropped her chin and bit her lower lip to let Eli know his wardrobe was having an effect on her. "Wow, Eli, that is a perfect fit."

"Almost," Davin interjected, "but not until I'm finished with him." He continued, "My dear, you're done, and you're absolutely gorgeous. Are you sure you don't want to model my gowns at my events?"

Mia stepped down and turned around so Davin could unzip the back of her dress for her. "No, no, Davin. I like to dress up, but only for special occasions, and I need to have someone's arm to hold when I walk in a gown," she said as she glanced at Eli.

She took the dress straps from her shoulders and pulled her arms through them as if she were about to just drop the dress on the floor. At the last moment, she held the dress up to keep her front covered, but allowed her back to be exposed as she walked off, peeking over her shoulder one more time at Eli.

"Come on up here, Detective," Davin said. "This shouldn't take long, but I do want to make sure we have all of you measured correctly."

Eli stood on the stool and looked over at Brad as if silently calling out for help. Brad smiled back and then covered his mouth with his hands to hold back laughter. He knew Eli was uncomfortable, and the more that became obvious, the more Davin was going to strive to make it even more uncomfortable for him.

It was fun for Davin, making straight guys nervous about being touched by a gay male, as if it would somehow infect them with his gayness. Davin knew it came from a place of ignorance, fear of the unknown, and often lack of exposure to homosexuality. But he wasn't offended in the least. He found it sporting to make innuendos out of every innocuous statement.

"Let's see how you measure up," Davin said as he pulled the cloth measuring tape from around his neck.

"You sure it's long enough?" Eli fired back, hoping to set Davin on his heels and maybe put an end to the sexual innuendos. It was a risk because Davin could certainly keep it going, or he could give up now that Eli was bantering back, no longer afraid of the joust.

"Touché, Detective!" Davin said proudly.

"Nice!" Brad burst out laughing and backslapped Eli.

"Listen, Brad, this is all crazy, right?" Eli said.

"What is?"

"That after us meeting only a couple of days ago, you're inviting me as your guest for this Sunday? I mean, there have to be a thousand people lined up wanting to go with you. Studio executives and people like that?"

"They've got their own tickets. But I get to decide who to take with me. I'll be honest, if my mom and dad were still around, they'd be going and not you and Mia. But since they aren't, I'd much rather enjoy your company than some phonies."

"Amen," said Davin as he chalked around the hemline of Eli's pants.

"I've got plenty of people who make themselves part of my world. I don't often get to choose much in my life. The writers tell me what to say. The director tells me how to say it, where to stand, walk, and sit when I say it. The studio tells me how I should look and what to wear.

The catering folks are on strict instructions regarding my diet so I don't get pudgy, and the list goes on. But I do get to choose who I take with me to the awards show, so I'm taking you, who has shown me friendship without asking for anything in return. It's nice to be able to do for others who aren't demanding that *I* do something grand for *them* and then pretending to be gracious about it when, in fact, they've been expecting my caretaking, compliance, and generosity."

By the end of his impromptu speech, Brad's face was slightly red, and he was breathing a little heavier. Being on the inside of the celebrity circle was an interesting spectacle. Brad was frustrated with the celebrity part of the life, it seemed. Who wouldn't be? At this point in his life, Brad couldn't go to any regular store or restaurant without being accosted by adoring fans, each expecting him to spend extra time with them, take pictures, sign autographs, and make them feel special.

Being famous must have had its drawbacks. The wealthy part was great, but to lose one's anonymity must be devastating. It seemed obvious that Brad felt isolated, like he was being quarantined for a disease. More often than not, when Brad had spare time, he spent it home alone.

"Well, well. You've been holding that in for quite some time," Davin said with a look of straight-faced concern.

Investigation Closing In

"All right, let's go over what we know and get this train moving on one set of tracks, please," Sergeant Kesling said to his team once they were assembled in the homicide conference room. About as plain as any other conference room in a county building completed in the early 1980s, the room had carpet in a wonderful shade of mauve, with dark blue carpeted walls for softness and sound resistance from adjacent rooms. The two colors together were befitting of a bygone era. Centered on three of the walls were large dry-erase boards that allowed for multiple case theories to run concurrently.

Kesling's team had their coffee cups and breakfasts of choice. Artie loved his donuts, aka "power rings," especially if they were Krispy Kreme, whereas Nate was more of an Egg McMuffin kind of guy. Eli didn't eat a morning meal. He fasted intermittently, so he typically only ate two meals a day between noon and eight p.m. He was sticking to just black coffee. He'd had a strong workout this morning, which allowed his body to feed off his stored fat cells and get him motivated for all-day action.

"Well, Shelly is definitely our guy," Artie said. "She had motive, opportunity, and the evidence is mounting against her in more ways every day."

"Let's list them," Kesling prodded.

"Okay, first," Artie said, "the fact that she *may* have a physical alibi doesn't concern me. She could have had one of her parolee turds do the deed for her. Five hundred dollars is a king's ransom for them guys. Second, the victim's car was found up in Chinatown where she has a bunch of people on her roster. The car was oiled down."

"Oiled down?" Eli asked.

Kesling chimed in. "Yeah, after two days of not moving, we snatched it up and brought it in. CSI worked it as a priority. Every printable surface of the entire interior was wiped with baby oil or vegetable oil. Whatever they used guaranteed we didn't get any fingerprints."

"No shit?" Eli said with raised eyebrows and a thrust of his lower lip. That was actually ingenious.

"No shit," Artie continued. "Yeah, I forgot you missed a couple days around here, hanging out in Hollyweird. So, get this, under the seats, an accordion-style folder contained the Browers' wallets, passports, wedding rings, and watches."

"So why would the suspects do that?" Eli asked.

"Sarge has the best theory so far. Sarge?" Artie asked with a smile.

"I think they planned it perfectly," Kesling said.

"Really?" Eli was curious how much of his theory was about to come out of his boss's mouth.

"Yeah, nothing else makes sense. The killer or killers were trying to make them look like they fled. They took their wallets, passports, their fluffy little dog—all the important stuff that the Browers would have taken had they really been fleeing. I think they dropped the car in the parolee's neighborhood hoping it would get stolen, chopped, and vanished before anyone ever got the wiser. It would not have been entered as a stolen vehicle if we didn't find the dog and the bodies. I think the suspects wanted the Browers' IDs and credit cards to be used by whoever stole, or I guess, re-stole the car. Think about how many parolees we'd be shaking down right now. We would be living in Chinatown trying to solve this."

Eli was fascinated to hear his case theory regurgitated through his sergeant. He looked at Nate, who shot him a knowing smirk. But the problem with Kesling's rendition was that he hadn't thought things all the way through. "Wait, but no, that doesn't make total sense," Eli interjected. "The suspects forgot that stuff. Has to be. It wasn't intentional. Remember, the Browers are found dead in spite of their plan. In order for this whole thing to work correctly, the suspects certainly did *not* want us chasing down people using the vic's credit cards, which would demonstrate signs of foul play. I think the killers were banking on the parolees chopping the car, sure, but they didn't want anything personal from the victims located that might indicate they were dead instead of fleeing the country."

"But they are dead," Artie said.

"No fucking shit, Artie, but can't you see this wasn't a straight murder? If someone wanted to seek revenge, then fine, kill them, go to their house, bust down the front door, shoot them in the head, and leave. Enjoy the revenge. But instead, to make it look like they fled overnight, driving two dead bodies, or two alive and bound bodies, across two counties and burying them deep in a ravine, ensuring they would have never been found, takes great planning and an industrial-strength set of balls. Had it not been for Teddy, none of this would be going on. Not for at least several months. No, no. This was done by someone who needs them to still be alive but missing."

"Shelly has the will and thus control of their estate," Nate said.

"Well, what about the dog, smart-ass?" Artie asked Eli.

"Mistake number two. Or really, it was mistake number one if you take them in order. Didn't you say the coroner and the vet both concurred that the dog died of exposure and not trauma? That the only injury was a bruise to the eye?"

"What are you saying, Eli?" Kesling asked.

"I'm saying that for all the thought that went into this, two simple mistakes, two critical mistakes, were made that have us working this case as a murder in the first place. I think the dog was intended for the hole with the Browers but slipped away. Probably was barking his head off or tried to bite the bad guys and got smacked for it. Probably ran off and hid in the dark. They hoped the coyotes would get it, but instead, he lay upon his masters' graves so they'd be found. Kind of a Lassie-type story, but it really happened."

"What kind of idiotic bullshit—" Artie was saying before Kesling cut him off.

"You know, kid, you may be onto something." Kesling wrote on the board with a marker.

Artie was pissed. He crossed his arms and grabbed a neighboring chair to put his feet on. He leaned back in the chair and was visibly pouting like a six-year-old who got called out trying to steal second base.

"Let's work the mistakes, then work backwards," Kesling said.

Nate jumped in, "Well, leaving the computer and all the paperwork will likely be a big mistake when we get through examining it all."

"Yeah, but if the vics are supposed to be missing, then anything else missing from the house in the first few days would seem suspicious, right?" Eli countered with excitement void of attitude. Now that Artie had shut the fuck up, an intelligent conversation could commence without his ridiculous interference.

"So, who had control of the residence?" Kesling asked.

Nate said, "Shelly for sure. She's the executor of the will."

Eli added, "And that one couple had a key, but I don't have a shred of belief that they're involved."

"Me either. They're not near the suspect list for now. I mean, anything is possible, but let's work on the probable. What does Shelly have to gain?" Kesling asked.

"Well," Nate said, "all their assets, money and otherwise, would be under her control. After the court case was resolved, she could keep as much as she wanted and disperse a little to the beneficiaries, of which there was only Abby's half brother and Bill's sister. No one would really know how much money was left besides Shelly."

"What about the lawyer?" Eli asked the room.

"Now that's the stupidest thing you've said," Artie barked. "Why would a lawyer kill his clients? Isn't that killing the golden goose? Or I guess, gooses?"

Nate, Eli, and Kesling all simultaneously shouted, "Geese!"

"Whatever, goose and geese, moose but not meese, who the fuck made up this language?"

"I'm not saying he's our suspect, but he did have access to their lives. He wrote the will and is friends with Shelly. In fact, it was Shelly who introduced the Browers to Harold in the first place," Eli finally added.

"All right, let's do this. Nate, you start on a series of search warrants for all of the Browers' known bank records and safety deposit boxes. Track the money and let's find out exactly what Shelly has or doesn't have. Eli, get with intelligence to work up a profile on Shelly. We've watched her for a few days without anything to report. She leads a seemingly normal, if not ultimately boring, life. I'll let the narcs keep tabs on her for a few more days, but in the meantime, if she doesn't deviate, I'm going to call it off. Both of you work through all the files we got from the Brower residence."

"What about me?" Artie asked. "It is my case, you know."

"Yeah, I know. I didn't forget about you. Road trip. There's an extradition to Chattanooga, Tennessee, which is about a three-hour drive from the county where the Georgia land deal was being developed. Locate and interview Kurt and see how that actually turned out. You leave tomorrow afternoon. We've scheduled an extra day so you have time to get the interview done and get the extradition to court and back here on a plane.

"Questions?" Kesling asked.

"What about Dimitri and the spindles thing? Lot of people ripped off and pissed."

"Yeah, but that doesn't fit either," Artie said. "They'd want their pound of flesh. Them farmers come looking for the Browers, they'd probably pitchfork them to death rather than spend all the time and thought that went into this."

Eli had to agree they didn't fit the profile. In fact, those wronged might be able to get some recompense from the estate now that the Browers were actually dead and not hiding from them.

"Oh, Nate and Eli, since you two are so well-versed with the LA freeways now, go out tomorrow and interview Sgt. Weller and see what you can dig up on Shelly."

Eli was happy to go back out to Los Angeles. If luck were on his side, he'd get a chance to see Mia again. If he was really lucky, he might be able to spend the night. But that wouldn't work if Nate came with.

"Um, boss, can I, well—" Nate stammered.

"Spit it out, Nate," Kesling said.

"Well, I was going to ask you later, but I might as well let the kitten out of the bag. Ruth and I have an appointment tomorrow with our OB-GYN. She's twelve weeks along now."

The sudden announcement that the Parkers were going to have a third child certainly lightened the intense mood in the room. With all the death and destruction that homicide detectives faced, babies and puppies still melted the most hardened veteran cop.

"No way, a new baby Parker?" Eli shouted and high-fived his partner. "Boy or girl?"

"Won't know for a few more weeks."

"Why the fuck would you want a third carpet monkey draining your bank account?" Artie said as if it weren't meant to be offensive.

"Why, thank you for your congratulatory sentiments, Artie. It never gets old hearing the warmth pouring from your soul," Nate shot back, shaking his head.

"Congratulations, Nate. Seriously, that's awesome," Eli said. "All is well so far?"

"Yeah, thanks. Ruth is great, no issues. I just love hearing the heartbeat and hearing the doctor say all is well in person."

"Well, Eli, looks like you're on your own to Los Angeles again. Think you can handle it, or do you want me to come with?" Kesling asked.

Eli's excitement that he'd be able to visit Mia crested with the first half of his sergeant's statement, but his hopes were nearly dashed by the second part. Trying not to sound too eager to leave Kesling behind, he said, "Naw, I'm good." But he couldn't hide the emotional response and grin that came and went across his face when he thought about some alone time with Mia after hours.

"What's with the smile?" Kesling asked.

"Oh, I was just thinking about whether or not I could get more of the coffee from the lawyer's office. Tell him, Nate."

"Best coffee you've ever had, sarge. Swear," Nate added enthusiastically.

"I want to talk to Harold again about what we've learned so far with regard to Shelly and the estate," Eli said.

"Trust him?" Kesling asked.

"Not sure. He's an arrogant ass—"

"Then you two should get along great," Artie said with a laugh. Kesling and Nate even chuckled at that one.

Eli ignored the interrupting comment and continued, "He does have the most inside knowledge to the whole story about the Browers."

***

It was truly quite nice to have their set of cubicles to themselves without Artie's negative influence or his pretending to work, which actually slowed Eli and Nate down. Artie usually got to work a little late, so he made up for it by leaving early today, claiming he needed some time to get ready for the trip to Chattanooga. Eli and Nate were alone to work, think, and talk.

With the search warrants completed and emailed off to the repositories of record for the Browers' bank accounts, it might take only a day or two to get the records emailed back in a zip file. Technology was terrific. What used to take hours, days, or weeks of work for a bank clerk to copy bank records, box them, and then ship them across the United States now only took a few keystrokes, print-to-PDF commands, and then a reply to the original email.

Throughout the day while reading through stacks and stacks of tax records from what appeared to be average citizens with normal jobs and small businesses, Eli was sending the occasional text to Mia, asking her questions about the Emmy event that was coming Sunday. Eli hadn't told a soul, nor was he planning to. What he did with his own time, as long as it wasn't breaking the law or violating sheriff's policies, was no one's business but his.

He couldn't stop thinking about her. Not only was she gorgeous with a smoking-hot body that fit perfectly with his, but she also seemed kind and caring. She laughed at his jokes and seemed genuinely into him. He was still waiting for her to respond to his text asking if she had time to meet tomorrow when he was out in LA to interview the sergeant and the lawyer.

He just hoped that nothing would happen between now and the weekend to force a change of plans and keep him from going. He wasn't sure if they were going to be asked to work on the case on Saturday. It was his plan to make it out to Brad's on Saturday and spend the night with Mia and experience all the pre-ceremony bliss.

Unless they were on call, not even the meanest sergeants forced detectives to work on Sundays. Everyone held to an unwritten Sunday Code. After years of patrol where weekends didn't exist, making detective came with a fairly normal schedule, with Sundays off for church, football, or doing absolutely nothing. The Sunday Code was sacred.

"Hey, check this out," Nate said excitedly.

"What is it?"

"Remember that Harold King said that the Browers sold their condo in San Diego?"

"Yup."

"Well, guess who got the proceeds from the sale, which netted three hundred and eighty-three thousand dollars?"

"I would have said the Browers, but obviously, that's not correct."

"Nope. Shelly."

"What? How?"

"Seems she loaned them the money as a second mortgage with no interest or payments. Just the loan repayable upon the sale of the residence."

"Whoa, whoa, whoa. How the heck did a fifty-thousand-dollar-a-year parole agent come up with that much cash to loan to them, and why would they need that money? Man, this is good! Where'd you find that?"

"It's right here in the escrow papers. And check this out. The loan was executed four months ago, before they sold it."

"They got a loan from Shelly, to do what?"

"It looks like the loan from her basically shored up all the equity in the home. The principal balance on the first and the second from Shelly equates almost dollar for dollar to the amount of the sale of the condo minus expenses and fees, etcetera."

"Why?"

"That, I do not know. Good question for Harold, I'd say. He probably knew why they did that."

"Good idea. I can ask him that tomorrow when I see him," Eli said excitedly.

"Wow, aren't you the eager beaver to head out to LA? Last week, I had to practically beg you. Now you can't get enough. Is this girl you barely mentioned out there?"

"She might have something to do with it."

"Did you meet her at a gas station or what?"

"No, but that's funny. I'll let you know more later. Now isn't the time."

"Why not? Usually you blab your sexual exploits to me the next day. What? Do you actually care for this woman?"

"Maybe. Yeah, I think I do."

Sgt. Weller

The next morning, Eli drove out to LA County Sheriff's Headquarters and made his way to the Special Projects Bureau. "Hi, I'm looking for Sergeant Weller?" Eli asked a harried-looking man who was sitting behind a desk and rubbing his eyes with the palms of his hands.

"That's me, unfortunately," Eric Weller said with some frustration.

"Unfortunately?"

"Well, today, yes. I'm the one they put in charge of our new policies and procedures manual. If that doesn't sound boring enough, we have a killer deadline and we're not ready. Never mind. Totally not your problem. You sure are dressed nice for a narc."

"I'm from homicide. San Bernardino County Sheriff's Department. I'm Eli Hockney. We spoke on the phone."

"Oh, yeah, oops. I forgot about you. I'm expecting a narc from Tustin who has a whole set of policies and some forms...never mind again. This project is going to kill me. I swear, if I ever hit the lottery big, they'll get my badge and ID sent to them in the mail from some tropical island. A man can dream, huh? What can I do for you? You said something about the Brower murders on the phone."

"Yes, sir, that's right. How well did you know them?"

"Gosh, it's been, what, ten, no, wait, twelve years since I've seen them or any of Shelly's other friends. Once we divorced, there wasn't much need for contact. I got a call from Bill once to see if I still wanted him to do my taxes, but it was too weird, so I got someone else. I don't have any

176

assets or make much money like Shelly and her friends, so really, anyone can do them. I only started using him out of mutual friendship to Shelly."

"This desk job pretty dangerous?"

"Huh?"

Eli pointed to a healing injury on Sgt. Weller's hand.

"Tree trimming. I can't afford a gardener. Shelly has made sure of that. She makes the same amount as me, plus she gets overtime as a field agent, whereas I'm stuck here nine to five as if I were salary. I love the hours, but I miss the OT from working detectives. That's where the real money's at, right?"

Eli smiled and nodded, but said nothing.

"Well, every couple of years since our daughter was four, Shelly goes in like clockwork and gets the courts to bump my child support another two hundred per month. Between the initial alimony and the ever-increasing child support, I'm damn near tapped out. She gets to live in her late parents' Burbank home worth three-quarters of a million dollars and I'm living in a shithole in Van Nuys just to stay afloat. Do you have any idea what kind of god-awful commute that is?"

"I can only imagine," Eli said in a soft, empathetic tone.

"Well, young man, be glad that you only have to imagine it. I'm living the fucking nightmare, and it's real. Anyway, there I go complaining again. Sorry, but I am totally stressed out by all the shit I gotta get done before I can get out of here."

"Out of here?"

"Yeah, I'm trying to push the deadline so me and a couple buddies can make our annual fly-fishing trip to Idaho Falls. Supposed to leave Friday, but I'm guessing that isn't going to happen."

"Wow, sorry, sir—"

"No worries. Have I answered all your questions?"

"Pretty much. Just one simple one left, I guess."

"Shoot." Eric Weller stood with his hands on his hips in anticipation.

"Know anyone who'd want to kill the Browers?"

"Besides Shelly?"

"Wow, that was fast."

"Look, I'm assuming the fact that you want to talk with me has something to do with Shelly being a suspect in their murders, right? Don't forget, I'm in the business too. Just because I'm an admin-weeny right now doesn't mean I don't know how to work a case and connect dots."

"Sure. Yes, of course. I guess everyone who could profit from the Browers' disappearance or death is a suspect at this point. It wasn't a robbery homicide, that I can say for sure."

"Well, I know that a few months ago, when I went to Shelly's to piss and moan about the recent raise in child support, I saw some real estate papers on her kitchen table. She saw me peep at them before she snatched them up. Looked like she was getting a loan at first, but from what I read on the docs, it looked like *she* was loaning the Browers three hundred eighty thousand. I totally flipped out on her. I asked her why in God's name was she stiffing me for more and more child support if she had that kind of cash to lend." Weller's emotions had been riding near the surface since before Eli got there, but now, they were overflowing.

"Now, I know she sold her first house after her mom died and she moved into the Burbank home. Way back when, when we were more civil, she said something about investing the equity from the sale of her home—the one I bought for us—into some rental homes or an apartment. Since then, I know from talking with our daughter that Shelly is a landlord of several homes, but I don't know what 'several' means. But to toss around three-eighty seemed a bit much. Shelly told me it wasn't her money, that she was just helping Bill and Abby. I didn't understand what that meant, but she made sure not to provide any details."

"Interesting."

"I don't know if that's helpful or not, but it's all I can think of that may hold some relevance to all this. Tragic, really. I liked Bill and Abby. Hated to see them hurt like that."

There was a moment of silence that seemed appropriate under the circumstances.

Eli broke the silence. "I've heard from everyone they were really nice folks. As you have also been. Thank you so much for your time. I hope you meet your deadline and can make it to Wyoming."

"Idaho."

"Right, Idaho."

Eli tossed out the wrong location to see if Weller told the truth about his fishing trip. When people lie, they often forget the details of their ruse. By confirming the intended location of the trip, it was more likely than not that he was indeed telling the truth.

The evidence was mounting against Shelly the more people Eli talked to. The more he learned, the more questions he had. It was definitely time for another conversation with Harold. Certainly, he would know about the loan from Shelly to Bill and Abby.

Judgment proof

"Hi, Harold, thanks for seeing me again, and on such short notice."

"Long drive for you. I probably could have helped you on the phone, but since you're here, would you like a cup of coffee?"

"That's why I made the drive," Eli said with a grin.

After a fresh cup was brought into the office for the two men, Eli leaned forward to put his cup on the saucer after taking a wonderful first sip. He still couldn't believe the difference between this coffee and others he'd tried at various coffee shops. Obviously, the station house coffee was some of the cheapest on the market, but it did the trick for boosting alertness on the graveyard shift. But for flavor, nothing beat what he was drinking in Harold's office.

Eli rested his forearms on his thighs while sitting at the edge of the couch cushion. This afforded him the ability to keep his coffee cup on the table next to his open padfolio, and, maybe more importantly, leaning forward toward someone while conversing with them was a very visible and obvious sign of active listening. "So please help me out here, Harold. I'm trying to figure out the reason Skip would have sold his condo in San Diego shortly after getting a second mortgage on the house."

"Well, that's easy. He was making himself judgment proof."

"I don't understand."

"Okay, let's say that you're being sued for, say, fifty thousand dollars. You own a home that's worth two hundred and fifty thousand and you only owe one hundred thousand. That leaves one hundred and fifty thousand in equity, right?"

"Right."

"So, if you were to lose the lawsuit and be forced to pay the plaintiff the fifty thousand in a judgment, and you didn't have it in your bank account, the court could force you to sell your house, refinance it, or put an interest lien on the house so that when you did sell it, the plaintiff would be paid off the original amount plus accrued interest for the time that has passed. Either way, with those assets available, you would be forced to pay the judgment."

"Oh, okay."

"Bill had lots of assets he could have been forced to liquidate to pay back a large sum of money to the plaintiffs in the primary case, both David and his secretary."

"So, he sold his condo to simply get rid of his assets?"

"Yes, sir," Harold said as he sipped from his coffee.

"But what about the equity?"

"Well, if there's no equity, then there's nothing to attach, now, is there? It is now a worthless asset to the plaintiff. Only current assets are attachable during litigation."

"But haven't they been in litigation for a while?"

"Yes, indeed. Little over two years now."

"But they only sold the condo like, what, six months ago?"

"Sounds about right."

"So...?"

"Right. You're wondering how it was that they were able to liquidate their assets during litigation and not have it held against them."

"Yes."

"You're indeed an intelligent young man, aren't you?"

"Thank you, but wasn't it illegal for them to sell their condo and dispense with the proceeds?"

"What proceeds?"

"The equity from their house went to Shelly."

"Yes," Harold said with a smile, and sipped from his cup.

Eli stared a moment, then took a sip from his cup, not only for taste, warmth, and caffeine, but to allow him to process his thoughts.

"Come on, Detective, you're getting there," Harold said, sounding like the patient tutor who used to help Eli with his awful algebra homework.

"Wait, so, that wasn't technically the Browers' money, then?"

"Not just technically, but legally. As far as I know, that loan from Shelly was a private matter between parties that had nothing to do with the lawsuit. The condo sale paid off the first mortgage to the original lender, paid off Shelly's loans, and after the Realtor fees and transaction fees, I think the Browers walked away with a little less than five thousand dollars."

"But couldn't the plaintiff put some sort of lien or stay of sale, if there is such a thing?" Eli scrambled for legal words he didn't have in his lexicon.

"It's not called a 'stay,' but yes, the plaintiff could have requested an order from the court that the defendants in this case not sell, relinquish, or otherwise liquidate their assets until a settlement was reached or a judgment rendered."

"Why didn't they?"

"You'll have to ask them that, Detective."

"Would you have, were you the plaintiff's attorney?"

"Sure, first thing. But I'm a helluva lot better lawyer. That's why the plaintiffs were never going to win and were frustrated."

"Frustrated enough to kill?"

"You'll have to ask them that, Detective," Harold repeated with a grin.

Eli picked up his coffee cup and sipped a couple of times, savoring the wonderful aroma and flavors, then put the cup down gently while he thought another moment.

"All right, let me see if I've got this. The Browers sold their condo so it wouldn't be seized, sold, or otherwise taken from them if they lost the case. But what about their other assets? Their primary home in La Cañada Flintridge and other holdings they may have had?"

"They didn't own the house they were tragically killed in. That was a rental. Their new car was a lease to Bill's company. In fact, at the time of their death, they owned nothing on paper. All the jewelry, the 1957 classic Corvette, and artworks were all gone as far as the court was concerned."

"Your idea."

"A guided decision on the part of the Browers, but also payment."

"Payment?"

"Yes, my time does not come free or cheap. If a client has worldly assets they're willing to part with, I'll give them current market value in trade of services. Bill and Abby paid me with the Chevy and some beautiful works of art. Plus cash, of course."

"What about safe deposit boxes? I recall something about boxes stuffed with cash."

"Well, I wouldn't really know anything about that. If they existed, he never told me, and I would surely *never* ask."

"Who would know if they did exist?"

"Other than Shelly? I'm not sure."

"What other methods or means were there for judgment proofing?"

"All lawyer retainer fees are judgment proof."

Eli had his coffee cup in one hand and rolled the other one in a backward circling motion to request Harold keep explaining.

"You see, rather than billing a client weekly or sporadically, clients will hand over a check to the lawyer to be deposited in a trust account, like an escrow. Let's say you're getting a divorce. I'd ask you for ten thousand right up front before I made one phone call. Then I'd send you a weekly or monthly bill showing the draw down with documentation for hours spent and any expenses incurred."

"Did the Browers give you a retainer?"

"Two hundred and fifty thousand."

Eli nearly spit out the coffee he'd just sipped. "Two-fifty? Wow, that's a helluva retainer."

Harold leaned in and lowered his voice an octave. "It was a helluva case."

"How much is left?"

"I don't know, I'd have to check my records, but those numbers are attorney-client privileged as well."

"Interesting," Eli said before he realized it came straight from his brain and passed his lips before he could censor himself.

"Interesting, how?"

"If my math is correct, between you and Shelly, you two have around a half a million dollars in cash from the Browers."

"And then some."

"*And then some?*"

"Listen, that may sound like a lot of money to you, but these people dealt in million-dollar deals all the time, and with Southern California real estate prices being what they are, your average citizen who twenty years ago bought a run-down condo by the 405 is now sitting on a half a million dollars."

Eli was stunned. He didn't even know what else to ask at this point. This was all going to take a while to process. He had to make a quick decision regarding how much further he would take the questioning. Delving deeper now might lead to an interrogation, which was exactly where Eli did not want to go with Harold.

Eli closed his notebook, stood, and put out his hand. "Well, Harold, you have absolutely enlightened me today. It's why I love this job so much. You learn something new every day. Thank you so much. You've been really helpful."

Harold matched his stance and reciprocated with a warm handshake. "My pleasure. Are you getting any closer to finding out who killed my clients?"

"A little bit every day," Eli said with a stoic expression. "It is difficult, you know. So many people wanted revenge or were harmed financially by them, it's going to take a while to determine who had the most to gain by their deaths."

"Yes, indeed. Thank *you* for what you and your team are doing."

Eli took note that Harold seemed to be pleased with himself and how the meeting went. But Eli really didn't know him well enough to determine what was real and what was fake. With a lawyer who'd spent his entire adult life making underhanded deals, conning people, saying just enough without lying, it was certainly tough to tell. Harold was quite practiced.

Dinner with Mia

Eli got to the restaurant ahead of Mia, who said she was excited to see him. They were to meet at 6:00 p.m., but Eli really had nowhere to go to kill time, and he surely wasn't going to get himself jammed up in traffic by driving around sightseeing. He had gotten himself a beer and played on his phone, patiently waiting for Mia to arrive.

He saw her the moment she entered. Wearing a light-yellow sundress with spaghetti straps across her bronze shoulders and deeply cut down the front nearly to her navel, accentuating her breasts, the mid-thigh length of the ruffled bottom flowed as she spun first in one direction and then another. The sun beamed in through the glass door of Lenny's Casita, a Mexican restaurant Mia said was her favorite. As she turned back and forth, scanning the restaurant, the sun lit up her dress and shone through the light fabric just enough to expose her curves.

Mia's eyes finally found Eli, who was waving at her from a booth near the front corner. She smiled brightly when she saw him, and it warmed his heart. He smiled back just as brightly and stood as she approached, something his father taught him when he was very young.

"What a great surprise that you had time to get together today," Mia said as she slid her way into the half-circle booth.

"I'm just so glad you were able to make it. I really wanted to see you. And with that dress you have on, wow, am I glad I got to see you."

Mia laughed and maybe even blushed a little as the waiter came up to the table. "Another cerveza, señor?"

"Yes, please."

"And a margarita for the señorita?"

Mia replied in what Eli could only guess to be perfect Spanish.

"Gracias. Uno momento, por favor," the waiter said as he smiled and walked off toward the bar.

"So, hey, this Sunday," Eli started.

"Yes?"

"I was wondering, hoping, actually, that if my schedule permits, I could come stay with you Saturday night? You know, save the drive and all?"

"Well, I don't know…"

"Hey, sorry if it's too much, too soon."

"Of course you can, silly. I was hoping you could. In fact, do you have to go home tonight?"

"Yes, I do, unfortunately. I can't stay tonight. Trust me, I wish I could. But I really have to get back to my place tonight. If I don't get caught up on some of my paperwork, I might have to work Saturday. That would totally suck!" If Eli could have, he would have quit right now to stay with Mia. But until he won the lottery, as Sgt. Weller put it, he'd have to keep working. Too bad Eli didn't have an inheritance to look forward to. Maybe then *he* could spend his time fishing or doing whatever he wanted.

Microsoft Theater

Massive crowds had formed up and down the street in front of the Microsoft Theater in Los Angeles, California. The red carpet was in full action, with TV show personalities being photographed and stopped for interviews by all the American and foreign press that could squeeze into a small roped-off area. Limousines lined Chick Hearn Court as they dropped off their A-list guests to be fawned over.

A stretch limousine stopped at the drop-off point, and from the right rear passenger door, out stepped Brad to the squeals, shrills, and yells of his adoring fans while he assisted his lovely date in climbing out of the car.

Eli and Mia got out of the limo on the other side and received some quick glances, but the media and crowd instantly realized they weren't stars or famous people. They moved across the red carpet past Brad and many other stars who were being photographed and had microphones shoved in their faces. They both waited at the entrance for Brad and his date to catch up after the countless interviews and handshakes.

When Brad caught up with Eli and Mia, he remarked, "Intense, huh?"

"Yeah, how do you deal with that all the time?" Eli asked.

"First, *that* isn't all the time. Besides, when they stop stopping you, then it's a problem in my business." Brad motioned for the four of them to go ahead and enter the main lobby. "But I do miss just being able to walk into a store and simply buy socks," he added.

"Socks?"

"You know what I mean!"

"Yeah, I do. So, what now?"

"Guess we mingle inside, tell lies, and pretend to like everyone who's competition or who has stabbed me in the back a dozen times or more."

An unknown man's voice shouted, "Brad!"

Before the guy could cross the crowd and meet up with them, Brad leaned over to Eli and said, "And so it begins."

Without actually remembering who the man was, Brad smiled brightly and replied, "Hey, buddy! How are you?"

Mia pulled on Eli's arm to move them both away from Brad and the small crowd forming around him. "You get used to it," she said.

"What's that?"

"Being two steps behind Brad and his adoring fans. It's all part of the package." With that, Mia handed Eli his ticket with their table number and seating assignment.

***

Nate was lying facedown on the carpet while his kids climbed and jumped on his back. They played Slay the Dragon, with their daddy, of course, being the dragon.

"You think you've got me? I'm the biggest dragon in the whole land!" Nate shouted and growled as he flipped over, spilling his children onto the floor. "And this dragon tickles all who try to slay him!"

The children squealed with delight at being tickled and wrestled with. In the background, the Emmy Awards show was playing while Mrs. Parker was once again folding the never-ending laundry.

"Hey, hon, I think they're going to announce Brad Clark's category next. You know I told my sister you two have met, and she was crazy jealous, asking me all kinds of questions."

"Honey, we met him once. Eli did, really, but it's not like we're hanging out with the guy."

On the television, a well-dressed famous couple came to the microphone and read cold from the teleprompter one of those horrible back-and-forth attempts at humor that make everyone in the audience and at home cringe. When the camera showed a wide pan of Brad Clark for his reaction, home viewers, including Nate and Helen, could clearly see Eli sitting two seats away, with Mia sitting between him and Brad.

The Emmy Award presenters continued reading names and showing titles until they reached the final nominee. They then ripped open the envelope as the five nominees' faces were put into their little Brady Bunch squares. The couple announced simultaneously, "Bradley Clark!"

The TV show cut to a close-up of Brad smiling and reacting with sheer joy. He hugged and kissed his date, then high-fived and bro-hugged Eli and got a kiss on the cheek from Mia.

From inside the Parker living room, Nate and Mrs. Parker stared at the screen with mouths wide open while they watched the scene on the television play out. The silence was finally broken by Nate's exclamation of "Holy shit!"

Helen immediately scolded, "Nate!"

"Oooohhhhh! Daddy said a bad word!"

"Sorry, kids," Nate said. He stared at the screen, then rewound the footage to confirm what he knew he saw but couldn't believe to be true.

Helen smirked and shook her head while looking back and forth between her husband and the display on the screen. "This is going to make for a very interesting week at work," she summed up.

Without another word, Helen picked up the stacks of folded laundry, put them in the basket on top of the remaining unfolded laundry, and got up from the couch with the basket. "Come on, kids, help me put away your clothes. Daddy needs a few minutes alone to talk on the phone."

Just then, Nate's mobile phone rang. He looked at the screen to see Sgt. Kesling's name.

"Mommy, how'd you know Daddy's phone was going to ring?"

"Because I've been in the department a long time too," Helen said as she walked the children out of the room while Nate answered his phone.

"Hey, Sarge," Nate said.

"Did you see your idiot partner on television just now?"

"Yeah, I saw him."

"Did you know he was going to be there?"

"Hell no, I didn't know!"

"How long has he been connected to Brad Clark? What's the deal with that bullshit?"

"Honestly, I don't know. Lemme try and reach him and see what the hell is going on."

"Do that and call me back." Nate could hear the deep sigh of his sergeant. "Shit, the captain is trying to ring through. Gotta go!"

"Okay, boss, I'll call you back." Nate hung up with Kesling, then dialed Eli's mobile phone. The television was on a commercial after Brad Clark's acceptance speech, where he thanked the usual people and was self-deprecating and gracious in his appreciation for winning the award.

***

Inside the theater, people stood around chatting and stretching their legs. A man dressed in a tuxedo came up to Eli and asked where Brad was seated.

"Why, what's up?" Eli asked him.

"Oh, I'm a filler for the seat when the award winner is behind stage doing post-acceptance press. He won't be back before the next segment. TV doesn't like empty seats."

"Ah, well, that makes sense."

"Yeah, if you need to use the restroom or be relieved, we can get someone to fill your spot from commercial break to commercial break."

"Cool, thanks." Eli felt his phone vibrate and saw that it was Nate.

"Hey, Nate, I've only got a second. What's up? Where are we meeting tomorrow?"

"Oh, I don't know, I was thinking maybe the Oscars would be next?"

"Aw, shit, you saw me?"

"The whole fucking department saw you, dickhead!"

"Well, listen, I haven't done anything wrong. He invited me to go. I'm helping him out by keeping someone else from sitting with him that he doesn't like. It's not like..."

192 – DEREK PACIFICO

"Like what? Like you're compromising our case by colluding with a material witness?"

"Colluding? Hey! It's not like that."

A male announcer came over the theater speakers to warn everyone to take their seats because the commercial break was nearing its end.

"Hey, I gotta go. Commercial break's over in a sec. Can't be on the phone or out of my seat or I lose it to a filler. We'll chat tomorrow."

Eli hung up and then put his phone on airplane mode.

Nate answered back to a dead line. "Are you kidding me? Commercial break is over? Chat tomorrow?"

After-Party

It was well after midnight, and there were a dozen cars parked in Brad Clark's driveway along with limousines lined up and down the street. The party inside Brad's home and out by the pool was in full swing. Champagne flowed from countless bottles, along with the bar service that had been rented for the night to celebrate the win. Much as in the professional sports world, personalized party favors had to be pre-ordered in case Brad won. Had he not won the award, with one phone call by Mia, the home would have been cleared out before he arrived. But in this case, not a dollar was wasted on Emmy-related swag.

Brad stood in the living room holding his Emmy award and taking pictures with people who wanted to be associated with him and the golden statue. Mia sipped from her glass of champagne while Eli drank his second rum and coke courtesy of the hosted bar. These bartenders were told not to hold back on the liquor. They obliged their customers with pours that would get them in trouble if they were tending a restaurant bar.

Eli liked being with Mia, who seemed to like him for more than just the sex. She clung to his side, and he was happy to wrap an arm around her thin waist and hold her close. He knew if he wasn't careful, he would totally fall for this woman. Or hadn't he already? Maybe it should have been too early to tell, but the strong feelings he felt for Mia were also not just about dynamic sex. There was more.

A few people recognized Eli from the dinner at the producer's home and came over to say hello and chat for a few minutes. Some of the people who came over to him brought with them new people for Eli to meet. He was once again holding court, regaling people with action stories from his law enforcement career. He collected a few more business cards and invitations to call in the coming weeks and set up appointments for meetings to discuss story options.

Brad came over with two glasses of champagne, one in each hand. "I'm not sure how I wound up with two of these," Brad said with a slight slur. He offered one to Mia, but she declined, showing Brad her nearly full glass. Eli had a nearly finished drink in one hand, but he readily accepted the champagne.

"A toast to your win. Congratulations," Eli said with a smile. They clinked their glasses, and both knew by looking at each other that it was a race to see who could guzzle their glass down first. Being the veteran drinker that Brad was, he beat Eli by a swallow.

"Ahh! You're going to have to work on that, my young friend, if you're going to hang out with the big boys of Hollywood," Brad teased.

Eli wasn't that much younger than Brad, but being called young by him didn't seem to bother him as it did when his sergeant said it, or especially if Artie mentioned it. Brad was different. He treated Eli like a trusted friend, and Eli knew the comment was meant in good-natured fun.

But for Eli, sadly, the party had to end, "Listen, I got a bunch to do at home and work early Monday. I have to head out."

"Yeah, all right. This is going to be nutty for a few days, anyway, and I won't be able to hang out with all the press junkets I'll have to go to."

"Oh yeah, for sure. No worries. Catch you later. Next week or so. Congrats again!"

"Thanks, brother," Brad said back before being pulled by a woman to take some pictures with him.

Eli looked at Mia with sad puppy dog eyes. He didn't want to leave her, but there was only so much time he could be away from home and expect his neighbor to take care of Ranger. But leaving the party, leaving Mia, was the last thing he really wanted to do.

Mia walked Eli to his Taurus, which he had strategically parked at the bottom of the driveway by the gate so he wouldn't be blocked in by other guests' cars. They held hands as they walked, not saying a word to each other. When they reached the car, Eli leaned up against the driver's door. He pulled on his bow tie and released it and opened the top button.

"You know, I have to say, I've always wanted to do that," Eli said. Mia grabbed each end of the bow tie and pulled Eli forward to kiss her.

"So, hey," Eli whispered after their lips parted.

"Hey, yourself," Mia said back softly.

"I gotta head back to my place and catch up on my life a little, and there's a pile of work waiting for me. Plus, maybe a pile of something else."

"And?" Mia asked while looking up into his eyes. Her hands had moved from the ends of his bow tie to the sides of his waist. She pulled herself closer to him, grinding her front against his, reminding him what a sexual being she was and how well they fit together.

"And I thought if you have some time, you might want to make it out my way maybe sometime this week."

"There'll be a lot going on here, with Brad winning the Emmy and all," Mia replied. "My life is behind the scenes of his, and there'll be a crazy amount to do for a while to come, I'm afraid."

Eli was embarrassed to have asked and been shut down. Maybe she wasn't fully interested in being with him, but just having great sex. "Yeah, sure. I was just..."

Mia shut him up with a deep kiss. "When you have time, I'll be right here."

"You sure?"

"Go home, Detective."

"Yeah, okay."

Eli got into his detective unit and drove off through the gate. More cars were still coming up the drive as he left. The golf cart service used to bring guests from their limo parking place was also in high gear, ferrying partiers back and forth.

The long drive home would give Eli time to think about how he was going to deal with being seen on television with a material witness from the murder case. If the bosses also knew Eli spent the night at the actor's house and got involved with a woman working there, the trouble might be more than he could imagine.

DUI Traffic

After driving down the hills of La Cañada Flintridge, Eli was stopped at a red light. Just ahead was the sign for the freeway showing he was one mile from being able to get on the 134 and head due east on straight roads. The champagne on top of the two rum drinks had caught up to him. Plus, now that he'd left the excitement of the party, the quiet of his car plus the adrenaline of the night wearing off was a perfect recipe for drowsiness to set in.

He'd driven home plenty of times while tired after being up for a couple of days straight working a murder, but this was a little different. Usually when it came time to go home, there was a shorter drive from headquarters, where they'd just booked their crook in the jail across the parking lot at Central Detention Center. This night, his trip would take well over an hour in spite of driving at a higher rate of speed that he wasn't afraid to exercise in his official county vehicle.

But the red light wasn't changing, making the night even longer. Frustrated, Eli looked back and forth and saw that no cars were coming through the intersection from cross traffic. He got more tired waiting for the light to change on its own, and it seemed ridiculous to wait. After double-checking, he jumped on the gas pedal and sped on through the intersection.

What Eli didn't notice in his tired and slightly inebriated state was the California Highway Patrol officer who was sitting in the parking lot of a closed strip mall, filling out a report and sipping coffee from a ther-

198 – DEREK PACIFICO

mos he'd brought from home. Truth be told, the officer wasn't looking for a traffic violator. He was actually trying to hide for a moment on what had started off as a quiet night. He needed to get his paperwork done from the night before, which included three fender-benders and one major-injury traffic collision. Injury TCs took a little longer to prepare, and if he could get thirty minutes of uninterrupted time to verbally dictate his notes into the micro-recorder, he'd be almost caught up. It was Sunday, so it should have been relatively slow.

Eli didn't recognize the old pickup truck coming through the darkness. It had only one dimly lit headlamp working, and from a certain angle, the light appeared stationary and distant, as if it were from a far-off porch light. Just as Eli drove through the red light, the truck entered the intersection having the right of way.

When Eli barreled through the intersection, he cut off the truck and forced the driver to lay on his horn and brakes simultaneously. Eli looked at the wild-eyed driver, who flipped him the middle finger.

"Oops! Hey, fuck you too," Eli yelled through the closed windows as he returned the gesture.

CHP officers, lovingly or not so lovingly nicknamed "chippies," have the primary function of enforcing traffic laws. There was zero chance that this officer would let such an easy and blatant infraction go by the wayside. The interruption to his dictation would be worth it. This was a good ticket.

Eli looked up into the rearview mirror and saw the flashing red and blue lights of the CHP unit behind him. "Aw, come on," he said in exasperation, "not again."

He pulled into the parking lot of a corner gas station. The black-and-white CHP police unit pulled up behind close on his bumper and turned on the spotlights to shine brightly inside Eli's unit. The uniformed officer got out and walked up to the driver's door of Eli's car.

Eli opened the driver's-side window for the approaching officer. He'd already pulled out his badge wallet from the inside breast pocket of his tuxedo jacket.

"Good evening, sir. My name is Officer Ackerman with the California Highway Patrol."

"Hi."

"The reason I pulled you over was for running the red light back there. You almost caused an accident. I wanted to make sure there wasn't anything interfering with your ability to drive safely."

"Sorry, no, Officer, I'm fine," Eli said with a smile. Then he opened the wallet to display the seven-point gold star with the word "Detective" in a banner connecting the two top star points.

"May I see that?" Officer Ackerman said while holding out his hand.

"Sure. I'm Detective Hockney with the San Bernardino County Sheriff's Homicide Detail."

"Not James Bond?"

"Huh? Oh yeah, the tux. Actually, truth of it is, I just left Brad Clark's house. You know, the famous actor guy who plays cops all the time? He won the Emmy for best actor in a drama, and there's quite the party going on up there. If you want to meet him, I can get you in to meet him if you'd like to meet him." As the words came out of Eli's mouth, he knew it sounded bad. The thickness in his head was increasing.

"Nah, I'm good."

"Sorry for the trouble, but I've been crazy busy on an investigation out here, and I'm just headed back home. I've been out late and without sleep for a couple days now. I'm just tired and was careless. I'm sure you know how that goes after a long shift and court call," Eli said, laying the brotherhood on pretty thick.

"Sure, sure, yeah, I do. So, listen, Detective, you haven't been drinking, have you?" The officer's light shone brightly into Eli's eyes, which were red, glossy, and a little lazy on reaction.

"I mean a little, but not enough... Sure you don't want to go to an awesome party? I really can get you in. It's no trouble."

"Mm, nah, that's okay. How about instead, if you wouldn't mind, stepping out for a minute so I can make sure you're safe to drive home."

"No need, Officer. I promise to be more alert. You have woken me up for sure, and now the traffic is an easy zip home. If you'll just give me back my..." Eli said with a dismissive tone.

"I'm afraid I can't do that. I really need you to step out of the car and take a few tests with me."

"Is this really necessary?" Eli lowered his volume as if protecting his speech from others who might be listening, even though they were alone. With a chummy tone, he said, "Whatever happened to professional courtesy?"

"I am courteously asking you to get out of the car," Ackerman said with a firm yet professional tone. Then, much to Eli's dismay, the officer leaned his head over to his left side and grabbed the shoulder microphone for his HT and called dispatch. "7-Baker-16, can you have a Sam unit head my way, please? I have an off-duty SO unit needing FSTs."

Regardless of agency or jurisdiction, there was no confusing the term "Sam unit" to mean sergeant or supervisor. Either way, the situation had just gotten grim.

"Sir, I've asked nicely."

"FST? I'm not drunk! And I'm certainly not going to have some chippie treat me like I'm some nobody," Eli said in a condescending tone that was developed out of fear and alcohol.

Officer Ackerman's voice dropped an octave when he replied, "I know you're not a nobody. That's why I haven't ripped you out through your window yet. But the professional courtesy is starting to wear thin."

Eli pondered for a moment. Maybe he had been out of line. Maybe he should just get out of the car, do the stupid tests, and then be on his way.

"Fine. Fine. I'll get out. Geez..."

Eli swiftly opened the car door and stood up rather quickly, but then gravity took its toll. He lost his balance slightly and had to shuffle step and grab the door and place his hand on the roof of his car to maintain balance.

"You all right there, Detective?"

"Yeah, I'm fine," he said with a bowed head. Eli took a deep cleansing breath. Simultaneously, a second CHP unit approached. The CHP supervisor had arrived. This wasn't good news for Eli. He knew at this point, he was fucked.

Cite and Release

Eli's unit was still parked with the two CHP units at the gas station. Sergeant Kesling pulled into the lot with Nate riding in the front passenger seat.

The two men got out and were greeted by the CHP watch commander, Lt. Jeremy Briggs. Eli was seated in the rear of Officer Ackerman's patrol unit. He wasn't handcuffed, but he was sullen and defeated.

"Sgt. Kesling?" Lt. Briggs asked.

"Yeah, that's me. This is Nate Parker, one of my..." Kesling paused to briefly censor himself, "other detectives."

"Hey, Lieutenant. Sorry about my partner. He's usually not this stupid."

Briggs put up a hand to stop Nate. "Listen, we gotta do what we gotta do, and I hope you both understand the situation your boy put us in."

Kesling replied firmly, "Yes, we do. It is what it is. Are you going to book him?"

"No. That's the kind of professional courtesy we *will* extend. He has already been cited for the DUI. If you're going to take him back with you, and looks like you've got a sober driver with you, then I'm not going to make matters worse for him, and I certainly don't want to screw your agency with tow bills and such. I'll release him into your custody."

"Thanks for that. How was his 'tude?" Kesling asked.

Officer Ackerman said, "He was a bit salty at first, little cocky, but reality has hit him pretty hard, I think."

Eli's head was down, and he wouldn't look up at his partner or boss.

"You want this?" Briggs asked, handing Eli's badge wallet to Kesling.

"Oh yeah. Where is his duty weapon?"

"Front seat," Ackerman said, indicating Eli's Taurus.

"Was he wearing it?" Kesling asked. If Eli had been wearing his gun while intoxicated, that would have put him in deep hot water. Boiling as it already was, he didn't need to fan the flames and bubble the water completely over the edge of the pot.

But Ackerman relieved the sergeant by shaking his head. "Glove box."

Sergeant Kesling turned to Detective Parker. "Nate, you take his car and his gear back to headquarters. Put his weapon in the temporary evidence locker and go home. I'll see you in the morning."

"Want me to take Eli with me?" Nate asked.

"Nope. He rides with me. Get going, Nate."

"Yessir."

Nate shook hands with both CHP officers and then headed directly to Eli's Taurus.

***

Kesling and Eli hadn't said a single word to each other from the time Kesling plucked him out of the back seat of the patrol unit throughout the entire drive on the 210 and 15 freeways all the way to Eli's home in the Victor Valley desert.

"That was most silent car ride I have ever experienced," Eli said grimly.

"Would you have preferred I yell at you the entire way back?"

"Maybe."

"You know, Eli, you're the dumbest fucking smart guy I know. Your future is bright, or was, I don't know now. You have a lot to learn." Kesling wasn't yelling, but his tone was firm and animated enough that yelling wasn't necessary. "You're gifted, there's no doubt. But when you can figure out a way to pull your head out of your ass long enough to know that you don't know every fucking thing, that no one is out to get you or hold you down, the world may just get a little easier for you to navigate. But until you do, the biggest problem you have right now is you!"

Kesling took a beat to let that sink in. "Stop swimming against the tide, and you won't be so exhausted all the fucking time."

Eli didn't know what to say or what to do. He looked like he wanted to cry and get a hug of forgiveness from his boss, like a son from his dad.

"Go inside. Get some rest. Someone from IA will call you in a day or two, and things will move pretty fast after that. But for now, Captain told me to tell you're on admin leave until further notice."

"Okay, Sarge. Thanks. Well, not thanks, but, yeah, thanks."

Eli walked inside to find that Ranger had shredded the corner of the couch while being so lonely without him. She was happy to see her master and jumped all over him, but Eli yelled at her to get down and walked to the kitchen to check her food and water dishes. There was a note taped to the sliding back door at his eye level.

Eli, sorry but we couldn't watch Ranger every day, so I hope you don't mind I bought her some feeding dishes. I left you the receipt and you can pay me back when you get back from this case.

Eli crumpled the note and threw it on the table. He looked down and saw that the normal food dishes had been replaced with food dispenser systems that each held a couple gallons of food and water.

"Aw, fuck it." Eli stripped off the tuxedo while walking toward the master bedroom. Once inside his bedroom, he finished disrobing and then fell across the bed.

Ranger came into the room, dog tags jingling happily. She stopped and sat down with her ears perked, waiting for Eli to pat the bed and give her permission to jump up there. He let her cuddle up next to him while he repeatedly relived his arrest in his head before finally drifting off to sleep.

Run & Shower

Eli's breath was rhythmic and in consistent tempo with the pounding of his feet on the pavement. No better way to deal with a hangover than to sweat out all the toxins. The dehydration from alcohol the night before was barely reduced by the large glass of water Eli drank before starting his five-mile run. The headache would last most of the day, he guessed, but it was also penance for bad decisions. He might have to live with the consequences of his actions for the rest of his life.

Shirtless and wearing only shorts and running shoes, Eli stopped every so often to knock out an alternating set of thirty push-ups or thirty burpees, then right back into running. Blasting music into his ears helped drive him most days, but on this particular run, silent reflection was what he needed. Instead of the pumping rock music, Eli instead played the sounds of ocean waves to soothe his mind and soul.

His thoughts turned to Mia. He missed her already, and it hadn't even been a full day. How was this possible? Was it just the sex, or was there more to her than just the physical attraction? It worried him that he didn't know the answer. What if he was falling in love with her? She was way out of his league, living in what was, for all intents and purposes, a foreign country. He had only been a recent visitor, and that would end sometime soon with the resolution of the case.

But would he still be part of the case? Would he even have a job? So much uncertainty. So much worry. So much fear. Better drop for thirty push-ups to help settle the mind.

Sweat completely covered his body at this point, and he only had a couple of miles left before he was done. By the time he finished, he'd be dripping. He needed a good workout in the gym too, but that would have to wait until tomorrow. He needed a little recovery and a proper day of dieting to get himself regulated again after all the rich foods and copious amounts of alcohol he'd been sharing with Brad and his friends.

Being on administrative leave wasn't like being on vacation. It was paid leave while the investigation was being conducted, and it kept the accused party, Eli, in this case, from further damaging the circumstances by essentially grounding the deputy until a resolution could be determined.

The rules of admin leave were that employees were to be home between the hours of 8:00 a.m. through 5:00 p.m. on all weekdays. If anyone from IA or other parts of the administration or executive staff wanted to reach the deputy, they were supposed to be guaranteed that he would answer his home phone. But since he didn't have a home phone, Air Pods and an iPhone would do the trick if he got called on his exercise route. If they were going to be pissed that he was out for a run, well then, fuck 'em.

***

Wearing only a towel around his waist after a hot shower and shave, Eli leaned up against the kitchen counter, eating a bowl of cereal with the living room TV playing a live interview with Brad talking about winning the Emmy. After it ended, Eli picked up his mobile phone, scrolled through his favorites and paused on Nate's name, then scrolled past him. He chose another favorite, one he'd always been able to count on, no matter what.

"Hey, buddy," Eli said stoically into the phone.

"Hey, Eli. You all right? You sound down."

"Listen, I'm in trouble, and I need your help."

Avi Visits Homicide

After checking in with the receptionist, Avi made his way to Eli's desk. He'd visited before and had met the team shortly after Eli got settled in. But he hadn't really had any reason to come back since. Until now.

"Hey, Avi. Um, Eli's not here...right now—" Nate started.

Avi put up a hand to stop Nate's painful approach to delivering bad news. "He called me. I know what's up. He asked me if I'd come down and get his gym bag. He said his locker key was in his desk."

"Oh, yeah, sure. Yeah, go ahead."

"Thanks."

"How's he doing?"

"Pretty bad, actually. He's afraid he can't recover from this. Not all in one piece."

"Well, he wouldn't be the first guy on the department to get a DUI and survive. It isn't an automatic death sentence, but it will probably be some painful punishment. I just hope I'll be able to work with him again someday."

"You think he'll get launched out of here?"

"I don't know. Probably. This assignment is a privilege that he may have just lost."

"Yeah..."

There wasn't much else to say. Avi sat in Eli's chair for a moment and opened several drawers, pretending to look for the key. He found it in the top drawer in the sliding plastic tray just where Eli said it would be. But the second drawer down was where the disc was that Avi was actually there to retrieve. With Nate's attention back on his computer, he didn't see Avi slip the data DVD into his back pocket. "Found it!" Avi said as he stood and showed Nate the key in his other hand.

"Listen, Avi, tell Eli I'm not allowed to call him right now, due to, well, you know. But tell him I hope everything works out for him."

"I will, Nate. Thanks. I'm going to head out."

Mustang Ride

When the garage door opened to reveal Eli's Mustang, he hoped it would start. It had been a while since he'd driven it, and she could sometimes be a bit finicky. He got in behind the wheel, pumped the pedal three times like he'd done a thousand times before. The cranking noise and the smell of the engine exhaust reminded him of a more innocent time in his life. After a couple of seconds of sputtering, the engine turned over. As much as he loved this old car, he'd grown used to a new car and the confidence that it was going to start and drive without fail every time. He might have to consider getting a new car if he got bounced out of homicide and lost his detective ride.

Wearing jeans, boots, and a form-fitting golf shirt, Eli was ready to take his beloved car out for a spin, even though he was supposed to stay home on admin leave. He had more important things to do than sit around and sulk, waiting on others to decide his fate. Besides, if someone called, he would just say he ran out to get some lunch if they asked about the external noises.

Being midday and midweek, the traffic on the freeway wasn't absolutely awful, it was just thick. The windows of the Mustang were rolled down, and Eli was enjoying the Southern California sun and wind blowing through the car. The air conditioner had long since failed, but until he got over a few bills, putting a new AC unit in his Mustang was going to have to wait.

It was a hot day, but thankfully, it was a dry heat and not like the time he went with a friend to an Atlanta Braves game. There is no other way to describe the oppressive heat and humidity of the South in the summer other than to say Georgia is *fucking hot*.

Eli had reached a point where the traffic gods were no longer on his side and he was in typical stop-and-go Los Angeles traffic. His Mustang had been performing terrifically while traveling at freeway speeds, but the stop-and-go was wreaking havoc on his ability to maintain a good idle. She stalled once or twice and started up again, but the third time was the end of the road.

"Aw, come on! Are you kidding me? Not now!" Eli slammed the car into Park and tried to get her started, but she wasn't having it. Cars honked behind him and drivers waved their frustration out their windows at Eli as he sat there, trying to get the car to start and remain running. There was plenty of gas. This wasn't human error. Decades-old cars were just unreliable.

There was nothing he could do to coax his Mustang into running. She turned over and over to the point he was draining the battery and wearing out the starter. Without any other available options, it was time to get out and push. He was in the number two lane and therefore only had to move it through two lanes to get to the emergency lane. Traffic was nearly at a standstill, so it wasn't necessarily dangerous, but it was infuriating how many drivers wouldn't let him get over. As soon as traffic ahead moved a little, the cars to his right would speed up to close the distance, disallowing Eli to maneuver to the right. They enjoyed the space he'd created in front of him by stalling, and the traffic moved ahead slowly.

But finally, a man in a Suburban to his right stopped, put it in Park, and got out to help him. The SUV blocked the number three lane and thus allowed them to push Eli's car from the number two over to the number three. Just as someone was trying to slide into the spot created in front of the SUV, Eli and the man were able to get the Mustang partially into the lane. The oncoming car nearly ran into them, but instead of stopping to help, the driver cussed at them and honked the horn.

It wasn't until a big-rig driver in the number four lane, who could see all the action from his raised perch, stopped his rig, giving them the reprieve they needed to get the car out of everyone's way to the roadside.

"Thanks, man, I really appreciate your help!" Eli said sincerely to the SUV driver.

"Yeah, no worries. You got a cell phone?" the man asked.

"Yeah, I'm good now that I'm over here out of the way," Eli said. "Thanks again!"

With that, the rig driver had kept the lane clear and the SUV driver was able to get back to his car without hassle. Eli saluted the rig driver, then pulled out his mobile to call for help.

With almost nothing in his checking account after needlessly buy a new wardrobe, Eli's options to get himself out of this new jam were limited.

Brad & Harold

Mia's long black hair was pulled into a ponytail poking through the back of the white unstructured ball cap she wore. The white scooped-neck, three-button ribbed Henley she wore unbuttoned over her braless breasts showed as much cleavage as possible without her being topless. Her cut-off jean shorts were barely visible as the majority of the fabric was tucked underneath her perfect buttocks and the rest was hiding way up between her exposed thighs. Just looking at her had Eli hoping for some alone time today.

Eli rode in the front seat with her as she drove the Mercedes convertible up the driveway to Brad's house. He hadn't yet seen the garage and didn't know the extent of the car collection Brad had accumulated. The wooden two-car garage door opened into a cavernous underground parking garage that held a dozen or more cars as well as some motorcycles, and appeared to have all the tools a mechanic would need to work on any vehicle in the fleet.

Coming into the kitchen from the garage was a new experience for Eli. He'd only seen what seemed to be a quarter of the house so far. He hadn't been on a tour or explored on his own. He might have to do that if he stayed a little while as a guest.

Brad was in the kitchen getting some sodas from the refrigerator when Eli and Mia walked in together.

"A DUI, huh? You all right?" Brad asked with genuine concern.

"Suspended...pending IA and the courts."

"Man, that's rough." Brad opened the cans and poured them over ice. Then it hit him. "Wait, was this after you left here the other night from my party?"

"Yeah, guess I had a little more than I thought I did. I was enjoying myself."

"Now I feel responsible. You got a lawyer?"

"I'll get one from the union, I guess."

"Well, I know a pretty good one. And funny thing, he's sitting in the den right now working on a personal matter for me. Let's see what he says."

"Oh, I don't know," Eli said nervously. He wasn't sure what to think. If the lawyer was truly great, he'd be perfect, of course, but Eli could certainly never afford the kind of lawyer that Brad had on retainer.

"Don't worry about it. He's here on my dime. Let's get his opinion."

Sitting on one of the chairs with a laptop and files in front of him on a table was none other than Harold King.

"Ah, Detective, what brings you out...so casually?" King said with a grin.

Eli looked himself over and thought he was dressed rather nicely. But considering he would have normally been in a suit during business hours, this was indeed very casual and unexpected for Harold, who had to assume he was there on business.

"Wait, you two know each other? Seems I'm always one step behind in these introductions," Brad said with his hands on his hips.

"Hello, Mr. King. I'm not here on duty," Eli said.

"Indeed."

"Harold, Eli here got himself jammed up leaving my party the other night. Got pulled over for having a few too many, but I think he was just tired, and someone made a mistake. What do you think? Anyone over at CHP ever mistake a DUI for a real tired detective who may have had a drink but wasn't actually impaired?"

"Happens all the time. Let me look into it," Harold said.

"Wait, wait, I don't know." Eli wasn't sure he wanted something underhanded to play out on his behalf. He'd lied enough already to his partner. This was digging himself in deeper.

"It'd be my pleasure. Any friend of Brad's is a friend of mine. Did you submit to FSTs or make a statement?" Harold asked.

"Well..."

"Never mind. Let me make some phone calls and then we'll see what's what."

"I, uh..."

"Perfect!" Brad exclaimed with a loud clap of his hands. "Hey, Harold, we done with the other thing?"

Harold slapped his laptop closed and slid it into his briefcase, then scooped up the papers and dropped them in there too. He got to his feet while saying, "I've got what I need and I should have something for you to review by, say, mid next week?"

"Yeah, that's great. Thanks."

"All right, then, I'll see you both soon," Harold said. He turned to Eli. "Don't worry about a thing, Detective, I've got you covered."

With that, the lawyer dashed out the door. Brad smiled at Eli, who wasn't sure how to react to everything that just happened. It'd be great to have the charges dropped, which would guarantee that he wasn't going to jail, but it didn't automatically mean he wasn't going to get punished at work.

Just then, Eli's phone rang. "Hello?"

He covered the phone and mouthed to Mia, *It's the garage.* "Yeah, okay." Eli turned his back and walked away a little distance and hushed his volume. "Wait, four hundred and thirty dollars? Can I do something less just to get it running to get back to San Bernardino?"

Brad heard what he said even though Eli was trying to be subtle. "Gimme the phone," he said, putting out his hand to Eli.

"Huh?"

"Give. Me. Your. Phone."

Eli handed over his phone to Brad, who then deepened his voice slightly as if his own adult voice wasn't, you know, adult enough.

"Hello, this is Eli's father. Don't worry about the bill. Fix what needs fixing. When will it be done, do you think?" After a brief pause, he said, "That's perfect. Just please call back when it's done, and we'll come by to get it. Thank you."

Brad grinned, hung up the phone, and tossed it back to Eli. "Don't worry. You've got friends here, and like Harold said, we've got your back."

"I don't know how I'll repay you. Money is tight right now with student loans and—"

"Who said anything about paying it back? Friends help each other out, right?"

Eli was overwhelmed with relief and not sure what to say. He'd never had anyone so willing to help him without question and without expectation of payback. Mia closed the distance and came to Eli's side and put her arms around his waist. A tear welled in Eli's eye and he saw Brad smile before nodding slightly and looking away.

The moment of silence and reflection was interrupted by the front doorbell ringing.

"You expecting someone?" Eli asked.

"Nope."

"That's weird, huh?"

"Kind of. Gate should be locked."

"Let me." Eli stiffened up a bit, going into police mode, surveying the surroundings. He walked to the door and peered through a piece of clear glass to see Nate standing on the other side. He yanked open the door.

"Nate!"

"Eli?"

Together they exclaimed, "What are you doing here?"

Eli went outside and closed the door behind him to talk with Nate on the front porch.

"I'm here doing an investigation. Why are you here? What the hell is going on with you?"

Brad opened the front door to see what was going on. It was his house, after all.

"Hey, Detective...Parker, isn't it? Eli, you didn't say your partner was coming to visit."

"I didn't invite him, Brad."

"Oh?"

"That's right, Mr. Clark. I didn't know Eli was here, troubling as that is. I'm actually here to speak with you."

"You got a warrant, Nate?" Eli demanded.

"Hey, Eli, can I talk to you over here for a minute?" Nate asked.

"Um, no Nate. I don't think so. And you aren't talking to Brad either, not unless you've got a warrant, which I know you don't."

Nate shot Eli an evil eye, then looked to Brad, and just as he was beginning to make an obvious appeal, his words were thwarted by Brad, who said, "Well, Detective Parker, it was good to see you, but I think it best that if you would like to talk with me, or Eli, for that matter, you should make an appointment with my lawyer. I can give you his name and number if you'd like."

"Nope. Don't need it. I got everything I need."

Nate turned to leave and looked back one more time to see Eli closing the door from the inside. Nate retrieved his mobile phone from his interior coat pocket and place it to his ear while walking toward his car.

Captain Montgomery

Behind a large desk surrounded by homicide detail memorabilia, plaques, and pictures of a distinguished career, sat Captain Scott Montgomery. Dressed impeccably in a crisp white shirt and striped Brooks Brothers tie, Montgomery read from a file on his desk wearing his reading glasses. His broad shoulders belonged to a former football athlete, while his bright white hair and matching white mustache didn't make him look old as much as they made him absolutely dignified. Together with his booming voice, he wasn't a man who suffered fools lightly.

He looked up when he heard a light knock to see Kesling standing at the open doorway.

"Cap?"

"Come in, John. Sit."

Kesling sat in one of the two chairs across from his captain. It was a little intimidating, like being called to the principal's office in school.

"What are we going to do with the kid?" Montgomery asked.

"He's actually a damned good investigator, but after this last stunt, I don't know. I really don't know."

The captain kept reading through the file when Kesling continued, "Any word from upstairs?"

"Sheriff's pissed as hell at him. I am too. You should be too!"

"I am. But I don't have time to be pissed right now. I'm down to two detectives, and this is one of the biggest cases we've ever had. And, I can't believe I'm saying this, but I could use the kid right now. He's talented. An arrogant ass sometimes, but he's really talented."

Just then, Kesling's phone rang. He reached into his coat pocket and saw it was Nate calling. He showed the phone to Montgomery, who nodded at him to answer it.

"Hey, Nate." After a moment of listening, he said, "He's where? He's there? What the fuck? Are you kidding me?"

Kesling covered the mobile phone microphone and said quietly to the captain, "He's at the actor's house." Then back into the phone, he muttered, "Hang on, Nate, I'm sitting with the captain."

"Put him on speaker," Montgomery directed.

Kesling selected the speaker setting on the phone and put it on the captain's desk between them. "Nate, you're on speaker with me and Cap."

"Hey, Cap!"

"Is your idiot partner with the actor again?"

"'Fraid so."

"For being so bright as you guys claim he is, this is pretty goddamned stupid, don't you think?"

"Well, yeah. I don't know what to think."

"At this point, he leaves us little choice. You still out there in LA?" Montgomery asked.

"Yes, sir, I am."

"Good. Do your best to keep tabs on him until we can get IA and a full surveillance team set up," the captain boomed across his desk into the speaker. Then to Kesling in a lesser tone, he said, "We're going to run two ops on this. John, you stay point on the murder investigation with Artie and grab up some guys from Marshall's team if you need them in the interim." Then more loudly for Nate's sake, he said, "Nate, I want you to take point on the operation out there until we can get you relieved by IA and a surveillance team. I know this sucks for you, being his partner and all, and this may sting you a bit with those who don't know what's really going on, but I trust in your integrity to do the right thing."

Nate let out a deep sigh. "Yes, Captain. Anything else?"

"No. That'll be all, Detective Parker."

Kesling hung up the phone and pocketed it, then let out the only word he could muster. "Shit."

"Shit is right," agreed Montgomery.

The Chase is On

Brad didn't mind one bit that Eli was staying with Mia in her bungalow. In fact, Eli had helped around the house with a couple of minor repairs and tasks that saved Brad the hassle of calling in a technician. For the next couple of weeks, Brad was going on a trip to New York to film some scenes for upcoming episodes due out in the fall. Eli and Mia would have the mansion pretty much to themselves. Eli asked Avi to fetch Ranger from his house and let her stay with Avi. He knew Avi loved Ranger, as did Avi's girlfriend. Ranger would be in good hands until Eli would come home again.

Eli's email and remote access to his computer were severed by the sheriff's IT department. If it weren't for the disc Avi was able to slip out of the office for him, Eli would have been totally detached from the case. He put the disc into the laptop he borrowed from Mia and tried to read through all the bank records.

The amount of bank records one DVD could hold was incredible. The warrant had requested all bank records going back three years for Bill and Abby Brower, Davin Harris, Shelly Weller, and Harold King. Last week when Eli received all the forwarded emails from Nate, including the attachments from the multiple banks who electronically serviced the various search warrants, Eli made a DVD containing all the data to make it easier to review the information all in one source. Fortunately, Eli's need for organization allowed him to unofficially continue working the case without remote access.

Going through the bank records and trying to find the connection to Shelly and the Browers' money was what Eli had planned for the week in the office had he not gotten himself arrested and suspended. He didn't need to be in the office to continue investigating. Sitting poolside and working on his tan, taking a break to eat some of Mia's absolutely fabulous cooking, making love to her, swimming, and working out could all be mixed in with the financial investigation. He'd created a spreadsheet showing the linkage from one account to another.

Eli focused on the flow of money from Davin to Bill, who then split his money across several accounts, one of which he shared with Shelly. There it was. Bill had tens of thousands of dollars in various accounts spread across several banking institutions. Over a period of several months, Bill had moved money in denominations of ninety-five hundred dollars. He couldn't move several hundred thousand dollars at once without alerting the banks, who were required to report transactions over ten thousand dollars.

The shared Bill-Shelly account receiving payments of nine thousand five hundred every two weeks would appear just as if they were being paid as high-end consultants. After the payments went into the shared account, Shelly would transfer the money to another account solely in her name. It was this account that was used to "loan" Bill and Abby the three hundred and fifty thousand dollars for the beach condo. It was, in fact, Bill's money all along. Well, it was really Davin's money that Bill had embezzled.

It was all starting to make perfect sense. One of the accounts, however, surprised Eli. It was a large account with nearly seven hundred and fifty thousand dollars in it. Trying to trace the transfers was tricky. He couldn't find the money in Shelly's account.

Then he realized the problem with his thinking. He was trying to force his opinion onto the evidence rather than letting the evidence show him the truth. When Eli listened to the evidence, he discovered something surprising.

Confronting the Lawyer

With Brad out of town, he wouldn't have minded that Eli borrowed the Mercedes convertible. Eli had practically been living there for a week, enjoying his administrative leave like it was a Sandals vacation. He and Mia had hardly been separated. Being with Mia, both in and out of bed, was the most intense and best time of his life. But there was still work to do.

When he pulled up to the front of the Waldorf Astoria in Beverly Hills, he handed off the car to the valet. Wearing the Davin Harris suit again, Eli looked like he belonged to the car, the hotel, and the whole lifestyle.

The IA surveillance team that had been following Eli for the past week, or more accurately taking shifts parked down the street from Brad Clark's house while Eli stayed inside, was now parked directly across the street from the hotel. Neither detective was dressed for the Waldorf, so they decided instead to remain inside their white panel van with magnetic signs reading "Sam's Flowers" posted on the side. They'd wait there until they saw Eli come back out to get his car.

Eli made his way to Jean-Georges bar to meet Harold, who called him earlier asking to meet for a drink. Harold sat at a small round hideaway booth against a back wall, sipping a drink. Wearing a navy blue sweater and white chinos, Harold looked like he'd just stepped out of a Tommy Hilfiger magazine. He saw Eli approaching and stood up as he got close to the table. "Ah, Detective!"

"Hey, Harold. You know, you should really call me Eli."

"Very well. Please, have a seat."

"Nice place."

"Nothing but the best. For both of us. What'll you have?"

Eli looked at the menu and saw that there wasn't a price listed by the items, which meant he couldn't afford it if he were paying for it himself. When the prices were this high and the clientele this exclusive, a server was essentially waiting in the wings per table. The waiter saw the nod from Harold and rushed over to take a new order.

"Jack on the rocks?" Eli asked.

The waiter replied with a respectful and hushed tone, "Sir, we don't serve Jack Daniels, but we do have a variety of others to choose from."

"Well, that's fine, pick one for me. I'm sure it will be great."

"Right away, sir," the waiter said, adding a slight bow. He then looked to Harold, who pointed to his own drink, indicating he'd like another.

"Listen, I want to thank you again for your help with the DUI. It seems the CHP no longer has no interest in pursuing the charges against me. The case is gone before it went active. Nicely done. I just don't know how I'll ever be able to repay you."

"Hey, what are friends for?" Harold drank down the remainder of his drink. "I'm sure there will be a time real soon when the favor can be returned."

Right on cue, the waiter reappeared with a drink for them both. After taking a sip of the smoothest whiskey he'd ever had in his life, Eli said, "I could get used to this."

"Be careful, my young friend. This place is a more expensive habit than heroin."

"I should have gone to law school."

"It does pay well." Harold smiled as he took a sip from his fresh drink.

"Is that why you do it?"

"So that I can eat here?"

"No, I mean all this. Being a lawyer in Los Angeles. The Hollywood connections, the big-name clients...all of it. It's got to make all the sacrifices worth it, right? The tough decisions on who gets paid and who doesn't. Who gets what they deserve and who doesn't? Who lives and who doesn't?"

"I'm not sure I follow."

"Well, as far as I can tell, you were friends with the Browers, defended them in lawsuits, wrote their wills, established their estate executor as Shelly, a friend from your district attorney days, who conveniently happens to be a parole agent," Eli said before being interrupted.

"The fact that I know a great many people in this town makes me very good at what I do."

"Well, of course, sure, but when it comes to this case, every time I turn around, the dots are connecting through you." Eli took a decent swig of whiskey to punctuate his point. "The Browers' car was found in a dirtbag parolee neighborhood, but none of those guys or that particular district are in Shelly's jurisdiction. But you really couldn't have known that," Eli said, looking Harold straight in the eye. The lawyer didn't flinch one muscle. "Shelly is the executor of the will, and that really made her a great suspect. But there's a problem with Shelly."

"Interesting. Please go on, Detective."

"Since the victims weren't supposed to be discovered dead and instead were supposed to be missing, that'd cause her years of dealing with their absence before they could be declared legally dead and she could move forward with dispensing their estate. Yeah, it really doesn't make any sense that she would have killed them, hidden them in a deep, faraway grave, and then waited around for seven years to collect. If greed is the motive, then bang-bang, dead and collect, no?" He took another sip of the whiskey.

"This got me thinking, whoever wanted them killed didn't want them dead. They needed them alive but missing for as long as possible. What is that, seven years? That's a long time for someone in control of their *lives* to make things happen. Make things disappear. Now, who would most benefit from that?"

Eli took a big gulp from his drink and arrogantly motioned to the waiter for another. "Because, while they remained missing persons, their lawsuits would drag on and on. And so would your billing. Pretty nice little gambit."

Harold leaned in and condescendingly said, "Oh, so you have this all figured out now, do you?"

"Not all of it, but it's becoming more clear to me. But something still doesn't fit."

"What's that?"

"Honestly? I'm not completely sure yet. But I'm sure I'll figure it out soon enough."

"Ah, thank you my dear," Harold said as he welcomed Mia to the table. She'd intercepted their two drinks and brought them over to the table. "I understand you've already met my daughter."

Surprise and confusion could not in any way describe the way Eli felt at that moment.

Harold leaned back, smiled with his perfectly purchased teeth, and with a raised eyebrow said, "Take a drink, Detective. I think your mouth has gone dry."

Eli took a large gulp of his whiskey. He was indeed speechless.

"Would this be the puzzle piece you were searching for?"

"Nope. Not anywhere on my radar." Eli took another large swig. "But I'm guessing I wasn't supposed to see this coming."

"Eli," Mia said, "don't be upset. What we have together is fun, but this is family."

Eli's head was spinning. Two whiskeys in a few minutes might have caused a buzz, but the way he was feeling was well beyond tipsy. It wasn't a drunk feeling. It reminded him of the aesthesia he got when he had his wisdom teeth removed.

"Mia..." Eli slurred, just before his head fell forward and he slipped into unconsciousness.

The Boat Ride

The silence of the darkness was destroyed by the roar of an engine going at near full speed. Eli was seated on the main cabin floor with his hands duct-taped around a center table post. Waking from a deep unconscious state, his body swayed to the rhythm of the boat ride, and his head bobbed as he came to, blurry and confused.

Harold sat across from him, holding a pistol in a relaxed manner, watching Eli wake up. The boat engine slowed and turned off. The sound of wake water slapping up against the hull was matched by the swaying of the boat as it pitched and rolled while adrift.

"De-*tec*-tive," Harold said in a singsong voice. He turned to Mia, who came down from the bridge. "I thought you said he could handle his liquor?"

"I said he could handle himself in bed. He's actually a cheap drunk."

Hearing what was said but not yet having opened his eyes, Eli muttered, "As far as reputations go, I guess I can live with that." He lifted his head and tried to focus his eyes, which were still crossing uncontrollably.

"Now, what are we going to do with you?" Harold asked rhetorically.

"Well, if I had to guess, you plan to kill me and dump me overboard. Doesn't take a rocket scientist to grasp the cliché that has become my life."

"Not necessarily. I believe in long-term solutions rather than short-term gains."

Eli shook his head back and forth trying to rid himself of the cob-webs occupying his skull. The pounding headache was not being eased by the onset of the nausea that was either from the drugs or seasickness. His mouth felt like he'd just rinsed with a cup of Elmer's glue. "Uh-huh. And how does me being tied to a table work into your long-term solution?"

"Well, I guess that would be the short-term solution, wouldn't it? Listen, you're an industrious young man who now has experienced the pleasures of the finer things in life. I—we—could use you." Harold pointed to Mia and the boat. "But you're stuck in this quandary of good versus evil, or so you think. They aren't that different. You and I aren't that different."

"And how is that?"

"You claim to detest the Hollywood lifestyle, yet you spend every free moment you have with Brad, his friends, and all that comes with it. You're happy to accept a get-out-of-jail-free card from the lifestyle from me, but here's the rub," Harold said as he leaned in as if to tell a secret. "You don't have much time left."

"So, you *are* going to kill me."

"No. Well, yes. Maybe. It depends."

"On what?" Eli asked incredulously.

"On whether or not you know how to tell time."

"Okay, maybe it's the alcohol or the shit you put in my drink, but now you're not making any fucking sense."

"The time you have left is all about your usefulness. Right now, you're a novelty plaything. But soon, Brad and his friends will tire of you. Tire of you not being able to provide any new value."

"Now I'm a plaything?"

Harold looked to Mia, who smiled back at him. But then her glance at Eli gave away a little more than she might have hoped. Was it regret he was seeing in her eyes? Was it fear? It was such a quick gesture, and Eli wasn't yet able to focus completely.

"Well, for the moment, yes. But don't be troubled, Detective. Life's a game, and we are all merely players."

"So, Brad *is* in on all this?"

"No, no, no. He can't know about any of this. It's him we have to protect."

"Protect? From what? From whom?"

"Nice. 'From whom.' My, my, I do love your command of the language."

"This is the craziest fucking conversation I've ever had. And with what I do for a living, that's saying a lot." Eli looked around and found that his vision had stopped drifting and he was able to focus both eyes at the same time. "So, at this point, I guess it's fair to assume I got it right about you offing your clients. But what I want to know is why. They seemed like the cash cow."

"They were. Until Bill decided to settle."

"Settle?"

"Bill worked out a deal behind my back to settle the whole thing with Davin for a measly two hundred fifty thousand dollars and cover the cost of his secretary's losses."

"So?"

"I spent the money!"

"What money?"

"All of it. Bill's money. He liquidated everything and put it in a trust account with me as his lawyer, which made the money judgment-proof. Anything Davin or anyone else could have won through a trial verdict would have been effectively zero, since we got rid of all their assets. I told Bill this! But he wouldn't listen!" Harold took a deep breath and continued more quietly, "I invested his money in a pharmaceutical company that was supposed to deliver on some state-of-the-art new drugs...and, well. It got shitcanned. The whole investment!"

"How much?"

"What does it matter?"

"How much, Harold?"

"A *million*, okay? A million."

"And then some?"

"Yes, and then some, you little prick!"

"Not according to your daughter."

Harold's face turned red and the veins on the side of his neck pulsed as he jumped up and kicked Eli square in the ribs. Eli could hardly breathe afterward. Harold continued, "There was nothing to give back to the Browers after the case was over, so I couldn't let it settle."

Eli coughed and wheezed through the pain of what he could only assume were broken ribs. "So, hang on, what does this have to do with Brad?"

"Nothing! I just can't afford to lose another client. If he were to find out about my involvement in the Browers' murders, then surely he wouldn't trust me. And he is worth twice as much as the Browers in contracts and residuals, along with all the new ventures he has brewing. Hell, I was even looking forward to what you two were concocting. That was going to be another show that might go five to seven seasons."

Harold was doing that lean-in-and-whisper thing again. "You know who lives in all those glorious houses in the Hollywood Hills? Mostly lawyers for the entertainment industry." Harold stood up and paced back and forth. "No, no, no, sir! There is no way you're ruining all that I've worked for because of one lousy mistake!"

Eli was stunned at the confession and wished he had a pocket recorder going. "Wow, that is some of the most babbling bullshit I've ever heard. So basically, you're just a thief with a bar card."

"As opposed to all the thieves wearing badges?"

"Yeah, well, I'm not going to argue that one with you."

Harold stood tall and waved the gun at Eli to emphasize his question. "What's it going to be, Detective?"

"I'm not sure I follow," Eli said with genuine confusion that had nothing to do with alcohol or drugs.

"Are you on board with our program? You'd have to resign, of course, but since you won't be brought up on charges, you can get a private investigator license and work for my law firm. I could use a bright, intelligent, and resourceful man like you. Mia seems to like you too. From the moment she met you at Brad's, she's talked nonstop about you. She's no doubt smitten with you, as you are with her. That much is obvious. So what do you say? Join our team and become a major player?" He turned to look at his daughter. "What do you think?" After a moment passed while Mia just stared at the deck in front of her, Harold nearly shouted, "Mia?"

"Yeah, Dad? Um, yeah sounds like a great plan," she said without much conviction.

"You're out of your mind!" Eli exclaimed.

"So, that's a no?" Harold asked.

"That's a *big* fucking no!"

"That's all right, Detective. We weren't really going to let you live through this. People go missing all the time. They commit suicide. Distraught people whose careers just took a sudden turn for the worse. Who'd blame you for ending it all after 'fucking up,' as you so eloquently put it." Harold turned to his daughter. "Mia, cut the tape from his wrists. It's time for the detective to make his departure."

Mia retrieved the scissors from a kitchen drawer and bent down to cut the silver tape from Eli's wrists. "I'm sorry," she whispered.

"Don't be. I should have known it was too good to be true," Eli said solemnly.

After freeing his wrists, Eli crawled out from under the table and massaged his sore wrists one at a time. The fact that he was about to be killed didn't stop him from wanting to relieve the tension and soreness. He stood up and faced Harold, then threw his head back and forth to adjust the vertebrae in his neck and heard the popping sounds that went with the momentary relief.

He thought about rushing the older man, but the distance between them was far too great. Harold would have easily been able to fire a couple of rounds before Eli could close the distance. Harold was a greedy and arrogant ass, but he wasn't stupid.

"Well, let's get you outside and put an end to all this," Harold said. Eli stared him down and didn't move. He hoped the lawyer would be bold enough to close the distance and put the gun within arm's reach. Eli's extensive training on the sheriff's department plus many years on his own time training in the martial art of Aikido would surely give him the edge if the two got close enough. No amount of physical fitness or weaponless defense techniques worked when the man with his finger on the trigger was ten feet away, though. Harold knew to keep his distance.

"Yeah, I don't think so, Harold," Eli said in defiance. He crossed his right hand over his left and put them in front of his belt line. He stood there with his hands down in the faux appearance of being noncon-frontational. In reality, having one hand over the other, fingers not laced together, would allow him to quickly react with his hands and arms without getting them tangled up.

"Come on now, Detective, you know how this ends," Harold said.

"Maybe, maybe not," Eli replied.

"I've got the gun. Now walk outside before I shoot you right here," Harold demanded.

"Then go ahead and shoot! What are you waiting for? I'm tired of your phony threats. You're nothing but a fucking thief and a wannabe."

Eli trained on a police range to shoot calmly through all the adrena-line, recoil, muzzle flash, and noise. But he'd always experienced firearms from behind the weapon, never from the front. The sights and sounds when Harold pulled the trigger were shocking, as was the instant pain. Eli buckled and fell to the deck, writhing in agony and gripping his left thigh.

"Daddy! What are you doing?" Mia cried. She ran to Eli's side and held him in her arms while he growled in agony, holding his bleeding thigh. Based on the volume and force of the blood, Eli was fairly certain the femoral artery wasn't severed. Had that happened, there was no chance of survival out at sea with someone who wanted him dead. This wound, however, was a through-and-through and survivable if treated within a reasonable amount of time.

"Now you can crawl outside, Detective!" the lawyer growled. "Lis-ten, I'm trying to save cleaning up the inside of my boat, but if I have to spend the next four hours picking brain matter out of the cabinetry, then so be it!" Harold raised the gun and pointed it at Eli's head. "Mia, come here!"

"No, Daddy!"

"Mia, don't be a fool. Get over here! You knew this was going to end this way. I was never going to let you be with a cop from methamphetamine county!"

Mia rose to her knees in front of Eli, shielding him from her father. Eli tore open his shirt and yanked it over his head. He quickly folded the shirt in half lengthwise, putting the shoulders together and the arm lengths down at the sides. With one hand on each end of the arms, he twirled and twisted the shirt in a circular motion like prepping a towel for snapping it at someone in the locker room. He wrapped the shirt around his thigh, covering both gunshot wounds, and then secured it with his dress belt to try to stop the bleeding.

With shaking hands gripping the gun, Harold pleaded, "Get out of the way, Mia. I have to do this. You don't understand."

"No, Daddy, you're right, I don't understand!" Mia cried through the tears welling in her eyes. "How could you do this? I mean, did you really kill those people? I thought you were their friends!"

"It's not that simple!" Harold shouted, sweat beading on his forehead.

She stood up, but still blocked Harold's direct line of sight. Harold reached out so he could pull her to him and away from Eli. She refused to take his hand, so he moved a couple of quick steps forward and grabbed her by the arm. She pulled back until they were in a tug-of-war. Harold lost his grip on her arm, and attempted to grab her with both hands, forgetting for that split second that he was still holding a 9mm pistol.

When he tried to secure his hold on Mia, his brain crossed signals, and he tightened his grip with both hands, causing him to accidentally pull the trigger and set free another explosion of gunpowder to shock and deafen everyone on the boat.

More frightening was Mia's horrified expression as she stood in momentary shock. They both looked down to see the tight white dress that clung to her perfect form begin to paint itself red on the right side of her abdomen.

Harold was frozen, still holding Mia's right wrist. She was no longer pulling away from him. Tears poured from her eyes at nearly the same speed that her dress soaked up the bright red arterial blood flowing from the wound that entered the side of her torso, just above the hip.

Unable to control the weight on her legs due to the pain, shock, and blood loss, Mia slumped to the floor into Eli's arms. Eli barked, "How the fuck did you kidnap and kill two people and transport them across the whole goddamn Southland and bury their bodies in a nearly flawless execution, yet you fuck this up so badly?"

Harold stood there speechless with his mouth wide open and the smoking gun hanging loosely from his right hand. He stutter-stepped backward, then fell to his knees. "Look at what you made me do!" he screamed at Eli.

Holding Mia in his arms, Eli applied pressure to her wound, leaving his own wound unattended.

"Daddy, why?" Mia cried and winced with pain. As she went into shock, she was becoming disassociated with the pain. Shock made the pain manageable, but her level of consciousness was waning quickly.

"Mia, I..."

"Turn this boat toward shore, now!" Eli demanded.

"But, I didn't..."

"*Now*, Harold!"

"What?" Harold fell to his knees only four feet away from them both, his hands on his thighs, still holding the pistol.

"Get up there and drive this boat back to shore, or she's going to die!"

"Right." Harold stood and moved toward the captain's chair, but then stopped and turned around. "I can't let you live."

"What? Harold! What the fuck is wrong with you? Get up there and get us back to land. To a hospital. For Mia, for God's sake. You can still kill me later, but help me save her!"

"No, no, no, no. I need a new plan," Harold walked in circles, waving the pistol as he mumbled his internal thoughts out loud. "Okay, this should work!"

"What are *talking about*?" Eli shouted.

"All right, you took me and Mia hostage. Yes, yes, okay, here we go. You were in a rage of frustration after learning that Mia wanted to end her relationship with you. She was to meet me on the boat for a dinner cruise, but you tried to stop her, to talk with her one more time."

"What the fuck?"

His eyes twinkled with devilish delight as he bent forward slightly and held a finger across his lips before continuing, "Shush! This is good. Listen, you'll like this part. The employees at the bar will be able to tell the investigators how drunk you were, how you needed help getting into the car. No one will have trouble believing me that in your distraught state after Mia telling you for the umpteenth time that there was no relationship, coupled with your recent DUI that has ruined our career, you couldn't take one more failure."

"Oh, come on. No one's going to believe this pile of shit." Eli wanted to scream but the pain of his injury was stealing his energy.

"Convincing people what they think is the truth is what I do for a living, Detective. Lest you forget. Now, quiet. I'm thinking," Harold replied in a soft an eerily cam tone.

"Yes, but you're the one who got me out of the DUI. Remember?"

"Yes, indeed. Well, that's because I was protecting Brad."

"Huh? Brad? What's he got to do with this?"

"Everything. You see, you threatened to broadcast to the world that he was a latent homosexual, a charge you know could ruin him. Even though being gay in Hollywood isn't the sin it used to be, not all action stars are ready to come out of the closet."

"Brad is gay?"

"No, you fool. But your fake accusation would be such a distraction and damaging to the show, and his macho persona that he spent a decade building, that I agreed with your demand to make your DUI charge go away with a little bribery."

"So, now Brad *is* in on this!"

"Hmm," Harold brought his right hand up to the top of his head to scratch his scalp. It seemed he'd forgotten he was still holding the pistol. Eli hoped he'd shoot himself in the head, but instead he only bounced the metal barrel off the side of his scalp. The new scheme apparently realized, Harold said, "Luckily, I learned about your extortion plan from Mia, when you didn't yet know she was my daughter." He smiled broadly, "Oh, yes, this is perfect. When you told her of your plan, she was disgusted and broke it off with you. Had she not informed me of your deviant idea, I wouldn't have been able to cut you off before ruining a man's career. But clearing you of your crime wasn't enough—"

Just as her psychotic father was about to launch into his next lie, Mia convulsed in Eli's arms then went limp. "No, no, no, Mia, don't go! Stay awake! Stay with me!" Eli clutched her close, pulling her to his chest and rocking her back and forth, willing her to stay awake. Mia drifted in and out of consciousness, taking shallower and more rapid breaths with each minute that passed. "Harold, get up there and fucking drive!"

The Rescue

The spotlight shone down from the sky, and the noise of the engine and rotor blades whipping through the air was music to Eli's ears. He knew those sounds belonged to a helicopter. "This is the LA County Sheriff's Department. Cut your engines and come out to the rear deck with your hands up!" came so loudly from the public address system that it was clearly heard over the roaring engine, wind, and crashing seas.

Underway at full throttle, Harold wasn't making it easy for Eli to hold Mia. The floor had become slippery wet with both of their blood. But there was another liquid sloshing about, and it wasn't water. Eli reached back with one hand, touched the liquid, and brought his fingers to his nose to confirm what he feared was true. Gasoline.

The bullet that passed through Eli's leg had a downward trajectory that went through a cabinet at the rear portion of the main deck. The extra marine bladders were stored there as reserve fuel tanks. The pierced container was leaking high-grade gasoline, which first filled the cabinet floor, but now overflowed onto the wooden deck.

Mia was alive but unconscious due to the extreme blood loss and shock. Unable to walk, Eli gripped her under her arms, laying her limp body on the left side of his torso and his left leg, and fought through the pain as he used his right foot to push against the floor and slide backwards toward the rear deck.

The bright light of the helicopter's spotlight shone through the windows of the main cabin and up into the flybridge where Harold was piloting the boat.

"Turn back toward shore and cut your engines now!" the helicopter's speaker announced.

Turn back towards shore? From Eli's position, he could only see out the windows into the darkened sky. He couldn't see which direction they were headed. He had assumed, apparently wrongly, that Harold had cared enough for his daughter to make a speed run toward land. He should have called ahead to have an ambulance waiting at the dock. But if the LASO were ordering him to turn around, was the boat headed farther out to sea?

Eli was hardly able to get his rubber-soled shoes to catch a grip on the wet surface. The wooden deck was now covered in blood, gasoline, and even some seawater from the tremendous swells and rolls the boat was smashing and splashing through.

Inch by inch, he made progress, but the gasoline soaked into his clothing and reached his leg wound. The burning intensified with every moment he spent effectively swimming through gasoline and blood to get himself and Mia to the rear deck. He needed to show the crew of the helicopter that he and Mia were injured.

He desperately needed them to switch from assault mode to rescue mode. But wait, he thought, *Why is LASO here in the first place? Why are they trying to get the boat to stop? Are they after me? But why? They can't be after Harold, can they? They certainly aren't here for Mia.*

Eli stopped a moment. The drugs and alcohol hadn't yet completely worn off, and he was exhausted from trying to pull Mia along with him while only able to use his right leg and right arm to move along the floor. His position wasn't unlike the rescue swimming he'd learned as a teenage life guard when he worked at community pools for a few dollars a day.

He remembered back to those summer afternoons with envy and a bit of regret that he hadn't taken more time to enjoy the privilege of being young and free from any real burden other than high school.

He remembered how much he enjoyed being gawked at by the girls, young and old. He had to laugh to himself that back then, he considered twenty-five-year-old women old.

He'd already been working out regularly and enjoyed a young man's physique, not the skinny thistle sticks that most sixteen-year-old boys possessed at that age. He wore his solid red lifeguard shorts with pride, never wearing a shirt or shoes so that he had the perfect tan at all times.

He even used to worry that the whistle lanyard might leave a white line across the back of his neck, so he either had it pocketed or he carried it from wrist to wrist, twirling the lanyard around his fingers until it spun itself tighter and tighter running out of slack, then repeating the maneuver in the opposite direction.

How young and carefree those days were. Eli lay back, resting his eyes for a moment, thinking to himself that he if he could just rest thirty seconds, he could struggle some more. But he was so tired. The boat slammed against the waves, and sea mist landed on his face. Eli was hot, injured, tired, and the seawater, which might have otherwise been shockingly cold, was instead quite refreshing. Just a minute's rest.

Eli thought back to the academy when a drill instructor shouted at them during Will to Survive training. "You never give up! You keep fighting! I don't care how hurt you are. I don't care how tired you are. I don't care how scared you are! *You! Never! Give! Up!*"

Eli shouted out a growl and then, with more force and vigor than before, continued his backward trek toward the rear cabin. It was only six feet away. *Come on, Eli, it's only a body length to go.* He pushed with his heel, reached back with his arm to grab furniture legs, and pulled himself and Mia backward, two feet, four feet, and then finally reached the rear cabin entryway. There were three steps down to the rear deck. If he didn't get himself and Mia fully outdoors, the crew of the helicopter wouldn't be able to see them, see the blood, and make the assessment he needed them to make.

There was no chance he would be able to stand and walk Mia and himself down the stairs. There was one choice. The drop was only about four feet. He hoped all this tugging and pulling on Mia and the fall ahead of them wasn't causing more damage to her internal organs and making her coming surgery and recovery that much more difficult. He also hoped when he got them both over the side and into a gravity fall that he wouldn't knock himself out hitting his head on the fiberglass deck.

The boat continued to roll and slam against the waves, not slowing. Eli tried to time himself to the rolls so that he didn't shove off the upper deck at a time when the boat was dropping and thereby making the fall that much more precarious. He lay on his back and looked upside down directly behind and saw something odd from his inverted position. He leaned up on his right elbow and looked back over the stern to see an LA County Sheriff rescue vessel in full pursuit. When Eli and Mia came into view, the boat's spotlights lit up and shone directly at them.

This was the moment Eli needed. The lighting helped too. He pushed a little farther, then realized he could reach out and grab the silver rail with his right arm and keep Mia attached to him with his left arm. He pulled them both about fifty percent out of the doorway and then took one last breath to ready himself.

Mustering all the strength he could, he reached higher up the length of the handrail and pulled them both upright into a seated position in a one-armed pull-up that kept their torsos and butts hovering outside at upper floor level and their legs and feet still inside the upper cabin.

Eli held them both above the deck with his right arm, fighting against the rolls and swells of the boat, gravity, and increasing fatigue as he pulled Mia fully out of the doorway. Her feet now dangled and then softly touch the lower deck.

His right bicep shook with the strain. He slightly loosened his grip on the rail to allow his hand to slide down the rail and lowered them both,. He released Mia to the deck without dropping her from more than two inches. Eli then maneuvered himself out of the cabin and onto the deck to lie with Mia.

The aircraft crew trained their spotlight onto Mia and Eli. It was obvious that both the man and woman who came out of the main cabin were injured and needed help.

The aircraft announced, "This is the LA County Sheriff's Department. You are considered armed and dangerous. Cut your engines and prepare to be boarded." As if it was on a feedback loop, the message repeated about every ten seconds.

Eli looked back at the crew, who had gotten themselves close enough to board the boat if they weren't at full speed in choppy ocean water outside the channel of Marina del Rey. Eli waved at them to help, pointing at Mia. He got the thumbs-up from the two deputies in wet suits and masks.

There were four personnel on board the rescue boat, a driver and three rescue swimmers. In this case, two rescue swimmers and one gunner armed with an AR-15 assault rifle with laser sights. A rescue swimmer put his foot on the edge of the starboard bow and was about to jump onto the rear deck, but just then, Harold yanked hard to port and nearly rammed the rescue boat. Only the swift actions of the rescue boat driver saved them.

Eli held Mia in his arms, resting her back on his chest. The centrifugal force of the swift left turn had them sliding to the opposite side of the deck. If it weren't for Eli's quick thinking to reach out and grab the handrail once more, they would have crashed against the starboard-side deck wall.

Eli would have to take control of the rescue mission himself. He would have to trust the rescue swimmers and the actions of the entire team for his plan to work. It was a simple plan. So simple it should work, but if not executed with all parties in agreement, it was certain death.

Eli hooked his arms underneath Mia's and then stood up on his good right leg, but nearly lost his balance from the swells and swaying of the boat. For the moment, Harold kept them on a steady course, at full speed and straight forward.

Harold came down from the bridge to find Eli was standing and holding Mia's limp body. The blood stain on her white dress had now consumed her entire abdomen and right thigh, dripping beneath her feet into a diluted mixture of blood and seawater. Both Eli and Mia were soaking wet. Mia's hair clung to her face and dress in disarray. Eli's shirt-tourniquet was a band of dripping blood around his thigh, loosely held in place by the belt. Eli's hands and chest were stained in blood, the splashing seawater not enough to wash him clean.

Harold hid from the helicopter's view. obscured from the boat by Eli and Mia. He pointed the gun at Eli and yelled, "Stop, Eli! You'll never know who else helped me."

"What?" Eli couldn't hear over the rotor wash and yacht's engines.

Harold came out of the cabin and down the stairs to the lower deck. The pistol he had earlier was nowhere in sight. "Don't you want to know what really happened in this case? I didn't work alone. You must know that!"

"Fine! Who'd you work with? Who helped you? Brad?"

"I won't tell you if you don't call them off!"

"You're bluffing!" Eli shouted as he maneuvered closer to the stern.

"Is Brad really your friend, Detective? Or is he part of my team?" Harold shouted. The spotlight from the helicopter was now trained on him. He climbed back up into the main cabin.

Stunned by what Harold just said, Eli stopped in his tracks. Could it really be true? Had Brad worked with Harold to help him kill his friends?

Eli couldn't do anything but watch as Harold opened the tiny cabinet right next to the exit and removed a flare gun. Harold cocked it, then stepped back outside just long enough to fire it. The sheriff's helicopter was barely one hundred feet off the water and so close that when the flare shot out at rocket-like speed, the pilot had no time to react before the projectile hit the transmission housing, catching the starburst in the venting slats. The hot ball of potassium chlorate burning at nearly three thousand degrees melted the metals and fiberglass of the airframe, dangerously close to the pylon, on top of which spun the rotor blades.

The pilot had no way of knowing if the flare would burn itself out with only cosmetic damage or whether they were about to experience a catastrophic engine failure, fire, or worse, full fuel explosion. Helicopters are essentially flying gas cans with seats. As important as helicopters are to law enforcement, they are equally as fragile under the wrong circumstances. This was one of those times.

The helicopter was forced to peel off and head directly for land, smoke billowing from its side. Harold dropped the flare pistol and pulled the Glock from his waistband where he'd had it covered with his shirt.

He pointed his weapon at Eli, who still held Mia in his arms. Eli had made it to the rear edge of the boat holding the limp woman. His eyes were wide as he looked in Harold's direction. But what Harold noticed was that Eli wasn't looking at him or the gun he held, but more through him. His confused thoughts were interrupted by the flicker of yellow he saw out of the corner of his eye.

The cabin was on fire. The sparks from the ignition of the flare gun fell into the puddle of gasoline that had been pouring from the ten-gallon bladder. A small fire at first burning only the fuel itself led quickly to the wooden cabinets. The wooden floors themselves ignited once the fuel had created enough heat to burn through the sealants and lacquers that kept the wood from becoming water stained under normal circumstances.

Now Harold was the one with choices to make. Save the boat and himself, or try to keep Eli from saving himself and taking Mia with him. In the time it took Harold to survey the growing fire, Eli had carried Mia to the end of the swim deck. The rescue boat was still in pursuit. Eli looked over his shoulder at the boat operator, then back at Harold.

Harold saw what Eli was about to do and yelled, "Don't you do it!" But it was too late. Eli leaned backward and pushed with his right leg to create extra distance. Just as he started to fall backward, he heard two gunshots from Harold's gun and a bullet zipped by his head, missing Eli by inches.

Eli fell out of view of Harold, who was still shooting at where he'd stood. Now he aimed at the rescue boat. The LASO gunner fired a three-round burst, striking Harold in the chest with two of the three rounds. The third round went high and right and drilled through the cabin wall and into the kitchen inside the main deck galley. Harold was knocked backward and onto the ground. He dropped the pistol on the floor near him but out of reach.

As Eli and Mia landed in the ocean, the two LASO swimmers dived into the water within feet of them while the driver and the gunner maintained a momentary pursuit. One diver took Eli and the other took Mia. The water was cold but survivable for several minutes. The salty water burned in his leg wound, which had lost its compress during splashdown.

The flames grew higher and stronger, fully engulfing the upper cabin, blocking Harold's access to the bridge. The rescue boat came full stop and turned around swiftly to retrieve the swimmers and their victims. Not much could be done for the burning boat at this moment. But bleeding victims didn't need hypothermia added to their problems.

Eli watched as Harold and his boat continued to speed away. He'd heard the gunshots from the rescue boat and wondered if Harold had been shot. Eli feared that Harold would get away, that somehow, he'd be able to extinguish the flames and drive the boat to financial freedom somewhere else.

Eli was frustrated that his and Mia's need for medical attention might be the reason Harold was going to escape. But none of that mattered right now. Surviving was the only immediate goal. The repercussions would come as they would for Eli and hopefully for Harold too, one day.

"Let's get you on board," said the swimmer rescuing Eli.

"Mia first! Get her on board first," Eli demanded.

The second swimmer, the one holding Mia, looked at Eli and nodded. He took a couple of hard back strokes and got himself into position to be hoisted onto the emergency deck and lifted into the boat. Then Eli and his swimmer came up next.

The pain in Eli's leg returned to a shocking level. Without the need to focus on survival any longer, his mind and body reunited upon his own injury. Hot agony throbbed through his leg. He lay on a backboard, and the deputies, cross-trained as paramedics, put an oxygen mask on his face and cut through his pants and socks. He'd ditched his shoes on the rear deck before jumping, knowing he'd need his bare feet to help him swim.

They examined his wounds and rolled him back and forth, looking for other gunshot wounds. Finding only cuts, scrapes, and bruises, they focused on his leg.

"How is she?" His question came muffled through his mask.

"Let's focus on you right now, sir."

"Besides your leg, does it hurt anywhere else?" the other deputy asked.

"I don't know. I don't think so. Maybe. But I was only shot once. I was drugged, and I've got a killer fucking headache."

The unknown sound of grinding metal drew everyone's attention toward the speeding yacht. No one knew exactly what it was when they heard it the metal sound of the engine coming to an abrupt, seizing stop, but the explosion and the bright yellow glow were unmistakable. Eli sat up and watched the black-and-amber mushroom cloud as it slowly rolled vertically toward the night sky. The fly bridge and half the upper deck were gone.

A few seconds later, large chunks of the boat splashed down in the water around the rescue boat. The driver had no choice but to throttle up toward shore to avoid the raining debris, even though it was making initial patient assessment that much more difficult.

While Eli was being forced to lie back by the paramedic tending to him, he saw the other paramedics performing CPR on Mia with an Ambu bag while simultaneously giving her chest compressions.

"Mia! No, Mia! Please, God, help her!"

"Sir, please lie back. I need to get this bleeding under control."

The paramedic stuffed both holes with gauze pads, then wrapped a bandage around his leg very tightly, covering both gunshot wounds. The bleeding was slowed but not stopped. If treated in a reasonable amount of time, Eli wouldn't lose the leg. The paramedic then covered him with first a white sheet, then a wool blanket. Lying in the nude, wet, and buffeted by the wind from the moving boat, he didn't realize just how cold he'd gotten until the blanket was put over him. That was when the shivering started. He looked over and saw another man on the boat he hadn't seen earlier. He thought he recognized him, but his vision was blurred with tears. Exhausted, he closed his eyes and let his fifty-pound head fall back on the litter.

"Control, Rescue-five," the driver called into the microphone.

"Rescue-five, go ahead," replied the dispatcher.

"We have one patient with a GSW to his left leg; approximate thirty-year-old male; critical but stable condition; requesting life-flight meet us at Charlie Beach."

"Ten-four, rescue five. Second patient?"

Eli couldn't hear the radio response of the medic tending to Mia. All he knew for sure was that he was exhausted, cold, and in severe pain. He couldn't keep his eyes open.

Recovery

Eli lay in bed, his left leg wrapped and elevated post-surgery. He had an oxygen tube feeding air into his lungs and IV tubing attached to his left arm. As he awakened, he first heard sounds before he could see anything. The sound of hushed male voices was obscured by a reporter talking on the television.

"According to the Los Angeles Sheriff's Department, no bodies were found aboard the vessel and none were recovered from the water. The police are refusing to comment or explain the nature of the incident or how this involves a prominent Los Angeles attorney, Harold King, who this station has confirmed to be the attorney representing the Browers, the missing La Cañada couple found murdered and buried in a desert grave in San Bernardino.

"King was defending the Browers in several lawsuits regarding millions of dollars of allegedly embezzled funds. We cannot yet confirm all the details that connect the dots in this maze we've all been trapped in for several weeks now.

"Also on the boat was Harold's daughter, Mia Lopez, who is recovering at USC Medical Center from a gunshot wound. Finally, and this has really spurred curiosity, a San Bernardino County Sheriff's homicide detective was also among the injured. It is believed he survived being shot and is recovering at an undisclosed location. His name has not been released by his department.

"We will continue to investigate, and as we learn more, we will bring it to you.

"This is Adam Jenkins reporting live from Los Angeles Harbor. Gene, back to you in the studio."

The news anchor took the toss from the field reporter, *"In other news, the city council is looking at ways to fund park restoration..."*

Eli tried but couldn't open his eyes right away. They felt swollen shut and burned a little bit. He finally got one, then the other open, but they burned and watered the more he tried. He desperately needed to wipe his eyes to clear away the fog and crust that had developed while he slept, but his arms felt like they were tied to the bed. He lifted his head to look down and see that his hands were indeed free, but it felt like they each weighed a hundred pounds.

Hushed male voices finally came into focus. They belonged to Avi and Nate, who were sitting on guest chairs watching the news, drinking coffee, and eating Eli's hospital breakfast.

"Hey," Eli whispered.

"Holy shit, he *is* alive," Avi said. "Doc wasn't lying after all."

"Hey, partner. How are you feeling?" Nate asked.

"Like I've been shot and blown up."

"Well, that's convenient," Avi said.

"Hey, wait." Eli tried to sit up, but even his level of physical fitness wouldn't allow him to move this quickly after all the trauma his body had been through. "Aw, shit, everything hurts. Where's Mia? How is she?"

"Slow down, buddy. You've got a lot of catching up to do. So, she is *the* girl you talked about?" Nate asked.

"Yeah, bro, sorry I didn't let you in sooner. It was all happening so fast. Too fast. Now, I don't know," Eli said with still a bit of lingering fog. "So, wait, how did you two wind up here? Wow, I'm really fucking dazed and confused. And how did—"

Avi and Nate exchanged looks.

"Settle down. We'll explain everything," Nate said.

"Okay," Avi began, "so after you called me to be at the meeting with Harold, what I didn't know is that Nate and the department also had you under surveillance. You saw me at the bar, right?"

Eli thought back. "Actually, no."

"Well, that's because you rarely see me in a suit. You told me you were meeting Harold at the Ritz, so I put on my court clothes and beat you out there by an hour. In fact, I think I need to go back and tip the shit out of that bartender for pouring me a dozen waters with lime. But anyway, I saw you come in and sit with Harold, who is old as fuck, by the way. Then Mia showed up, and dude, I had no idea she was that gorgeous. But anyway, I saw you get a couple of drinks, then get super drunk, which I knew had to be something else, because, well, I know how much you can drink, and it usually takes at least three for you to fall out."

"Bullshit, Avi," Eli snapped back. "I can hold my liquor just fine."

"Ha, no, you can't!" Nate chimed in. "But it does make for a fun night after your third beer."

Both Avi and Nate were chumming it up pretty good at Eli's expense, but what could he say at this point? Not only were they right, but this story was also surely going to lead to learning how they wound up saving his life.

"Yeah, yeah, yeah, go on, Avi."

"Okay, so Harold called over the waiter and threw him a C-note to get some help from a couple other servers to walk you out of there through the rear of the hotel. He told them you were avoiding your wife or some shit, and these two servers helped carry-walk you through the kitchen. I bolted out the front door and ran around back to see you get tucked up into a Suburban."

"This is where I come in," Nate said.

"Not yet, actually," Avi continued. "Now, I don't know where you're going, so I run over and get my car and do a one-man surveillance without getting caught. Good thing I'm driving a car that blends in, I guess. I was able to follow you guys without causing too many road hazards until you guys got to Marina del Rey. That's when I called Nate," Avi said as he looked to Nate to take over the story.

"Yeah, so our guys on surveillance didn't see you go out the back. They're still playing video poker in the van, waiting for you to pick up your car," Nate started.

"Wait, wait, wait. What does 'our guys' mean?" Eli asked.

"Internal Affairs."

"Dude!"

"Listen, Detective Schmuckatelli, ever since you went to the fucking Oscars—"

"Emmys."

"Whatever. Ever since that day and then when you tossed me out of Brad Clark's house—"

"Hey, I never tossed you out. Just never let you in. But I was-"

"Yeah, how was I supposed to know you were doing your own Dick Tracy bit? So, if you'll let me tell the rest of the story..."

"Fine, go ahead. Geez, when did you get all sensitive?"

"So, *anyway*, the IA guys are sitting on their thumbs playing video poker and are miles behind and totally unaware of you being kidnapped like a little bitch. So, when Avi here calls me and runs down the game you two have been playing—which, by the way, I still don't know how this is all going to play out—I figured I'd better call Sarge, who then ran it up and down the chain of command and they diverted IA to meet up with Avi, but...you take it from here," Nate said, throwing the conversation back to Avi.

"Yeah, so I'm at the docks sitting down the road watching the Suburban not move. Then all of a sudden, this big fucking boat shows up at the pier and the Suburban engine shuts off. Now, I'm not a super detective like the two of you, but I can spot a clue when I see one. I called Nate back with the update. He called LASO command and got their Harbor Patrol guys tuned in that a SBSO homicide detective was kidnapped by murder suspects. Told them to meet with me and IA at Marina del Rey—"

"IA was supposed to be there any minute, but apparently, they got their wires crossed and went to Santa Monica Pier—" Nate interjected.

"Which doesn't make any damned sense because you don't launch boats from the Santa Monica pier. You fish from the pier. You get ice cream at the pier. You don't launch yachts from the pier," Avi griped.

"Well, that's IA for you," Eli threw in.

"Yeah, right? So, the boat takes off, LASO boat dudes call me, and I get them to meet with me. We wait as long as we can for IA, but once we learn they're in Santa Monica, we take off to go find you. The rest, shall we say, is history."

"You were on the boat?"

"Yup."

"Wait, yeah, so that was you." Eli remembered back to right before he passed out. He thought another moment in silence. "Now what?"

"Well, last I heard, Doc said you could go home tomorrow," Nate said.

"Can you guys get me up to see Mia?" Eli asked.

Avi winced and said, "Well—"

"Wait, where am I? The news said she was at USC Medical. Am I here too? Or—"

"Eli, buddy, I hate to break this to you and hoped we'd have more time before we had to." Nate paused.

Eli looked at his friends. Neither of them was smiling any longer, their jovial faces turned to stone. "What, guys? Did they fly me all the way to ARMC to save county funds?" Eli's eyes shifted from Avi to Nate. "Guys, come on!"

Avi looked at Nate, who then dropped his head. Avi knew it was up to him to break the bad news. "She didn't make it, bro."

"What the fuck?" Eli tried to sit up again, only to be thrown back onto the bed by his own pain and weakness. "Why did the news just report she was recovering at USC Medical?"

"Because that's what we told them," Nate said.

Eli's eyes filled with tears, "Why?"

"Because we still have a job to do, Eli. There's another killer out there, and we need to flush him or her out of hiding. There's no chance one person did in the Browers on his own."

Eli didn't speak. He laid his head back, closed his eyes, and took it all in.

"You want us to go?" Avi asked softly.

Eli sniffled hard as he took a deep breath and then palmed tears from his eyes. "No."

"Listen, buddy, we hated to have to tell you about Mia, but I have to ask you some questions," Nate said.

"Like what?"

"Tough as it is for you right now, I need you to think back and tell me if you think Mia was part of the plot and planning before the murders, or just afterward."

"What? No way she knew any of this." But even Eli couldn't defend her completely, not after what he'd learned on the boat. What good would it do to try to protect her now? This whole thing had blown up in his face, quite literally, and the only way through it all now would be with complete honesty with the department, his friends, and, at some point, himself.

"Harold was primary for sure, but he had help," Nate explained. "Who else had the access? No offense, but why else was she so willing to hook up with you so quickly? She was using you for inside information. We did a data-dump warrant on her phone. She took pictures of your notebook with her iPhone and sent it to her father when you were hanging out with her in LA."

"She said she was helping her dad with info to speed up the case, and yeah, it was sort of spying, but you should have seen her on the boat. She was devastated to learn her father was involved in the killing. She thought he was just their lawyer. She really had no idea. I swear, it wasn't Mia."

After a short pause filled with tension and sniffles, Eli continued, "You were right about one thing, Nate."

"What's that?"

"Harold had help. He even said so. But he didn't say who. But I think I know."

The Last Witness

Darkness in a hospital room was essential for good rest, as was the blanket that covered all extremities to ensure that warmth wasn't something the body needed to focus on instead of healing.

When the elevator dinged and the door opened to the fifth floor, the man got off the elevator and reviewed the wall for directions to the proper room. Wearing a dark blazer and a light-blue button-down shirt over khaki pants, he looked like every other husband who'd just gotten off work and was coming to visit his wife.

He hoped no one would recognize him, but at this hour and with how busy everyone was, no one was paying him any attention. He didn't look up and did his best to avoid eye contact with anyone. When he reached the room with Mia's name on it, a sign read, *Keep Room Dark*.

He slid open the glass slider and pushed aside the curtain enough to gain entry, then let it fall back in place and slowly, quietly closed the door. All the light he had to work with came from the blinking indicators on the breathing machine. He didn't dare turn on a light and draw attention. He didn't need to see clearly. All that was required was to inject the solution into the port on the IV tube and let the next thirty minutes after his departure take care of the rest.

He reached into his interior coat pocket and retrieved the syringe he brought with him. It didn't take medical training to know how to uncap the protective cover of a disposable needle, stick it into the rubber stopper, and inject solution into the IV tubing that led right to the patient in the bed. He took a deep breath and slowly exhaled as he injected the needle and pushed the plunger all the way to the end, emptying the barrel of fluid. He removed the needle, flipped the protective cap back on, and put the empty needle back into his interior coat pocket.

"I hope that was vitamin C," Nate said after turning on the light and nearly making the man pee himself. "Sergeant Eric Weller, isn't it?"

Stunned, Weller moved his hand toward his right hip. Nate's weapon came on target quickly, having already been hiding in his hand. "Don't do it, Sarge!"

Weller stopped, put his hands up, and dropped his head. Within a second, two uniformed deputies and Sergeant Kesling, who were hidden outside around the corner, slid open the door and came in to find Weller with his hands up and Nate pointing his pistol at him.

"Triple-check him for weapons. But first," Nate said, putting on rubber exam gloves, "I need something from him." He reached into his pocket and retrieved the syringe. While still holding it, he turned the glove he was wearing inside out, which cocooned the syringe inside. "This comes with me."

"And give me his badge and guns," Kesling said.

The uniformed deputy removed a Beretta 92 FS from a side holster and handed it to Sgt. Kesling. The badge wallet from the inside breast pocket, and a clip-on, folding lock-blade knife were removed from his right front pocket. The deputy nodded at Nate.

Nate said, "10-15." The deputy walked behind his suspect holding handcuffs and placed them on both of Weller's wrists. Then Nate said, "Eric Weller, you're under arrest for the murders of Bill and Abby Brower, and for the attempted murder of Mia Lopez. You have the right to remain silent. Anything you say can be used against you in court. You have the right to an attorney before and during questioning. If you cannot afford an attorney, one will be appointed for you, free of charge, before questioning."

Weller took a deep breath and threw his chin in the air.

"Do you understand the rights I have just read to you?"

"Yes."

"With these rights in mind, are you willing to speak with me?"

"I want a lawyer."

"That's cool, but you'll need a new one." Nate leaned in to get his lips close to his right ear while he double-locked the handcuffs and semi-whispered, "I think your last one blew up."

"Boys, take him straight to West Valley Detention Center. Do not pass go, do not collect two hundred dollars. Go," Kesling ordered.

"Yessir."

The deputies exited the ICU room, passing Eli, who sat in his wheelchair by the nurse's station. When Weller passed by, Eli couldn't help himself. "Gardening, huh?"

"Fuckin' dog," Eric Weller muttered as he was walked off in handcuffs.

The Funeral

Eli didn't join the crowd gathered for Mia's interment at Forest Lawn Memorial Park. He opted to lean on his crutches under a shade tree, hoping to obscure himself from her friends and family. Except for Brad, who wasn't there due to paparazzi concerns, no one would have recognized Eli, but he didn't want to approach the group and have to introduce himself. Even though he didn't pull the trigger, and tried all that he could to save her, he nevertheless felt guilty for Mia's death.

After the weeping crowd dispersed, Eli felt safe to make his way up close to her gravesite to say his goodbyes and mourn his loss. Eli had fallen hard for Mia. At least he thought he had. He was so unsure now. He loved the Mia he had come to know over a couple of weeks, but maybe he'd never really known her at all. Her actions on the boat—not just taking a bullet for him, but the way she reacted to learning that her father killed the Browers—was real. She hadn't known. Her shock was genuine, as was her display of disgust at the betrayal she felt for her own father. She'd chosen Eli and tried to protect him.

His thoughts were interrupted when he heard his name called quietly from behind. When he turned, Brad stood five feet away from him, wearing a floppy fishing hat, T-shirt, cargo shorts, and sandals. "Oh, hi, Brad. I almost did't recognize you."

"That was the point. Well, not you, but the media. How're you holding up?"

"I'm not. I can't believe she's gone," Eli said softly.

"Me either," Brad said.

"Did she..." Eli started, but he couldn't finish the question.

"Did she love you?"

With tears in his eyes, still looking at the grave, Eli nodded. He sniffled and wiped his nose with his forearm and took a deep, shaky breath.

"I don't know for sure. But I do know this. She never seemed happier. The other guys she dated never impressed her like you did. She talked about you all the time, to be honest. I really don't recall her talking much about other guys she dated. Complained was more like it. But not with you."

"Did you know she was Harold's daughter?"

"Of course I knew. That's how I came to hire her. I needed an assistant, and Harold suggested I try Mia and see how it worked out. It did."

"Why didn't you tell me?"

"I never really thought about it. I know a lot of people and don't usually introduce them to a person including their lineage."

"Did you know...?" Eli hesitated to finish his question.

"Know what?" Brad asked.

"About Harold? About what he did?" Eli turned to look directly at Brad to read his body language.

"Hell no, I didn't! I can't believe you're asking me this right now."

Eli was satisfied with his response. He'd gotten to know Brad enough to establish a truth-telling baseline long ago. "No offense, but you know I had to ask. No matter how this turns out, I'm still a cop at heart. It's in the blood."

"Speaking of that, what's the department going to do with you?"

"I don't really know. Probably fire me."

"Well, listen, why don't you come out and rehab at my place? We can take some time to design this new show, and it should take your mind off things."

"I appreciate it, Brad, I really do. But I think I'm going to stick close to home. It's time to regroup with my friends and family. Get back to what's really important."

Brad said nothing and just nodded, clearly a little put out that Eli didn't jump back at the chance to come out and live the Hollywood lifestyle again.

"I really hope the department doesn't can me. I need to finish what I started. I really can't thank you enough for all you did for me. I'll work to repay you—"

"Stop, stop. Listen, the money is nothing. I'm glad I could help you. Don't worry about it," Brad said with genuine kindness. "If you ever change your mind and want to do some work out my way, you've got my number."

"Sure, thanks."

Brad reached out, and they shook hands before Brad walked off toward the parking lot, leaving Eli to himself.

Epilogue

Six weeks later.

The San Bernardino County Sheriff's Department Homicide Detail buzzed with normal activity. Detectives sat at their desks dictating into recorders for secretaries to later type their words into reports, while others clicked away at keyboards listening intently to their headphones of recorded interviews they were transcribing for court.

Nate sat at his desk, talking on the phone. Artie sat at his desk next to him, trying to work his computer and read a case file. The desk across from Nate sat empty.

Walking with a cane, Eli entered his cubicle area and stood before his desk. Captain Montgomery had been walking with him, but then peeled off to head to his own office. Sergeant Kesling was a step behind.

Nate looked up and then excitedly sat straighter. "Hey, Mrs. Herbert, I gotta go. I've got a problem with a missing person who just walked in and needs my help finding his way. Okay, thanks, you too." Nate hung up the phone.

"Hey," Eli said.

"How are you?"

"Well, I hope I'm not missing, but—"

"Worse? You got fired?"

Before Eli could answer, Artie peered over his reading glasses, "He's too pretty for them to fire. Me, on the other hand, if I did half the stupid shit you do, they'd run me out of here like I was a Jew in Germany."

"Gawd, Artie!" Nate exclaimed.

Artie just laughed. Eli just watched Artie as he giggled and seemed amused at himself for always finding what he thought were the right words.

"So, not fired?" Nate asked just to be sure.

Kesling walked up and stood next to Eli. "We couldn't get so lucky. No, they didn't fire him. Worse, they left him here for us to deal with."

"I keep my rank, but I've been reduced to deputy sheriff trainee pay for six months."

Nate sucked air through his teeth and grimaced. "Ooh, shit, that's fucking brutal."

"Yeah, well, sheriff's pissed. Happy for the good ending, but pissed nonetheless."

"Hey, so Shelly. What was the deal with her?" Eli asked.

"We got total confirmation that she was in Disneyland—" Nate started.

"World," Artie interrupted.

"Yeah, well, Disney World, whatever. But it looks like she wasn't aware of what Harold was doing and was not involved in the murders," Nate said.

"Especially since she can't stand her ex-husband, who was more than willing to frame her it seemed," Eli added. "But the money—"

"Yeah, well it wasn't actually criminal money laundering since it was the Browers' money and no one lost anything," Nate explained. "She wound up paying it out to their estate. But she did get jammed up for a policy violation with the DOC, who didn't like learning that one of their employees was involved in what was definitely an ethical problem that sure looked like money laundering. She got dinged pretty hard, I heard, but kept her job and pension."

"For a while there, I thought for sure she was our gal," Eli replied.

"I never believed it for one minute," Artie said. "I knew all along it had to be someone else."

"How?" asked Eli and Nate simultaneously.

"I just did. That's how," Artie shot back. "When you've had as much time on the job as I have, you get a sick sense about these things. I'm still not convinced your boyfriend Brad wasn't in on it."

"Don't you mean *sixth* sense?" Eli asked.

"Whatever, smartass!"

Before the conversation could go completely off the rails, Kesling stepped in. "Doc cleared you for desk duty?"

"Yes, sir."

"Wait, so seriously, you *are* coming back to work here?" Artie asked.

"Yeah," Eli said, confused at how Artie had just missed the entire previous conversation. Eli, Nate, and Kesling stood silently a moment.

"Unbelievable!" Artie ripped off his reading glasses and tossed them down on his desk. He snatched his coat off the back of his chair and stormed out of the office. The rest of the team just stood there in amazement.

"Well, commercial break's over. Get back to work," Kesling said, then went back to his office.

Eli's desk phone rang, and he sat down to answer it. "Homicide, Detective Hockney."

The End

Derek Pacifico was born and raised in Southern California where he worked for over twenty years in law enforcement. His police career included working corrections, patrol, specialized investigations, where he spent six years as a homicide detective before ending his career with the San Bernardino County Sheriff's Department as a sergeant. He retired from active service and now consults with law enforcement agencies and fiction writers. (www.derekpacifico.com)

Married for twenty-eight years and with two grown children, he and his wife now live far away from the stress of the big city, trading in the concrete jungle for greener pastures where the pace of life has allowed Derek to focus on his newfound passion of writing novels based on his own experiences.

CPSIA information can be obtained
at www.ICGtesting.com
Printed in the USA
LVHW112322140721
692748LV00002B/23/J